Inauguration Day

Day

A Novel

Peter G. Pollak

"To me the great joy in writing a book is showing some small person, some ordinary person doing something in a moment of great valor, for which he would get nothing and which would be unsung in the real world."

Philip K. Dick

Acknowledgements

Many people contributed to the composition of this novel, including members of the Columbia (Maryland) Fiction Critique Group who suffered through early (and late) drafts. Thank you to Robin, Susan S., Susan D., Rissa, Mark, Eileen, Steve, Sarah, C.B., Amy, & Jo-Anne.

Thanks also to beta readers Barbara Baird Sullivan, Puja Guha, and Jim Duncan.

Researching the U.S. Secret Service is not an easy task. I benefitted from Ronald Kessler's *In the President's Secret Service* (Crown Forum, 2009), and two books by Dan Bongino: *Life Inside the Bubble* (WND Books, 2013) and *The Fight* (St. Martin's Press, 2016). Neither author is responsible for any miscues in my description of how the Secret Service is structured or operates.

All characters, locations, and events portrayed in *Inauguration Day* are fictional. The events have not happened . . . yet.

To learn about my previous and future novels visit *petergpollak.com*. There you can sign up for my quarterly newsletter and my book review blog.

Expendable Man Publishing is my personal imprint. As an independent publisher, I am appreciative of readers who help spread the word. If you like *Inauguration Day*, please tell your friends, recommend me to your book club, and post reviews on Amazon.com, Goodreads, Facebook, et al.

I love to hear from readers. So don't be shy about using the contact form on the website.

Friday, November 10

"Why are you bothering me so early in the morning?"

"I don't know how to tell you this, but . . . but I've got some . . . some bad news."

"What? Spit it out."

"Okay . . . Here goes . . . Your . . . Your son drove his car off the road."

"Where? When? Is he okay?"

"I didn't stick around to find out."

"You what!"

"I couldn't chance it. Another car was coming. I'm sure he called 9-1-1."

"Did it look . . . bad?"

"I'm afraid so . . . He was trying to get away from me. I was just trying to keep him in sight . . ."

Silence

"I have his briefcase."

"And his cell phone?"

"No. He had it on him."

"Bring me the briefcase."

Same Day
Washington, D.C.:

Headquarters of the United States
Secret Service

"Yes!" Tucker Daniels said to himself, pumping his arm like a golfer dropping a putt.

His retirement papers had come through. The official date was ten weeks away--January 22--the day Henry Garvin would be inaugurated President of the United States. That meant he could book a flight to Hawaii. Retiring and getting married the same week! Big steps, but after twenty plus years with the Secret Service and sixteen before that in the Marines, he felt he'd done his duty to his country and deserved a heaping portion of R and R.

There was a second item in his mail box that he hadn't noticed at first. He was more than a little surprised when he opened the envelope and discovered outgoing President Edwin Palmer had requested he be agent-in-charge of the team that would be accompanying him to his Nebraska farm over the coming weekend. He'd not been given a Presidential Protective Division assignment since being promoted to a management position in the investigations division a decade ago.

That evening he apologized to Maureen while packing. "Instead of a quiet ten weeks, it looks like they're going to give me assignments no one else wants."

She was sitting on his bed, a wine glass in her hands, probably unaware how sexy she looked in her Washington Commanders t-shirt. "That's not very nice of them."

"But," he said, zipping up his overnight bag, "in ten weeks, they won't have Tucker Daniels to pick on."

The trip out to Nebraska went smoothly. Saturday morning President Palmer announced he wanted to visit an elderly neighbor. Daniels sent a team ahead per standard procedure and assigned men to the three-vehicle caravan that would drive the President to the neighbor's farm and back. He didn't see the need to go with them. After they'd left, he headed to the kitchen of the old farmhouse in search of some fresh coffee.

Daniels was pleased to be retiring before Henry Garvin took office. From what he heard Garvin was mercurial and prone to changing his mind on a whim. President Palmer, on the other hand, had been outstanding during Daniels' years of service in terms of his treatment of the men and women of the U.S. Secret Service. He could have been like some other presidents--demanding, arrogant, and ready to blame an agent when his own behavior had caused the delay or whatever problem he didn't want to be held accountable for, but not President Palmer. Old timers compared him to Ronald Reagan--a man who was humbled by the office rather than one of those more recent presidents who expected everyone else to be humble in his presence.

On the flight to Nebraska day-dreaming about retirement, Daniels had reflected on the fact that he would be celebrating his 55th birthday in Hawaii. His father had died of a heart attack at age 55. George Daniels had been a man's man--rarely home, always working or hanging out with a small group of male friends. He rarely took his wife and children any place as a family--platoon picnics on the 4th of July were his idea of a family outing. Even then, he was likely to leave early with some of his drinking buddies without making arrangements for his wife, son, and daughter to get home.

Tucker had resented the fact that his father had been absent so much, but he had come to understand him when his own marriage had faltered and collapsed alienating him from his only son. Life didn't always offer easy choices. Now he was retiring while still in good health. It seemed like he was being given a chance for a different outcome, an opportunity to escape the cycle of black military men burning the candle from both ends.

It wasn't long before he got word Palmer was on his way back to the farmhouse. He pulled on his winter coat to meet the caravan. The wind, which had been fierce earlier, had died down, but the temperature had dropped well below freezing. As he stood at the edge of the front walk, he couldn't help wonder why he'd been chosen for that particular assignment.

"You didn't have to meet me, Agent Daniels," Palmer said as Daniels held the car door open.

"Just doing my job."

"I never got used to people doing things for me," Palmer said as he tromped up the walk towards the farmhouse, "but in ten weeks I'll probably get stuck someplace waiting for my car door to open."

Daniels laughed. "You'll be missed, Sir."

"I appreciate that, Agent Daniels," Palmer replied. "I suspect you wonder why I dragged you all the way out here."

"That did cross my mind."

"This isn't the time or place. I'm putting your name on my schedule for tomorrow. I'll explain then."

Daniels was so stunned he almost forgot to open the front door for the President. What could he want to talk to him about? He hoped it wasn't something that would delay his own exit from government service.

The next day fifteen minutes ahead of his assigned time Daniels arrived outside the barn in which an office had been built for President Palmer. He didn't have to wait in the cold very long before he was ushered inside by one of the secretaries who traveled with the president.

He was surprised when Palmer stood up, came around his desk, and offered him his hand. That was a first.

"I hope you're well, Mr. President."

The bags under Palmer's eyes were more noticeable than usual--a sign of the wear and tear of eight years serving as the nation's commander in chief. Although his posture was less straight than the day he'd been elected, his hair thinner, and his midsection rounder, those changes were offset by Palmer's steel gray eyes, which remained as penetrating as the first day Daniels had been in the man's presence. He'd never known anyone who was faster at zeroing in on what made a person tick.

"I'm fine, Agent Daniels, but I need some fresh air. Let's wander outside for a bit."

Palmer put on a fleece-lined coat, leather gloves, and a brown fedora and led Daniels through a door on the side of the office into the main part of the barn, across the straw-strewn floor and out a door at the back of the barn onto a dirt path cows and tractors had worn down over the years.

Once outside a blast of cold air hit Daniels in the face. Although his jacket was lined, he lacked a hat or gloves and hoped their walk would not last long.

President Palmer didn't say anything until they reached a tractor path that bordered a cornfield where the remains of that fall's corn crop peeked out of snow drifts.

"I apologize for the mysteriousness," Palmer said, adjusting his pace to the bumpy tractor path, "but we needed to be someplace where we would not be overheard."

Daniels had no idea where this was going, but kept his mouth shut. The surveillance cameras on the back of the barn would record their walk, but he wasn't sure if the NSA's listening devices could pick up their conversation. After Palmer told him why he wanted to speak to him, he prayed they did not.

"There's no easy way to reveal what I'm about to tell you, but I'd like you to listen to the whole story before you start asking questions."

"Certainly, Mr. President."

"As I'm sure you are aware, President-elect Garvin's son, Ethan, was killed Thursday morning in what appears to have been a one-car accident."

Like the entire country, Daniels had been shocked when he heard the news. Ethan Garvin, who at age twenty-eight had been a visible part of his father's campaign team, had been pronounced dead when his car was retrieved from a water-filled gulley in Fairfax County, Virginia.

"You say 'what appears to have been an accident.' Does that mean there's some indication it wasn't?"

Palmer stopped and turned to face Daniels. "Not officially, but please no more questions until I finish. This is hard enough for me as it is, as you will soon learn."

Daniels swallowed an apology, still wondering what this meeting was all about.

"Ethan Garvin was on his way to the White House with documentation of an extremely sensitive nature," Palmer continued. "I'll explain what the documentation was in a second, but when I heard about his death, I had my office contact the Fairfax County Police Department to see if the materials he had promised to bring me had been recovered. We were told no documents or digital media were found in the car--no briefcase, no laptop or tablet--not even a cell phone--nothing."

The president stopped again. "Listen carefully to what I'm going to tell you next because when I'm done I'm going to ask you to take on an assignment that may be a wild goose chase or it may be as vital as given any individual in my lifetime."

Daniels wanted to ask the president to repeat that last sentence, but Palmer resumed his story.

"Ethan Garvin came to the White House on Wednesday for the first in a series of meetings concerning the inauguration ceremony which he'd been assigned to manage for his father. I thought his asking to come by one day after the election to discuss inauguration seating was a little strange. When I told my staff to tell him there was plenty of time to take care of that, he insisted he needed to start, so I agreed.

"After his meeting with my chief of staff, Ethan asked my appointments secretary if he could have five minutes of my time. I was in the Oval Office in the middle of signing some not very important papers and thought it wouldn't hurt to hear what the young man had to say.

"When he entered the room, he looked uncomfortable, biting his lip and looking around as if expecting to find someone other than me. After I welcomed him, he thanked me and handed me a sheet of yellow legal paper. 'There is an issue related to the inauguration I feel needs your personal attention,' he said. 'I hope you can read my handwriting.'

"At the top of the page in capital letters he'd written 'CONTINUE TO ACT AS IF WE ARE TALKING ABOUT THE INAUGURATION.' I looked up and saw fear in his face, as if he expected me to have him thrown out on his ear."

Daniels tripped on a root and almost fell as he concentrated on the President's story. Palmer waited for him to regain his balance.

"Sorry, Sir."

"You okay?" Palmer asked.

Daniels nodded.

"Now where was I?"

"Young Garvin had given you a piece of paper."

"Right. He put those words in caps. Evidently he was afraid I'd say something that would give away the fact he was not there to talk about the inauguration. Most people think every word spoken in the Oval Office is recorded, but that's not the case. Ethan may not have known that.

"In any case, I had no idea where this was going, but I decided to give him the benefit of the doubt. What I'm about to tell you is the exact wording of what was on that piece of paper.

"It read, "My father must *not* be sworn in as president of the United States. He is under control of a high-ranking member of the Central Committee of the Chinese Communist Party. He will do whatever this man asks of him. I can provide incontrovertible proof. When you see what I've learned you'll understand why I say my father must not be allowed to take the oath of office.'

"You can imagine my shock at reading those words, but mindful of his initial instruction, I smiled at him and said something like, 'Don't worry, Ethan, vice presidents are always a pain in the butt about seating.'

"He chuckled and told me to keep reading.

"The next paragraph read, 'I have documented proof of my father's status as a Chinese agent, including the name of his handler. If you are willing to examine the evidence, ask me to come back tomorrow morning to continue inauguration preparations. I'll bring the documentation then. If our country's enemies learn what I'm doing, they won't hesitate to kill me. God bless you and God bless the United States of America.'

"Playing along I handed him back his sheet of paper and said something like, 'Can you come back tomorrow morning--say around nine?' He allowed himself a small sigh of relief, nodded, and said he would be glad to do so."

Why is he telling all this to me? Daniels asked himself, but he didn't interrupt.

"After he left, I sat there for a long time not knowing what to think. The idea that the man just elected president of the United States could be a Chinese agent--I wasn't ready to believe that. On the other hand, we've felt for some time that China had access to information they shouldn't have known about. We thought it was a function of advanced hacking, but what if it was as simple as someone's giving it to them?"

Palmer stopped to check if Daniels was with him, then continued his story.

"I ignored as long as possible the buzzing phones on my desk, knowing people were gathered outside the office with piles of papers needing my signature. Finally, not knowing whether Ethan Garvin was mentally ill or a patriot, I decided to do what he suggested. I notified my secretary to clear time for Ethan at nine the next morning.

"The next morning, nine came and went, but Ethan didn't show up. I wondered if someone discovered he'd gone over the edge and was on his way to a psych ward. Then, around ten thirty, my chief of staff buzzed me with the news--Ethan Garvin had been killed in a solo auto accident.

"When I got over the shock, I remembered the documentation he had promised to bring me. He hadn't said in what format the information was stored--on paper, a flash drive, or whatever. I had my chief of staff contact the Fairfax County police to tell them to let us know if they found anything that looked like it was intended for me. As I said, we were informed there had been nothing in the car for me or anyone else--no papers, no briefcase, no cellphone, no tablet, nothing."

The President stopped and motioned they should head back towards the barn. He didn't say anything for a minute as if struggling in his mind about what to say next. He took a deep breath and resumed his account.

"I've shared this with no one else until this very moment, Agent Daniels, for a reason. If Ethan was deranged, I don't want to embarrass his family--particularly now that he's gone, but . . . but if there's a chance what he said is even partially true and I do nothing, I could be aiding and abetting the arrival of an extremely dark day for the country that I love."

Daniels didn't know what to say. "That's some incredible story," he mumbled.

The President nodded. His face was grim. "The bottom line is the whole thing may be the result of a disturbed mind's run-away imagination and a terribly unfortunate accident, but we have to consider the worse case scenario. It's possible--no matter how improbable--that Ethan Garvin was killed for trying to save the country from his own father."

By the time they reached the barn, Daniels' mind was spinning so fast he forgot for a moment he was talking to the President of the United States and not to some college buddy sharing the plot of his next novel.

Before they parted, Palmer gave him an off-the-books assignment, although if Daniels had a second to spare, suicide mission might have been a better description.

"First," he said, "find out if Ethan Garvin was telling the truth about the existence of the documentation he promised to deliver. If you conclude such documentation exists, find out what happened to it *and, if possible, recover it*. Finally, and this is most important, you must determine the validity of his claim that his father is a traitor."

Palmer impressed upon him that the entire assignment had to be completed in days, if not weeks. "I'd like an answer by December 1 at the latest, Agent Daniels."

"I'll do my best, Sir."

"You understand why you can't show up the morning of the inauguration and tell me Ethan was right," he said.

"Absolutely, Mr. President."

"That's all the time I can give you today without making it look like this talk was about something other than two about-to-be retirees reminiscing," Palmer said as he motioned for Daniels to open the barn door for him.

As they stepped into the barn, Palmer handed him an envelope. "This contains contact information of someone I trust--someone who will do what he can to help you, including financing all necessary expenditures. The envelope also contains the keys to a furnished apartment in the District you can use if needed, as well as instructions for how to contact me with the results of your investigation. Thank you, Agent Daniels. I knew I could count on you."

After watching President Palmer enter the barn, Daniels stood there for a minute before the cold got to him. He was still in shock at what he'd been told and over what President Palmer had asked him to do.

Fortunately, as agent-in-charge for that weekend, he didn't have any duties the rest of the day and could avail himself of the office in the wing of the farmhouse that had been added to the main building for use by the Secret Service. The few people who came into the addition that afternoon were too much into their own worlds to notice Daniels' distress, giving him a few hours to try to wrap his mind around the President's request.

To begin to slow down his runaway thoughts, he jotted what he remembered of the conversation on a legal pad he'd found in a desk drawer. After an hour, he settled on a strategy. He was inclined to believe Ethan must have been mentally disturbed. If so, and if he lacked any proof to justify his absurd claim, perhaps he drove off the road intentionally. Maybe he only intended to injure himself, but miscalculated. Proving the absence of something, of course, is much more difficult than proving something exists or once existed. Either way, he wondered if he was up to the task. Although an experienced investigator, nothing in his background--either as a Marine or as a Secret Service agent--had prepared him to conduct the kind of investigation President Palmer had charged him with.

He recalled the President's answer when asked why he chose him.

"You're a trained investigator whose record speaks for itself. Further, I've been impressed with how you handle difficult situations."

"But Mr. President, shouldn't this be given to the FBI?"

"I wish it were that easy," Palmer replied, "but if I go through normal channels, call in the FBI, for example, Henry Garvin will find out and raise the worst kind of stink. This has to be kept between you and me until such time as we find out the truth."

Daniels nodded to show he understand the president's reasoning.

"There are only a handful of people to whom I could have entrusted this assignment," Palmer said. "The longer I thought about it, the more I was convinced you were the right choice."

Daniels hadn't known what to say at the moment and when he went to bed that night he was still trying to digest the implications of being given an assignment only he and the president knew about.

"The fact that you'll be retiring in ten weeks also contributed to my decision," Palmer had told him. "That means your replacement will be brought on board right away. That should give you the freedom and time to conduct this investigation. In any case, I'm confident you'll be able to wrap this up quickly."

"Let's hope so, Sir."

Palmer gave him a thin smile. "I understand what I'm asking you to do is unprecedented, but I think you can appreciate how crucial it is we learn the truth of the matter."

At the end of the afternoon, having memorized the contact name and phone number of the lawyer, he tossed the documents into the fire raging in the annex fireplace along with his notes-- not only the page he'd written them on, but the next two sheets on the pad, knowing the slight indentations could be used to recreate what had been written.

Finding it difficult to fall asleep, his mind raced through multiple scenarios. He had been trained to investigate a group of people known unofficially as 'loonies'--individuals who were off their meds, had illusions of grandeur, or had political axes to grind. Not that such people were harmless, as David Hinckley proved in nearly killing Ronald Reagan. It had been that near tragedy that changed Secret Service policy to eliminate public departures and arrivals and to take seriously even the most far-fetched threat. Every received threat had to be investigated and neutralized, either by convincing the culprit that she or he was not going to be allowed to come within a mile of the president or by taking legal action to put the person in a mental institution or in prison.

This situation was different in so many ways. The person being investigated was dead and the threat he voiced was not against the life of the current president, but a vague, seemingly irrational, accusation against his own father.

What made the situation even more difficult was Daniels realized he could not work through official channels, which meant he would not have access to the resources he normally possessed when looking into a "loony." Further, without Palmer's having said so, he knew the President would deny any knowledge of the investigation were it compromised in any way. Being found out could result in a prison sentence or worse, not just for himself, but for anyone he involved.

Daniels knew he should feel proud Palmer had selected him to investigate Ethan Garvin's claim, but there were so many unknowns about the situation. What if he wasn't able to prove that Ethan was mentally ill and do so quickly? He didn't want to think about the alternative.

Sunday Evening, November 12

Daniels was happy to discover Maureen waiting for him when he arrived at his apartment after the flight back from Nebraska. He told her she looked even more delicious in jeans and a frilly yellow top than the meal on the table or the open bottle of his favorite Malbec.

"If you want dessert," she said with a smile, "you'd better eat all of the steak I cooked for you."

Playing along, Daniels grimaced as if he was going to have a hard time doing that.

"So, did you learn why they sent you to Nebraska?" Maureen asked as they were eating.

"Yes, but it didn't apply to me," he replied, having made up the story he needed to tell her during the flight home. "The President invited me to be a supervisor for his retirement team. I told him 'thanks, but no thanks.' I explained I was retiring the same day he was leaving office."

"I was afraid he was going to ask you to stay on or to do something that would ruin our plans."

"Nope. Waikiki here we come."

The next morning he felt an urgent need to get to work on Palmer's impossible assignment. Fortunately, he had the next two days off as a result of having accompanied the President to his farm for the weekend.

The only problem was Maureen wanted him to go shopping with her to pick out some clothes for their honeymoon. Since it was Veteran's Day, he had a ready-made excuse. To go shopping on Veterans' Day would be an insult to the men who served our nation he told her. "Let's do it tomorrow."

Daniels thought long and hard on the flight back to D.C. about whether to tell Maureen what the President asked him to do. If it snowballed beyond a week or two, it would be hard to keep it from her, but he wanted to protect her at all costs. His head ached at the thought of his being responsible for her being strip-searched and clothed in prison garb instead of lying on a beach in a new bathing suit.

Once at his desk, he began to research Ethan Garvin, hoping to find some indication of prior mental illness. A search on his name resulted in pages of hits that it took hours to scan. The bulk of the news accounts covered Ethan's role on his father's campaign. He also found a few items going back to Ethan's college days when he made dean's list, earned other honors, and then graduated near the top of his class.

As he read each article, he jotted down unanswered questions and looked for names of reporters and others who might know something useful. Before long the list covered several full pages, but none of the material suggested any hint of mental health problems.

Next, he researched the accident. News stories reported a passing motorist discovered the accident about seven forty-five that morning. None of the reports touched on where Ethan was going or where he was coming from. How could he find out? Even if someone on his father's staff had Ethan's schedule, he couldn't just call up the campaign and ask without having to explain who he was and why he was calling them.

It was becoming abundantly clear that conducting an unofficial investigation put him at an enormous disadvantage. Not only couldn't he call up the Garvin campaign office to ask whether anyone knew where Ethan was going the morning he was killed, but he also didn't have the authority to obtain copies of the police accident report or the autopsy. The latter would reveal whether Ethan Garvin was taking some kind of medication or was under the influence of alcohol or a narcotic.

He was beginning to worry he couldn't find out anything useful on his own. He felt totally stumped and had no idea what to do next when Maureen knocked on his door and informed him she'd made him some lunch.

"You're an angel," he told her when he saw she'd heated up some minestrone soup from the local market and made him a ham and Swiss sandwich.

"You seem so wrapped up in whatever you were doing. I thought I'd stick around to help." They still hadn't decided which of their apartments they'd keep after they were married.

"I still can't believe the end is in sight," Daniels told Maureen after sitting down at the kitchen table. "Twenty years! Gone in a heartbeat."

She came over and started rubbing the back of his neck and shoulders. "What's got you so tied up, Eugene--instructions for your successor?"

He wished she wouldn't call him by his middle name--his mother used to do that when he was in trouble. "Maybe you can help me with an issue that's got me stumped."

"I'll try."

"What if my replacement needs to conduct an unofficial investigation? Say there's a rumor floating around and he needs to find out the truth, but can't use official channels."

"That could be a problem," she said after sitting down in front of a cup of minestrone. "Has it ever come up?"

"Not that I know of. Maybe I'm going overboard here. I just think our people ought to know how to do stuff that isn't covered in the manual."

"I'm sure you've thought of researching the problem on the Net."

"I have, but say the investigator would need to access something like police records, but without making an official request."

"I think I see," Maureen said. "Like if an agent had a DUI while off duty. That kind of thing?"

"That's exactly what I'm talking about," he said, feeling relieved the conversation was moving away from dangerous territory.

"What about hiring a private investigator? He could file freedom of information request without revealing who he was doing it for."

Daniels looked to see if there was any more soup on the stove.

Maureen noticed and filled up his bowl.

"Thanks," Daniels said. "How would you like to marry me?"

She laughed. Daniels still couldn't believe Maureen said yes when he asked her out the first time six years ago. No one believed him when he told people they met at the local self-serve laundry. The question had come up as recently as the flight from Nebraska back to D.C. Someone heard he was about to retire and congratulated him on the fact.

"And I'm getting married," he told the listeners.

"So how did you meet the soon-to-be Mrs. Daniels?" one of the agents asked.

"I was at my local laundry when I saw her struggling to maneuver a cart through the front door. So I got up and helped."

"Such a gentleman!" the agent quipped.

"Later, I noticed she was having trouble with the change machine. ' It always runs out on Tuesdays,' I told her. 'You can get change across the street. I'll watch your stuff.'

"She thanked me by bringing me a cup of coffee from Dunkin' Donuts. Then, after loading her clothes in the washer, she sat in the chair next to mine."

That had surprised him given most white women seem afraid to give a black man any hint they'd welcome a request for the time of day.

"I ran into her again a few weeks later at the local supermarket," he told his fellow agents. He asked her if she'd gotten a new washing machine yet and was again surprised when she didn't appear to shy away from his attempt to be friendly.

At that time he wanted to see if she had a ring on her left hand. Don't even think about it, he told himself. With her dark brown hair and large deep eyes, she was too pretty to be single, but he did look at her left hand the next time he encountered her and was surprised her ring finger was bare.

"It was probably two months later when I saw her seated by herself on a Saturday morning at one of those small tables they have at the Dunkin'

Donuts," he told his colleagues on the flight. "I ordered a breakfast sandwich and then told myself 'nothing ventured, nothing gained.'"

"That's an agent for you," one of the guys said.

"She told you to buzz off, right?" another jibbed.

Daniels laughed. "Nope. She looked up from her newspaper and hesitated just long enough for my heart to jump into my throat. 'Oh, I remember. The laundry. Sure, please sit.'"

"Why don't they react that way when I try that?" the agent said, getting laughs from the group.

"Now here's where I teach you guys a lesson," Daniels told them.

"Pray tell. What line did you use?"

He paused and leaned forward for affect. "She was doing the crossword from the *Post*. I asked her if she needed any help and she said she was stuck on one.

"It's sports so you probably know it. Three letters. 'Giants slugger.'"

"O-T-T, Ott."

"That fits. Thank you. I'm not particularly good at sports . . ."

"I never thought I was smart enough to do crosswords," I told her. "One day I found a book of them in the break room where I work and gave it a try. Now I'm hooked."

"Yah, right," one of the agents said. "Ever finish one?"

Daniels ignored the question. He was remembering an awkward silence prevailed that morning when they finished their coffees. He had checked out her left hand. No ring and she had told him her name. He took that as a sign that he could take the next step, but he was sweating despite it being a cold April morning.

"There's a new play at Arena Stage opening Saturday night," he recalled blurting out. "Would you like to go?"

She replied with a smile that floated him up to cloud ten. "I would, but I'm going to be out of town this weekend."

Daniels cringed remembering how he'd tried to hide how much coming down to earth hurt by saying something foolish like, "Maybe next time."

She cut a corner off the edge of the newspaper and wrote her telephone number on it. "Call me."

Taking the slip of newspaper didn't float him quite so high up he lost touch with earth. He suggested dinner the following Saturday. "When she said yes," he told his buddies, "you could have knocked me over with that corner of the paper."

Maureen's suggestions based on her years working for a K Street lobbying firm on how to conduct an unofficial investigation were great, except Daniels didn't know any private investigators nor did he think he could select someone at random when the consequences could be disgrace, loss of a job, or even a prison sentence.

Her suggestions did, however, reinforce a conclusion he was fast reaching--if Ethan Garvin was telling the truth, this was likely to grow into something much bigger than a normal investigation--one he doubted one person could even begin to handle.

Back at his desk after lunch, he started making a list of people who might be able to help.

Given that he wouldn't be able to use the computer in his office at the Secret Service to conduct the investigation, he needed an expert who might be able to find valuable details he hadn't come up with, and it just so happened he knew an expert in data analysis––one who worked for the National Security Administration to boot. The problem was they weren't on speaking terms. A reconciliation attempt three years ago had ended disastrously when his son told him not to contact him ever again. What would happen if he tried now?

Daniels sighed, but didn't make the phone call. Instead he plowed back into his Google search results.

Mid-afternoon, he came across a notice that Ethan Garvin's funeral would take place Wednesday morning in his father's hometown of Canton, Ohio.

Although a full team had been assigned to Henry Garvin since he declared himself a candidate for the Democratic Party nomination, a boatload of additional officers would be needed for the funeral given the likelihood that a large number of dignitaries would attend. If Edwin Palmer didn't attend in person, which Daniels assumed he would not, he'd certainly send someone no less important than the vice-president. Either way Daniels knew extra help would be needed. He called Personnel to let them know he'd be willing to assist. They thanked him and promised to send his assignment and travel details by the end of the day.

Late Monday evening, Daniels took stock. He hadn't found anything that suggested Ethan Garvin had gone off the deep end, but the story the young man had presented to President Palmer was too unbelievable to consider.

Tuesday, November 14

For the second time in two days Daniels had to tell Maureen a not-so-little white lie. "Personnel called. I'm needed for Ethan Garvin's funeral tomorrow."

"Another trip so soon?"

"It's a one-night thing. Things should quiet down after this," he said, knowing that was wishful thinking. "I'll get Thursday off. We can go shopping then."

"Where are you off to now?" Maureen asked as Daniels was putting on his jacket.

"To get my head shaved."

"I keep telling you I can do it for you."

"I know, but my brothers at the barber shop would miss me," Daniels said, giving her a kiss as he walked out the door.

Daniels' assignment for Ethan Garvin's funeral was to supervise the group stationed at the road entrance to the cemetery. He was disappointed not to be able to observe Henry Garvin and his family during the funeral service, but hoped to be able to pick up some useful information just by being on the scene.

Ethan Garvin was to be buried in Canton Ohio's Westlawn Cemetery, which shares an expansive park-like environment with the William

McKinley Presidential Library and Memorial. The cemetery entrance to be used for the funeral was off a one-block long residential street. A barrier had been erected at the intersection leading to the cemetery entrance in order to control both vehicular and foot access. A motorcycle brigade provided by the Ohio State Police would escort the hearse and official cars from the church to the cemetery. Counterassault teams would be stationed at key spots along the route looking for snipers, protestors, and suicide bombers. Daniels' team would be stationed at the barrier screening cars with a goal of preventing anyone not previously cleared from crashing the event.

A major concern was the possibility of a sniper who wanted to go down in history as the man who killed Henry Garvin on the grounds of William McKinley's Memorial. The access road to Interstate 77 would be closed during the ceremony, as would Stadium Park Drive, which parallels I-77 on the other side of the park. A combination of city and state police were given perimeter assignments while uniformed and plain-clothed Secret Service teams were deployed at strategic locations around the park.

In addition to checking each vehicle as it passed through the barrier to the local street that led to the cemetery, his team was to prevent sightseers from gaining access through that point on foot. The assignment was a disappointment in terms of observing the Garvin family up close, but he had no choice in the matter.

When he arrived in Canton the day before the funeral, Daniels could see the biggest problem was going to be holding back the crowds trying to access the cemetery on foot. Firm instructions had come down that only people who arrived in official vehicles were to be admitted onto cemetery grounds. That did not go over well with a crowd of sightseers who had already started to gather, forcing the Secret Service to maintain counterassault teams in the park throughout the night. Daniels got zero hours of sleep that night.

In addition to dealing the curious who showed up thinking they'd be able to enter the cemetery on foot, the media represented another problem. Fortunately, someone else was in charge with screening reporters and TV crews and controlling their movements. Daniels had enough to do and stayed busy right up to the moment late the next morning when he got word the funeral service was over and the line of official vehicles was about to roll.

It took longer than scheduled for the motorcade to maneuver from the church to the cemetery entrance where the screeners under Daniels' supervision checked each vehicle and the occupants. Once the final car had passed through the gate, he hoped the worst of it was over. His next problem was how he could justify going into the cemetery to observe the family at the gravesite.

While he was puzzling that out, a loud argument caught his attention. A young woman dressed in funeral black was berating one of the agents manning the barrier. Daniels hurried over to see what the problem was. His man looked relieved when Daniels arrived. "This young lady wants to be let in. She claims she is Ethan Garvin's fiancé and was left behind at the church."

Ethan Garvin's fiancé? Daniels could not recall reading any mention of a fiancé during the funeral briefing session the previous evening.

The young woman in question looked to be in her mid-to-late twenties. She wore an expensive-looking dark coat with matching mittens and hat and her dark hair was fashionably cut shorter on one side. Most people would consider her attractive, although at the moment her anger couldn't hide the fact her eyes were red from crying.

"I have a right to be at my fiancé's funeral," she asserted, daring Daniels to contradict her.

Daniels needed to diffuse the situation. "May I see some identification, young lady?"

She fumbled open her small pocketbook, took out her wallet, and handed him her driver's license. "After the service there was a line at the ladies' room. When I came out, all the cars were gone."

Her name was Sharon Washburn and she lived in Arlington, Virginia. The identification looked authentic and she clearly was the person in the license photo.

"Okay. Stay right here," Daniels told her. "I'll make a call and see what can be done."

Walking a distance away so he couldn't be overheard, Daniels called the officer in charge of the event. He had to go through three agents to reach him. "Agent Amerman, Tucker Daniels here. I'm at the Seventh Street barrier. I've got a young lady who says she missed her ride from the church to the cemetery."

"What's her name?"

"Sharon Washburn. She says she was Ethan Garvin's fiancé."

"Hold on while I check the list."

The young woman was wiping her eyes with a handkerchief. She looked more self-possessed than she had a few minutes ago. Daniels had to consider that she might be a threat to the Garvins. If Amerman okayed her going into the cemetery, he would use a metal detector to make sure she wasn't carrying a firearm or other weapon.

"Okay, I see the problem," Amerman stated when he got back online. "She was included in the funeral, but at the family's request was not on the list of people to be transported to the cemetery."

"Any explanation?"

"None."

"What am I supposed to tell her?"

"Just what I said."

Daniels walked back to where Sharon Washburn was standing to the side of the entrance barrier. She must have read the look on his face. "What? What did they say?"

"I'm sorry, Ms. Washburn, but your name was not included on the list of people to be transported to the cemetery. That means we can't let you in."

"That's ridiculous. There must be some mistake. I was Ethan's fiancé, for God's sake." She started back towards the barrier. "I'm going in there! You just try to stop me!"

Daniels had to do something. Several people with press badges on their coats had overheard her plaint and were paying close attention. In the past, Daniels would have stuck to protocol--no ticket, no admission, but this time was different. He had a reason for wanting to talk to this woman, which meant he needed to gain her trust. "Hold on, Ms.

Washburn. Let me try one more time before you do something you're going to regret."

She hesitated for a second, but then nodded.

He walked away again and buzzed Agent Amerman a second time.

"Now what?"

"How about this, I'll escort her in myself and see that she stays away from the family."

"I don't like it, Agent Daniels. What if the Garvins notice?"

"The problem is she's about to get herself arrested. There are a dozen reporters here with cameras paying attention to her. I think we're asking for more trouble if we don't let her in than if we do in a way that diffuses the situation."

"It's your call, Agent, but your neck will be on the line if anything goes wrong."

Daniels hurried back to where Sharon Washburn was standing. Once again she seemed to have read the look on his face. "Finally!"

"You're going to be allowed into the cemetery on the condition you do exactly what I tell you and do not do anything to call attention to yourself. Is that acceptable?"

She nodded. "What do you think I was going to do?"

"Let's not go there," Daniels replied. "Follow me."

Daniels commandeered one of the Ohio state police cars with one of their men to drive. After escorting the young woman to the car, he used the officer's wand to verify she wasn't carrying anything that could be construed as a weapon. Once he had her secured in the car, Daniels instructed the driver to follow the paved road through the cemetery to the burial site.

"Pull up to the end of the line of cars," he told the state cop. He turned to face the young woman. "I'm going to open the door for you, but you are to stay with me. I'll escort you as close as I feel is appropriate without interrupting the service or causing one of the secret service agents monitoring the crowd to become concerned. Is that understood?"

She gave a quick nod. "I'll be good."

"Other than some tissues, you'll have to leave your purse in the car," he told her.

She took out a package of tissues, and set her purse aside.

When they arrived at the back of the crowd, Daniels feared the Garvin family would notice if he tried to escort the young lady near the front and that's precisely what he needed to avoid.

"We'll have to stay here, Ms. Washburn."

"I can't see," she whispered. She stood five feet five or six inches in her heels, which were sinking into the damp grass.

Daniels put his finger to his mouth imploring her to remain quiet. She managed to find a spot where she could see and did as he asked.

The burial service was near its conclusion. Soon the crowd started to break up with people heading back towards their vehicles.

"I missed everything," she said, starting to cry.

Think fast, Daniels told himself. "If you wait here with me for a minute we can go down to the gravesite and you can say your goodbyes. Would you like that?"

She nodded, while trying to staunch the tear flow with a soggy tissue.

Daniels kept her away from the grave until everyone had left and then allowed her to move close.

She stood there a good five minutes tears flowing down her face. Finally, she turned indicating she was ready to leave.

They walked in silence to the car. "Do you need a ride to the airport?" Daniels asked before opening the door for her.

"My flight back to D.C. isn't until tomorrow morning," she said.

"Then to your hotel?"

"I don't have a reservation. Just drop me at any hotel near the airport."

Daniels suspected all of the chain hotels in the city were booked solid. Once they got back behind the barrier, he informed Agent Amerman that he was going to assist Ms. Washburn for a short time longer.

Daniels contacted the Secret Service travel office to see if they could find a suitable room. It took less than twenty minutes for them to book a room in a reputable locally owned motel seven miles from the airport.

The next problem was getting her there. Once again, Daniels enlisted a state trooper to drive them. The crowd had been slow to disperse and traffic crawled. When they got to the motel, he asked their driver to wait, thinking he'd have him drop him off at the airport, but when they were informed her room wasn't ready, Daniels rejected the idea of leaving Sharon Washburn in the lobby, recognizing he'd been given a golden opportunity to learn something about Ethan Garvin.

"You must be hungry," Daniels told her. "I know I am. There's a diner across the street. We can go over there, grab a bite, and have the motel call us when your room is ready."

"You don't have to trouble--"

"It's no trouble at all. Our job is not just protecting the president. It's making sure things don't happen that embarrass the White House. I hope you won't make a big deal out of what happened today."

"I guess I want to," she admitted. "I suppose it could have been a clerical error."

"I don't know if I should tell you this, Ms. Washburn, but Ethan's family purposely kept your name off the list."

"Why? What reason--"

"I was about to ask you the same question. Did they have reason to believe you might do something to call attention to yourself?"

"Of course not," she muttered. "It was his mother. I hate her."

Washburn eventually calmed down and ten minutes later they were seated in the diner. Daniels ordered a sandwich and coffee; she declined food, but picked out an herbal tea from a small selection, the names of which the waitress didn't even try to pronounce.

While they waited for their food, Ms. Washburn started to tear up.

"How long had you known Ethan?" Daniels asked, hoping to distract her from her thoughts. She would have plenty of time for that when she was alone in her motel room.

"We met in college and dated until our senior year, but then we didn't see each other until our fifth year reunion. We got engaged less than a year later."

"I can't imagine how difficult this must be for you," Daniels said.

She dabbed her eyes. "Thank you. I can't believe they'd prevent me from going to the cemetery. His mother never liked me, but I didn't think she'd do something so nasty."

Daniels shook his head. "It's possible there was a misunderstanding."

"There was no misunderstanding. She did it to hurt me."

"But you were engaged to her son."

"She never approved of me. When Ethan told them he'd asked me to marry him, his mother forbade him from making it official until after the election."

The waitress brought Daniels' sandwich and her choice of tea.

"His father must have counted on Ethan's undivided attention during the campaign," Daniels offered after the waitress left.

"That's what's so odd. His father didn't seem to trust Ethan. He told me his father took him off assignments and excluded him from key policy meetings."

"Did Ethan explain what he thought was going on?"

She sipped her tea and thought for a moment. "He went back and forth, sometimes making excuses for his father, other times saying his father was becoming paranoid."

"Did he explain what he meant by that?"

She shook her head. "Just that at times his father acted like he didn't trust Ethan."

"Anything else?"

"I didn't think much of it at the time, but the other day Ethan said he wanted me to know if something happened to him he loved me and had done his best to protect me."

"Did he explain what he meant?"

She shook her head. Daniels waited while she reached into her purse for more tissues. "They killed him. I know they did."

Had he heard that right? "You think someone killed Ethan Garvin?"

"I don't know, but I just know he didn't drive off the road. He was a good driver and knew that road like the back of his hand."

Their waitress interrupted to refill Daniels' coffee cup. Sharon decided to eat something and took a minute scanning the menu before deciding on a bagel with cream cheese.

Daniels held the question he'd wanted to ask until the waitress was gone. "Why would someone want to kill Ethan Garvin?"

"I don't know. I just know it wasn't an accident like they said."

She turned her back to him and blew her nose. Daniels hesitated, but then asked the question he'd been waiting for the right moment to ask. "Where was Ethan going the morning of the accident?"

She looked up as if she was seeing him for the first time. "Why do you ask?"

A half dozen lies went through his head, but then what did he have to lose by telling her the truth? "The White House was under the impression

Ethan was coming into the District to give the President some important information, but the police say there was no briefcase or documents of any kind in the wreckage."

She looked away for a second. "The night before he died he told me he was going back to the White House for a meeting that would change our lives. Those were his words."

Daniels perked up. "'Change your lives.' What do you think he meant by that?"

She shrugged and took another sip of her tea. "I assumed he meant we'd be able to announce our engagement."

"Do you know what Ethan was bringing to the White House?"

She shook her head. "I assumed it had to do with the Inauguration. He put some folders in the briefcase I gave him for his birthday. I don't know what happened to it if it wasn't in his car."

"Which raises another question. Why was he way out in Fairfax County? Is that where he lived?"

"Here's your bagel, Miss." The waitress slid a plate in front of Sharon. "Anything else?"

Daniels asked for a glass of water.

"Where were we?" Sharon asked.

"Why Ethan was living in Fairfax County? Don't his parents have a house in the District?"

She nodded. "It's a long story, but the bottom line is Ethan moved out to the family's farmhouse in the spring."

"And you spent the night there?"

"I did, but I left that morning before he did to get to my office by 8:30."

"Okay. Another question. I assume the police questioned you."

Sharon took a bite of her bagel. "No one asked me about anything."

"I wonder what would happen if you were to ask to speak to the person conducting the investigation into the accident."

"But Agent Daniels--that's your name, correct?"

"It is."

"Agent Daniels. You work for the president of the United States. Can't you ask those questions and find out what really happened?"

"We can and we can't. I know it sounds strange, but were this any other situation, we could certainly make official inquiries, but when you're inquiring about the son of the man who will be president in ten weeks time, that can generate the wrong kind of attention."

"I suppose, but I'm convinced someone wanted Ethan dead."

"Okay, but help me out. Why?"

She shrugged.

"There has to be a reason," Daniels said.

"I don't know. I just don't know."

"And you're sure it was not an accident."

"Positive. That section of the road was undergoing repairs. He told me he'd called the county to have them put up a guard rail before someone got killed."

Daniels considered that for a moment. The next question he was about to ask her might be telling. He hoped she'd answer honestly.

"Let me ask you a different question. Did Ethan have a history of mental problems-- depression, anxiety, or illusions--that kind of thing?"

She looked surprised. "Not at all. He was the most level-headed person I've ever known. He was patient, and fun-loving, and . . ."

Again the tears flowed. She blew her nose. "I'm sorry. I'm not myself at the moment. I hope that motel gets my room ready soon, because I'm about to crash."

"I understand. We'll get you back across the street." Daniels wrote his personal cell number and email address on a napkin and handed it to her. "Feel free to contact me in case you run into any further problems or think of anything else that would explain what happened to Ethan."

She accepted the napkin, but he doubted he'd hear from her.

On the way to the airport, he concluded the trip to Canton was a plus. Sharon Washburn had confirmed Ethan had been heading to the White House, but Daniels felt no closer to seeing a path to learning if Ethan was bringing President Palmer the smoking gun he promised or if he was the victim of his own delusions, and now there was one less day to find the answer.

Wednesday Evening, November 15

Daniels slapped himself on the forehead in the middle of the late night flight from Ohio back to D.C., waking up his seatmate.

"What's the matter, Tuck?"

"Sorry. I just remembered something I should have done."

The head slap was his reaction to realizing he should have asked Sharon Washburn to go back to the Garvin's farmhouse to search for the missing briefcase. Learning whether or not he'd taken the briefcase with him that morning would go a long way to settle whether Ethan was mentally ill or whether he was murdered to prevent him from delivering the promised information to the President. If she couldn't find the briefcase in the farmhouse and if it was not in the wreckage that would suggest Ethan's death might not have been an accident.

Daniels had no easy way to get in touch with her since he foolishly had not asked for her contact information. He could try the Internet, but private information was hard to find these days.

The next day Daniels couldn't come up with any excuses to avoid going clothes shopping with Maureen. She had him pick her up at her apartment and drive her to the malls in the Friendship Heights neighborhood to begin what he knew would be an all-day excursion. In between stops at H&M, Ann Taylor, and at least three fancy shoe stores, Maureen had him try on Bermuda shorts, golf shirts, and swim trunks. He wasn't particular about style--as long as the colors were navy blue or black--and would have bought the first ones that fit, but he knew better than to complain when Maureen couldn't decide which ones she liked on him until late in the day.

They had just finished perusing the clothing aisles at Saks Fifth Avenue and Maureen was deciding where they should stop for an early dinner, when Daniels' cell rang. He didn't recognize the number, but answered it anyway.

"Agent Daniels. This is Sharon Washburn. You might not be happy to hear from me, but you said I could call you if I had a problem and I do."

"I'm glad you called. What's up?"

"They won't let me into the farmhouse to get my clothes and things."

"Who won't?"

"They didn't identify themselves. I went there after work today and two guys in suits sitting in a huge SUV prevented me from going inside. I told them I just wanted to get my clothes and a few other things, but they said they had their instructions."

"Instructions from whom?"

"They wouldn't say. I don't have a lot of things there, but there's a necklace and a pair of earrings Ethan gave me that I just have to have."

"Okay, Miss Washburn. I'll try to help." He asked for her phone number and told her he'd get back to her.

First thing the next morning, Daniels put in a call to the lawyer whose name Edwin Palmer had given him to use if he needed legal advice or financial resources. Daniels told the receptionist his name was Joe Johnson, the code name on the back of Alexander Worthington's business card. "I need to meet with Mr. Worthington as soon as possible--preferably today."

"Mr. Worthington is not in today, and his schedule is entirely booked for the next several weeks, but we have an opening three weeks from--"

"I don't mean to be rude, miss, but would you please let Mr. Worthington know I called."

Although the receptionist took his contact information, Daniels didn't expect to hear from Worthington until Monday at the earliest. Less than an hour later, however, his phone rang from an unidentified number.

"Mr. Johnson. This is Alexander Worthington. How can I assist you?"

"Thank you for returning my call. I need to talk to you about a problem."

"What's the problem?"

"I'd rather not say over the phone."

"Very well. Can you come to my office this evening at seven?"

On the way to Worthington's K Street office, Daniels puzzled over how much to tell the lawyer. He decided not to make any references to the President. The fact that Worthington took his call and was willing to come in from wherever he had been strongly suggested he was ready to do whatever Daniels asked him.

Worthington was a partner in what was for D.C. a medium-sized law firm--one that would be the largest in many a city. It was obvious from the location and pictures on the wall in the reception area of men wearing wigs that they had been around for a long time. The sole female's photo was the wall's most recent addition. The furniture in the reception area was modern with lots of shiny metal, and it was not comfortable, which Daniels hoped meant he wouldn't have to wait long.

After ten minutes or so a heavy-set man of medium height in a white shirt with a red tie and suspenders came in the reception area. "Mr. Johnson, I presume."

Daniels stood up and accepted the man's handshake. He followed Worthington down a long corridor, surprised to see more than half of the offices occupied, despite its being after seven on a Friday evening.

Worthington ushered Daniels into a large corner office. The dark, mahogany desk in the center of the office was piled with books and folders. Framed family pictures lined the credenza behind the desk. Large photos of several recent U.S. presidents, including Edwin Palmer, were mounted on the wall. Worthington motioned to a couch under a large picture window overlooking K Street.

"Something to drink?" Worthington asked.

Daniels declined. When asked how he could help him, Daniels explained that Ethan Garvin's fiancé needed legal help to retrieve her personal belongings from the farmhouse in Fairfax County where Ethan had been living.

Worthington listened intently. "I can have a member of my firm meet with her tomorrow morning."

"Not you?"

"Since I'm known to be Edwin's personal attorney, it'll be better if my name isn't involved."

That made perfect sense.

To further protect their relationship, Worthington told Daniels to continue to use the code name whenever he called the office. He said he would start a file for the mythical Mr. Johnson as a person seeking guidance on setting up a trust. "But don't worry, you won't be billed."

Daniels called Sharon on his way to work to tell her he'd arranged for her to get legal advice about her problem. He also asked her to meet him at a nearby coffee shop after her meeting.

The next morning Daniels found a table near the back of the coffee shop where he was meeting Sharon Washburn. She came in looking somewhat agitated. Her navy blue suit looked out of place amongst the casual weekend crowd. She put her things on the table and stood in line for a soy latte and a ginger snap. Daniels was nursing a regular coffee to which he added a dollop of half and half--a concession to Maureen's warning that black coffee was probably the reason for his frequent acid indigestion.

"He's going to help me," she said when she sat down. "I told him I could pay, but he said it had been taken care of. Did you do that?"

"It's being taken care of by a friend," he responded.

"I'm not a charity case, Mr. Daniels."

"I didn't mean to imply you are."

"If you prefer we do it that way . . ."

"Let's see how things go," he told her. "Did the lawyer tell you what he's going to do?"

She nodded. "He said I have a legal right to recover my possessions and that he'll convey that to the Garvin family's lawyers."

"Good. Anything else?"

"He said we should have an answer in a day or two."

Daniels smiled trying to convey that sounded like a good outcome. "Meanwhile, I need to explain why I wanted to talk to you in person."

She looked up from her latte.

"The White House is very concerned about what happened to Ethan, but as I explained the other day, we can't go public with our concerns without risking a scandal which could mean we'd never find the truth, and the only way I can continue to help you is if you never tell anyone my name or that someone from the Secret Service is helping you."

"Oh, I didn't think of that."

"Did you already tell someone about me?"

"Not by name, but I told my boss the Secret Service had helped me go to the grave site when Ethan's parents tried to keep me away."

"That's it? Nothing about what happened afterwards?"

She shook her head.

"Good. If anyone questions you about that day, don't say anything about my talking to you at the diner, and certainly don't say anything about my helping you get your things back."

"Okay."

"We have to be careful about communicating with each other as well." Daniels took a cellphone out of his coat pocket and slid it across the table. "I added a second phone to my account today with its own number. I want you to use this phone whenever you need to talk to me. Never call me from your personal phone."

"But after I get my things, I won't bother you again. I promise."

"Miss Washburn--"

"Please call me Sharon."

"Sharon. I know you want to find out what happened to Ethan."

She started to tear up and for a minute, couldn't speak. "I can't believe he's really gone."

Daniels waited until she seemed to regain her composure. "I'd like to help you find the truth, but I can't be the public face for the reasons I've already explained."

"What do you want me to do?"

"Right now, let's see what happens with getting into the farmhouse. In addition to getting your things, I need you to see if you can find the briefcase you said Ethan was bringing to the White House. If it's missing, and if it wasn't in the car, that tells us something is amiss."

"What about his cellphone?" she asked.

"What do you mean?"

"He wouldn't go anywhere without his iPhone."

"I recall the White House telling me the police didn't find a cell either. So look for that too."

Before they parted, Sharon informed him she was leaving Wednesday to spend Thanksgiving with her family in Indiana, but would be back Monday night. It was unlikely she'd be allowed into the farmhouse before then, and that meant another week would probably go by before he knew where things stood with respect to the briefcase, and the president's deadline for his coming up with answers was less than two weeks away.

Late Monday, Daniels was surprised to see a call coming in from the phone he'd given to Sharon.

"Did you hear from the lawyer already?" he inquired.

"Yes," she replied. "The bottom line is they still won't let me in the farmhouse. I have to submit a list of items I claim I left there with proof such as a purchase receipt."

"What did the lawyer say about that?"

"He went to a local judge to try to prevent them from removing anything from the farmhouse until I've had a chance to get my things. A hearing is scheduled for tomorrow morning."

Daniels was pleased things were moving faster than expected. Maybe she'd be able to go into the farmhouse before she left for Indiana. On the other hand he needed a back-up plan. If she was not allowed in, he had to find another way to determine whether Ethan's death was accidental or intentional. What kept cropping up in his mind was "what caused the accident?" He needed to see the Fairfax County Police Department's accident report and, assuming one had been performed, the autopsy report. He doubted those documents were available to the public when the victim was an average citizen, much less the son of the President-elect. Further, given the Garvin family did not recognize Sharon as Ethan's fiancé, they'd probably get away with denying her access to the reports as well.

Could Attorney Worthington help? All he could do was ask.

Monday, November 20

Daniels was frustrated. When he tried to reach Alexander Worthington, he was informed Worthington had left for a family Thanksgiving in the Caribbean and would not be back until the following Monday. He left a message, but with no alternative in sight, he began to research online who to contact in Fairfax County to learn whether the public had any right to access police department accident reports and autopsies. While doing the research an email came in from Sharon. A free-lance reporter by the name of Randy Dodd contacted her through her lawyer to see if he could interview her after the next day's court hearing. She wasn't sure what to do. "Absolutely, do it," Daniels replied, "but let's meet someplace first and talk things over."

Daniels suggested they meet him at the Starbucks in Pentagon City, a short walk from the local Metro stop. Carrying a chai tea latte, Sharon had no trouble finding where he was seated at a small table near the front. "How did this morning's hearing go?"

"So, so. Can you believe this: the attorney representing Ethan's parents questioned whether I was Ethan's fiancé. He said no notice of engagement had been submitted to the regular or social media. Well, so what?"

"What did your lawyer say?"

"He argued the ring Ethan had given me seven months before his death was an engagement ring. To back that up, he submitted a statement taken from the owner of the store where Ethan purchased the ring. The owner swore that Ethan told him it was for his fiancé."

"Did that work?"

Sharon got red in the face. "Guess what that bastard said next."

"Their lawyer?"

She nodded. "He told the judge the fact I had a ring on my finger was not proof that Ethan and I were engaged. He even had the nerve to say I might have taken it without Ethan's knowledge."

Daniels shook his head. "How slimy can you get!"

Sharon's face told him what she thought of the lawyer's statement. "I almost stood up and demanded he take it back."

"I can't imagine the judge bought that line," Daniels said.

"She didn't. She took all of thirty seconds to make her decision," Sharon said with a grin. "She ruled I could keep the ring as well as the necklace Ethan gave me after his parents objected to our announcing our engagement during the campaign."

"What about accessing the farmhouse?"

She pursed her mouth in a frown. "Unfortunately, she accepted the Garvins' arrangement that requires me to submit a list of my belongings rather than enter the building."

"Too bad."

"I know, but she said I don't have to provide proof of purchase for items that are clearly mine, such as jewelry, clothing, make-up, and any item that has my name on it."

Sharon's being denied access to the farmhouse could mean he'd never learn whether Ethan had taken the briefcase with him that morning. The outcome of the hearing wasn't a total loss, however, since it had gotten a reporter's attention. Perhaps the reporter would get answers he couldn't get on his own.

"Let's go over how you're going to sell your story that Ethan was murdered," he said.

"I don't mean to be ungrateful, Mr. Daniels," she said, "but I do this all the time for my job."

He recalled she told him she was a communications specialist for a business association, but he had no idea what a communications specialist did. "Sorry. So, what do you plan to tell him?"

"I'll say Ethan told me if anything happened to him he loved me and had tried to protect me."

"That's good, but shouldn't you start off by telling the reporter when the conversation took place," Daniels interjected.

She gave him a stern look. "I meant after I told him that."

She sure is testy. "Right. When did he say it?"

"The Friday before the election. We were supposed to meet for dinner, but he called me at work to say he couldn't make it. That's when he said that."

"Did you ask him what he meant?"

"He said he couldn't talk, but he'd tell me the next day as we were planning to spend Saturday evening together."

"Did you ask him when you got together?"

"Not exactly. When I got to the farmhouse, he was pacing around like a caged beast. I asked what was bothering him. He hesitated for a moment, and it seemed like he was going to say one thing, but changed his mind. What he finally said was he was nervous because the polls had his father so far ahead."

"So, you never asked him directly what he meant by something happening to him?"

She didn't answer right away as two people settled in a nearby table. "I wasn't sure I wanted to know," she said in a quiet voice.

Daniels looked around acknowledging the fact they might be overheard. "Don't blame yourself," he said softly. "Is that the only reason you think he might have been killed?"

"I know he wouldn't have been speeding around that corner. He knew that section of the road was dangerous. You come up over a hill and make a sharp turn, but there hasn't been a guardrail since the county started doing some work in that area. He even called the county highway department about it."

"That's important. It's something the reporter should be able to check. Anything else?"

"Ethan's parents made it clear I wasn't allowed anywhere near the campaign, so on the night of the election I stayed at my apartment watching the results and occasionally texting with Ethan. He didn't get back to the farmhouse until after three a.m., but I had the next day off, so I drove up there around noon. When I arrived he was on the phone with his father. When he got off, he told me his father assigned him to coordinate the inauguration ceremony with the White House, and he was going to go to the White House that afternoon to get started."

Daniels sipped on his coffee. "Go on."

She put down her pen and looked up. "I just remembered something I thought was odd at the time."

"What?"

"When he called me after they'd won the election he was excited and proud, but the next day he was in a strange mood when I arrived at the farmhouse."

"How so?"

"I found him in the living room when I got up. The news was on the TV, but the sound was off and he was staring out the front window."

"What was he looking at?" Daniels asked.

"All you can see from that window is lots of trees."

"That doesn't tell me much."

"I'm trying here."

"I know."

"Wait," she said. "Now I remember what I was going to tell you. I offered him a penny for his thoughts. He turned and just for a second gave me this strange, sad look, which reminded me of the previous time when I think he wanted to tell me what was going on, but then he seemed to change his mind and suggested we go out for brunch."

That wasn't much to go on. "I don't think you should mention that to the reporter. Not unless Ethan said what was bothering him."

She nodded. "Of course not. I was just trying to remember if he said anything else . . ."

Daniels was concerned she didn't have enough to go on to get the reporter interested in pursuing the murder angle. "Did he ever talk about someone on the campaign who he didn't get along with or who didn't seem to trust him?"

She flipped a stray hair off her face. "Let me think. I remember Ethan saying Amy Marx, the campaign manager, didn't like it when his father included him on discussions of sensitive issues. Oh, and he couldn't understand why one guy was even there--"

"Whoa. Who did he say that about?"

"There was an Asian Ethan said everyone referred to as 'Mr. Z' because that was easier than pronouncing his name."

"He told you he couldn't understand why this Mr. Z was on the team."

She nodded. "More like why he was hanging around."

"Can you remember the man's real name?"

"That's the only name I heard."

"Okay. I'll see if I can find out who he is."

"Anyone else?"

"Can't think of anyone."

Daniels had another thought. "Did Ethan keep any kind of record of the things he did on the campaign or of the campaign itself?"

"Like what?"

"Like a diary?"

"I don't think so. He told me he had been warned not to post anything online their opponents could use against them."

Daniels pondered what to ask next.

"Are you thinking someone on the campaign may have killed Ethan?" Sharon asked.

"I don't have a theory at this point. I'm just trying to help you build a case so this reporter will investigate."

They sat in silence for a bit before he remembered he had something to tell her.

"By the way, I spoke to an attorney this morning. I wanted to know if there was some way we could get copies of the accident report and the autopsy. Unfortunately, they're not available to the general public. He said he'd check if you could see them being Ethan's fiancé, but he doubted it."

He waited while she wrote that on her note pad.

She looked up. "Do we know if they did an autopsy?"

"I believe it's mandatory. The accident report would reveal the cause of the accident; the autopsy would reveal the cause of death."

Daniels paused seeing Sharon had turned away.

She took a deep breath and reached into her pocketbook for some tissues. "I think I'm dealing with it, but then..."

"You don't have to apologize," Daniels said. He wondered if he should be discussing these things with her, but she was his only connection to the reporter, and he needed every bit of information he could get.

She wiped her eyes and took a deep breath. "Go on. I'm listening."

Daniels gave her his best warm smile. "Tell me if I'm going someplace you're not ready to talk about."

"No, please. I want to do this. I want to prove Ethan didn't drive off that damn road like a teenager."

"Okay, then. That's what you should tell the reporter. Say Ethan knew to go slow around that curve and you can't see how he would have driven off the road."

She wrote that down.

"He should also try to learn if they found any mechanical issues concerning the car. Was the accident caused by a blown tire, did the steering wheel lock up, or was there some other problem with the car? The point is you've got to convince this reporter until someone produces science-backed proof that it was an accident, you believe Ethan was a murder victim."

On his drive home Daniels thought about how he would react to Sharon's story if he were a journalist. It would be of interest because of the subject, but a good reporter would want to know why someone would want to kill Ethan Garvin. That, however, was the one subject Daniels didn't feel comfortable talking to Sharon about. He was still not convinced that Ethan was in his right mind and didn't want to consider what would happen if it got out the U.S. Secret Service was investigating a rumor that Ethan was calling out his father when later it was determined he was off his rocker.

Sharon called Daniels after she'd met with the reporter.

"Good news," she said. "Mr. Dodd told me he would look into the unanswered questions concerning Ethan's death. I could tell he didn't quite believe me about Ethan being murdered, but I think I gave him enough information to perk his interest."

"Let's hope this guy is good at what he does. Did he say when he would get back to you?"

"No. He just asked if it was okay to call me back if he had further questions."

"Good. Then all we can do is wait."

In truth, they couldn't wait. Nagging in the front of his mind was the fact that the inauguration would take place in eight weeks and he felt no closer to having an answer than the day he started.

Wednesday, November 23

"Not again!"

Even though he'd been smart enough to extend the phone an arm's length, Maureen's reaction to his telling her to put their Thanksgiving plans on hold almost burst his eardrum. He had just been informed that President Palmer had requested that he be part of the detail accompanying him to the nationally televised Thanksgiving Day football game between the Washington Commanders and the Dallas Cowboys.

"Again," was the only word he could muster.

"Well, you tell Edwin Palmer I'm not voting for him ever again."

"That's my girl," he said, relieved she saw the humor in the situation. He, on the other hand, didn't see anything funny in Palmer's request. He was pretty certain the President would ask for an update on the investigation and he hated to have to tell him he'd been working on it for nearly two weeks and hadn't made it to first base.

His suspicion was confirmed the next afternoon when he arrived at the Commanders' stadium. Palmer had agreed to do the coin flip at the start of the game and Daniels was one of four agents chosen to accompany him onto the field. Having four agents join the President on the field seemed to be overkill, given that the latest weapon-detecting magnetometers had been used to screen people coming into the stadium and counterassault teams were strategically stationed at various levels of the stadium some watching the stands, others focused on potential drone appearances.

Daniels suspected Palmer had included him to ask about the investigation, and he was right. On the way to the bullet-proof owner's box after he executed the coin flip flawlessly, the President told the other three agents to go ahead and asked Daniels to wait with him at the sub-basement elevator entrance for their all-clear.

"We've only got a minute," Palmer said after the others had left. "Tell me what you've learned."

"The bottom line, sir, is that I've yet to recover what Ethan Garvin was planning to bring you or find any evidence suggesting he was mentally unbalanced and made it all up."

"That's not good enough, Agent Daniels. I need to know one way or the other. What are you doing to figure this out?"

"For one, I'm going to try to persuade the media to investigate--"

Palmer shook a finger at him. "You can't tell the media what I told you."

Daniels raised his hands. "No, of course not, but--"

"Time's a wasting, Agent Daniels. Don't forget Alexander Worthington will finance whatever you need. Just get it done."

On the elevator ride to the owners' level, Daniels promised to have more to report to him the next time they spoke.

Just as the door was about to open, Daniels remembered a question he wanted to ask. "Mr. President. The first time you talked you said the police didn't find Ethan's briefcase in the car--is that right?"

"Correct. No briefcase, no computer, nothing."

"What about his cellphone? His girlfriend said he never went anywhere without it."

Palmer remained in the elevator for a second as the door opened. "I'm pretty sure none was found, but I'm not sure I can check without raising questions I don't have good answers for."

"I understand."

Palmer patted him on the shoulder as he exited the elevator. "I'm counting on you, Agent Daniels. America is counting on you."

As he drove home that evening, Daniels thought about Ethan Garvin's promised evidence. What had made him suspicious of his father in the first place? Perhaps he overheard an incriminating phone conversation. If he had evidence he was bringing to Palmer, there must be a paper trail. Given there was little chance he could access Ethan's digital devices, Daniels knew he'd have to find another way to discover what Ethan was planning on bringing to the White House. Not only didn't he know how he was going to do that, but there were other questions he couldn't answer--starting with why the police hadn't found Ethan's briefcase or cell phone in the wreckage?

Another problem was he couldn't access Ethan's personal digital assistant or computer. The family would have removed those items from the farmhouse by now, but he knew enough about information storage to know that it was difficult to get rid of all traces of information once it had been digitized. If only he had the authority to ask the FBI or NSA to do a search for him, but neither option was in the cards. As an alternative, Daniels needed to find a computer whiz willing to break a few laws.

By the time he pulled into his parking space, Daniels knew he had no choice but to make the phone call he'd hesitated making from the first day President Palmer had dumped the mess in his lap. Unfortunately, the person he knew who could help him with the research would probably not take his call. Daniels' last attempt to reconcile with his only son had been a disaster. His ears burned at the memory of being told never to try to get in touch with him again.

He knew it was past time he tried to re-establish contact, even if Trey Daniels were not employed by the National Security Administration. A graduate of Carnegie Mellon University, Trey had gotten into programming while in elementary school. He won all kinds of awards in high school and earned a full scholarship to CMU. The problem was his mother had left when Trey was eleven, and his relationship with his son had gone from stormy to under water.

He didn't know where Trey lived, nor did he have his phone number or his email address. The only sure way he knew to reach his son was through his ex. That meant he had to convince her to contact their son on his behalf. Given her reaction the last time they spoke, which amounted to a dressing down that would make Marine drill sergeants proud, he looked forward to that call as much as he looked forward to prepping for a colonoscopy.

"Ouch," he said, after slapping his forehead loudly. *I've got to stop doing that.* It was Friday morning and Daniels had just hung up on a conversation with Sharon Washburn. She had called from her home in Indiana where she was spending the Thanksgiving weekend to let him know she'd heard from Randy Dodd, the free-lance reporter.

"He asked me again who might have wanted Ethan dead. I couldn't give him a good answer."

It was as Daniels had feared. "We need to dig up something that we can give him."

"What?"

"Let's discuss it the next time we meet. Meanwhile, we can't just rely on one reporter. If I give you a list of names, will you call each one to try to get them interested?"

"Sure," she said, "but can it wait until I get back to D.C.?"

"Of course. It would be difficult to reach them this weekend anyway."

Daniels had already started researching the D.C. region news media. He'd come up with a list of newspaper reporters they could try to interest in investigating Ethan's death, then added the local TV stations to his list. They needed someone to start digging yesterday and couldn't afford to be choosy.

As he thought about finding who to contact at each station, it occurred to him rather than call the main number he should see if he could find the video clips of each station's coverage of Ethan's death. That way he could give Sharon the names of the reporters who had been on the scene.

Not surprisingly, all four local TV stations had covered the funeral. As he watched each of the segments, he copied down the names of the reporters, and then tried to look up their contact information on the station websites. In each case, however, the local stations had used feeds featuring network reporters rather than sending their own people to Ohio. He knew that was due to the restrictions the Secret Service had imposed on media presence at the event. If he wanted to give Sharon the names of local reporters who might be interested in looking into Ethan's death, he needed to learn who covered the accident. That's when he discovered that none of the stations kept news stories on their websites past one week.

At the end of the afternoon, Daniels called Sharon to report on his progress. "When I started calling the TV stations to see if there was a way to access older stories, the first two said no, but a receptionist at the third station told me to try a website that archived TV news stories."

"I could have told you that."

"In any case, I found links to dozens of stories about Ethan's death, including segments that reported from the accident scene that had been produced by the four local D.C. stations."

"Give me their names and I'll contact them," Sharon said.

"Will do, but one of them stood out. You might want to contact her first."

"Which one?"

"Cynthia Renfro from Channel 5. The segments from channels 4, 7, and 9 were pretty much the same. Each showed a reporter standing in front of the yellow police tape telling the audience the shocking news of Ethan's death. They focused on the fact that the victim was the son of the president-elect, but reported almost nothing about the accident itself.

None of them quoted any officials about the possible cause."

The segment from Channel 5, the local Fox affiliate, had prompted another head slap, but this one was not to punish, but Daniels' admittedly weird way of congratulating himself. The report by Renfro had included details the others failed to report.

"One of the officers here at the scene," Renfro told viewers, "told us from the tire marks it looks like the driver lost control of the vehicle. Therefore they are labeling the accident suspicious and will conduct a thorough investigation."

Not only had Renfro provided information none of the other stations had mentioned, but she had the camera zoom in on tire tracks. That didn't help Daniels since he was not versed in accident investigation, but it could prove valuable. It also strengthened Daniels' desire to get access to the Fairfax County Police Department's accident report. Knowing the accident was initially labeled suspicious gave him a shiny nugget he hoped would encourage Randy Dodd, Cynthia Renfro, and perhaps other reporters to dig further.

"The officer Renfro quoted did not appear in the segment that aired on the accident," Daniels told Sharon, "nor did she mention his name, but I know enough about journalism to know she must have written it down. It is even possible she followed up, although I haven't found any other on-air segments on the accident. Please try to reach her today if you can."

"I will," Sharon said, "but keep in mind it's Black Friday, Renfro is probably out at some mall interviewing shoppers."

Convincing the Fox reporter everyone had missed a major story was starting to seem like a long shot. Daniels didn't feel like he was making progress fast enough. It might take a half dozen reporters investigating before they started getting answers. On the other hand, public awareness that the president-elect's son was a possible murder victim could shake things up and might even get people who had the answers he was looking for to come forward.

He slapped himself on the forehead once again--gently this time. Maybe something's up there after all.

"I'm going to try to reach my son," Daniels told Maureen Friday evening after stuffing himself on a turkey, yams, and sausage stuffing--their Thanksgiving dinner a day late due to his having had to join President Palmer at the football game.

A piece of pumpkin pie sat on the coffee table in front of the TV waiting for his eyes to tell him what his stomach would deny--i.e., that there was room for seconds.

The TV was tuned to the opening minutes of a basketball game between the Washington Wizards and the Cleveland Cavaliers, but which teams were playing was the farthest thing from Daniels mind.

Maureen, who'd been putting food away, came and sat next to him on the couch. "What brought that on?"

She knew the history of his attempts to re-establish a relationship with Trey, like the time they were supposed to meet for dinner. He'd been held up at work, and had been unable to call. When he finally got to a phone, Trey had already left the restaurant. That was three years ago and they hadn't talked since.π

"I could have a grandchild by now," he said. "I deserve to know, don't I?"

Maureen gave him a sympathetic smile. "That's up to the parents."

"I suppose. Still I feel like crap every time I think about the fact my son didn't invite me to his wedding and now won't even talk to me."

"Then that's what you need to tell him."

"The problem is I don't have his number."

Maureen gave him a quizzical look.

"It's unlisted, which means I've got to try to get it from my ex."

"Call her," she said, taking his empty pie plate back to the kitchen.

She was right, but instead of doing so he sat there watching the game. At half time he took his empty coffee mug into the kitchen where Maureen was reading a novel. The coffee pot was empty. He contemplated brewing another.

"Did you call her?" Maureen asked.

Daniels looked at the clock on her stove. "It's probably too late. I'll do it tomorrow."

"Eugene!"

"Oh, all right," he moaned.

"Stop being such a cry baby. What's the worst she can do?"

"You don't want to know," he said retreating into the living room in search for his cell phone.

"Sharp residence," a man answered when Daniels finally dialed his ex's number.

"George? This is Tucker Daniels. Is my ex available?"

Silence. "Hold on, Daniels." Silence.

"What's it about? She's busy," Alysia's second husband, George Thompson, asked when he got back on the phone.

"I need to reach my son, but don't have his number. My insurance company needs some information." A lie, but he couldn't tell them the truth.

Silence. "Hold on." Silence.

After a couple of minutes passed during which Daniels could hear his ex-wife and her current husband arguing, Alysia came on the line. "What's this about, Tucker?"

"I need to talk to Trey. Can I have his phone number?"

"He doesn't want to hear from you. Can't you get that through your thick head?"

"Alysia. Let's not argue. Please just give me--."

"Stop! He doesn't want--"

"Okay, Alysia. How about this? Tell him I need to speak with him and ask him to call me."

Daniels relayed the substance of the conversation to Maureen.

"She hung up after I said that."

"She's a piece of work, Tucker. How did you ever--"

"Marry her? Good question. We were both young and we both liked dancing in the dark."

"Hmm! That hasn't changed."

Daniels had to laugh. He shook his head. "You must be God's way of paying me back."

"How's that?" Maureen asked.

"I got the raw end of the deal the first time; so, God sent me an angel."

Maureen looked at him like he'd lost his mind. "God's got more important things to do than balance the scales of your love life."

Tucker pulled Maureen over to him and kissed her on the forehead. "Still. I feel pretty damn lucky."

"The question is whether your son is going to call you."

Daniels sobered up with that reminder. "True enough." He realized he hadn't told Maureen why he wanted to talk to Trey. She probably assumed the holidays made him miss contact with his only offspring when the truth of the matter was that Daniels needed him desperately, the President needed him, the country needed him, and he didn't know what he'd do if Trey didn't return the call.

Monday, November 27

"That's the answer," Daniels told Maureen, but only in his mind. He couldn't say it out loud because then he'd have to explain later on why her suggestion didn't result in their being able to spend more time together before he retired.

What she had asked as he was leaving her apartment Monday morning, was didn't he have a lot of unused personal time. Bingo. He did, but he couldn't let her think they'd let him use it. "Normally they don't let you use personal time so close to your retirement date," he told her, "but I'll ask anyway."

Maureen had also mentioned that he looked like he hadn't been getting a lot of sleep lately, which was true. Not only was he putting in his daytime regular shift, but he was up late most evenings working at his computer or running off to some "important staff meeting," which was the excuse he used whenever he needed to meet with Sharon Washburn.

If he convinced Personnel to allow him to use some of his accumulated personal days--which indeed he had plenty of--he could work days on the investigation, except that created a different set of problems. If he worked from his apartment, it would be difficult to keep Maureen from wondering what he was working on and that was the last thing he wanted.

Daniels could just imagine the conversation. 'Honey, I'm investigating whether the man we just elected President of the United States had his son murdered so he could betray America to China.' She'd be out the door faster than butter melts on toast.

Maybe he could still make it work. If he took some of his accumulated time, he'd have to pretend he was still going to work, but instead of going into the office, he'd go someplace where he could work on the investigation.

As he mulled the problem over, answers started fitting together like the last pieces of a jigsaw puzzle. He did have a place he could go to work-- the apartment President Palmer had told him was available for his use. It belonged to Mrs. Palmer, but was listed under her maiden name. It was also in a great location--just off Dupont Circle in the heart of the District.

He would have to check out the apartment itself before committing to that plan. Just thinking over that scenario raised additional questions. Would a middle-aged black man going in and out of Mrs. Palmer's apartment draw unwelcome attention? Maybe calls to the local police? What would he tell them if they knocked on the apartment door? "The President of the United States said it was okay for me to use his wife's apartment." Now who would buy that?

Another problem was that he couldn't move his computer there without Maureen's wondering why. He'd have to buy a new one.

At least he wouldn't have to use his own funds. He could count on Alexander Worthington to cover the cost.

On another positive note, Sharon emailed that she was meeting with Cynthia Renfro later that day at the TV station. Daniels would have liked to go with her, but he couldn't figure out a way to explain his presence, even using his Joe Johnson alias. He could pretend to be her lawyer, but a good reporter would check. Nor could he go as a friend. What white twenty-something female has a black fifty-something friend?

Daniels felt encouraged that there might be a way for him to get more involved in the investigation by using his personal time, but it seemed that wouldn't resolve all of the obstacles he faced trying to make headway. He still would have to rely on Sharon to be the public face of the investigation in order not to compromise his position, not to mention the President's, and he still had to lie to Maureen to keep her out of the know.

Two days later, as he sat in front of the newly purchased computer equipment in Mrs. Palmer's apartment, not for the first time in recent days, he wanted to kick himself for being so fearful about contacting his son. He was on hold with Dell customer support in front of the system he'd purchased with the credit card that Alexander Worthington had provided him with "Joe Johnson's" bank account. The tasks that had to be performed before he could get to work, including hooking up to the wireless printer and getting online access, would have taken his son ten minutes or less. He'd been at it for the past hour, and despite having asked his ex to call Trey for him, he hadn't heard back.

He couldn't call his son at work at the National Security Administration. Not only had Trey told him never to do so, but what he wanted Trey to help him with might turn out to be traceable and therefore could only be conveyed in person.

Daniels was about to hang up the phone and ask the building super if he knew anyone who was good with computers, when his turn with Dell customer support arrived. Thirty minutes later he was online and ready to get to work.

He was still amazed at how fast Alexander Worthington had responded to his list of requested items. It seemed he knew what Daniels was going to ask before he did.

"Continue using the Joe Johnson alias," Worthington told him. "I've already set up a bank account in that name with a $25,000 balance. It also comes with a credit card with a $25,000 limit. Do you think that will be enough?"

Daniels didn't know how the lawyer had come up with a social security number that didn't raise red flags all over the District, and he didn't want to find out. He'd been nervous when he signed 'Joe Johnson' on the sales slip for the computer, but the transaction had gone through. Now he was sitting in Charlotte Palmer's furnished, but unoccupied, unit in a luxury apartment complex near Dupont Circle, about to take the next step in what still seemed like a hopelessly impossible investigation.

The next day he left a text for Maureen that he had an evening Secret Service meeting, when in reality, he was heading to the Dupont Circle apartment to meet with Sharon Washburn.

Instead of trying to find new meeting places where no one would pay attention to a fiftyish black male engaged in what seemed like an intimate conversation with a twentyish white female, she agreed to come to the apartment.

It seemed Mrs. Palmer's apartment might work out. Despite the time it took to commute from his apartment in Alexandria, the location was ideal in terms of anonymity. The building even provided underground parking--a huge problem in that area of the city. When he presented himself to the security desk at the building's entrance, they indicated they had been expecting his arrival and would do everything they could to protect his privacy. Another contribution from Alexander Worthington? If so, fine. As long as Mr. Worthington kept opening doors, he'd go through them.

While waiting for Sharon, he went over in his mind for the umpteenth time his recent conversation with Maureen in which he'd tried to finesse the personal time issue. He wondered if it could have gone any worse.

"I did what you suggested," he told her. "I applied to take some of my unused personal time, but was told I would only be allowed to take one day a week."

"Why's that?" she asked.

"They claim they're understaffed."

Maureen dropped the subject, but Daniels was worried that she hadn't bought his story. While it was consistent with the Secret Service personnel practices she was used to, he wasn't sure he presented it in as matter-of-fact manner as he intended. If his body language gave him away,

Maureen might start to wonder what he was up to and that would not be good.

Security called from the lobby. Sharon had arrived, but not only had she been forty-five minutes late, but before he could get her to sit down so they could talk business, she took the liberty of wandering around the apartment opening cabinet doors, gushing over the furnishings and peeking in closets. All he cared about was that there was a desk for his new computer and printer, a refrigerator, and a microwave. He found a single cup coffee machine in a cupboard, although he probably wouldn't bother buying coffee for it, as there was a coffee shop down the block that was open twenty-four seven.

He finally got Sharon to sit at the kitchen counter. He was working on a large coffee, and let her try out the fancy red tea kettle after choosing from an assortment of tea bags the renters had left behind.

"How'd it go with Cynthia Renfro?" he asked, impatient to get down to business.

"I went to their building and they taped the interview, but she couldn't tell me when they were going to air it."

"What kind of questions did she ask?"

"She started out asking me why I wasn't satisfied with the police version of what happened to Ethan. I explained about his knowing about that curve where his car left the road and that I didn't think he'd be speeding. At the end, she said it was up to her editors as to whether they'd play the interview on the air. When I asked her about researching some of the unanswered questions, she said it would be up to her assignment editor. In the end, she said to call her if I came up with any more details."

Daniels waited until Sharon poured her tea and came back to the table. "Did you ask her if she followed through on her initial report that the accident had been labeled suspicious?"

"She said her editor told her not to bother."

"I wonder why? In any case, did you tell her someone else was already looking into the accident?"

Sharon shook her head. "I didn't think that was a good idea. I thought she might go with the story if she thought she had an exclusive."

"You may be right," Daniels replied, finishing off his coffee, "but if her editor knew someone else was investigating your claim, that might convince them to air the interview to beat the competition."

Sharon pushed a strand of hair out of her eyes. "In any case, she said the list of stories she was working on was already pretty long, and even if she got the okay from her editor, she doubted she'd get a chance to do anything for a week."

"Damn. We can't wait that long."

"Why?"

"Why what?" Daniels had been thinking what to do next.

"Why can't we wait?"

It occurred to him she didn't know why time was critical, but he wasn't ready to tell her and had to make up a reason. "The further away from the event the harder it is to get people's attention, especially now with the holidays coming up."

"I know all that. I thought there might be some other reason."

He had to change the subject. "Did you make the calls to the other reporters?"

"Speaking of which I've got some news."

"What's that?"

"I took a leave from my job."

Surprised at her decision, he didn't know what to say.

"It's not that I didn't enjoy the work. I truly did, but this is more important."

"I see."

Sharon seemed to sense he needed further explanation. "I couldn't make or receive calls from my office. That made it hard to reach people."

"True."

"Aren't you pleased?"

"Pleased that you want to work on this fulltime? Of course."

That didn't seem to satisfy. "You don't sound it."

"I just didn't expect it. That's all."

Sharon got up and walked over to the stove to pour more hot water over her tea bag.

"Really, I'm glad to hear it," he said. Privately he wondered whether having her around all the time would be an asset or a hindrance. He didn't need to have to explain every detail and find things for her to do while he was conducting the investigation, but she had a strong incentive to find answers he reminded himself. Of course, that could cut both ways. Being so emotionally involved, as she was, could be dangerous. A good investigator has to be impartial to distinguish fact from fancy.

Sharon truly believed Ethan had been done in by other than his own foibles. Daniels wasn't convinced, but he didn't see how he could deny her the opportunity to prove her case.

She came back and sat down. "It means I can come here every day and make phone calls and do things like go to offices to file freedom of information requests."

He was beginning to see the potential. Wasn't he complaining the other day he needed help? He decided to be supportive. "That will be a big help, but . . ."

"But what?"

"We need to work as a team. No free-lancing."

She looked at him like a teenager who'd just been told her curfew was ten p.m. He needed to make her feel more like a team member. "Just check with me if you want to pursue a lead."

"Of course," she replied, although her face was red.

"Welcome aboard," Daniels said raising his coffee cup.

She raised her tea mug in response and gave him a half smile. "By the way, did you see the story in today's *Post* about Henry Garvin?"

"Which one?"

She pulled a page from the *Washington Examiner* out of her purse and unfolded it in front of him. She had drawn a big circle around the page-three story. "It seems he has been letting his wife and his staff set up his government."

"Why do you think that is?"

"I don't know, but I wonder if it's because he hasn't gotten over Ethan's death?"

He knew Sharon hadn't either. "I guess everyone deals with grief in their own way."

"Listen to this," she said, reading from the article, "An unnamed source says that Katherine Garvin--not her husband--is making key personnel decisions."

Daniels thought about that for a moment. "Do you think that could be right?"

"It sounds like Ethan's mother. She's a first class b-i-t-c-h. She was extremely cold to me, but then again I wasn't the person she hoped her son would marry."

"Why was that?"

"My parents are big-time Republicans. When we were dating in college, I didn't think those things would matter, but my father had a run-in with Ethan's mom over the choice of commencement speakers. I always thought that was why Ethan didn't call me after graduation, even though we'd been dating since our sophomore year."

"So, he stopped dating you to please his mother?"

"I never asked him outright, but I always wondered if that wasn't the reason."

"And the story in the *Examiner*. Are they implying that Henry Garvin is so shook up by Ethan's death that he can't function and his wife is taking over the show?"

"Not in so many words," she answered. "That's me speculating."

"But why? Of course it was devastating, but he's got a country to run."

"What if he holds himself responsible?"

"Again, I have to ask why would he feel that way."

"I can't give you a rational answer, Mr. Daniels, but remember I told you they had a strange relationship this past year."

He thought about that. "Both were under a lot of pressure."

"I get that, but wouldn't you experience more than a few sleepless nights if you felt you did something that contributed to your son's death?"

"You're right, of course," he said. "Let me think about it. Meanwhile, let's get down to work. I've got a list of additional newspaper and TV reporters I'd like you to contact."

Sharon waited for him to hand her the print-out. "Is it okay if I go into the other room when I make the calls. I'd be nervous with you listening."

"Sure, I've got my own work to do."

After less than two hours she said she was too tired to make any more calls.

Daniels didn't object. He didn't want to chew her out the first day on the job. "Can you meet me here tomorrow at eleven?"

"Why so late? I can be here at nine . . . or nine-thirty."

He tapped his pencil on the desk. "I've got to stop at headquarters to sign some papers. They've granted me the right to take some of my accumulated personal time. Turns out I'm working fulltime on this as well."

Sharon brightened. "With both of us working on it, we're sure to get to the bottom of this, don't you think?"

He smiled broadly, although in truth he wasn't so sure. All the lies he'd been telling to prevent people from being harmed by their involvement in what might turn out to be a wild turkey chase were beginning to drag on him. It seemed the old bromide about little lies gradually becoming big ones meant he was spending too much time covering up and not enough time getting answers.

Monday, December 4

More frustrations. The goal of that morning's Internet searches confirmed what a lawyer at Alexander Worthington's firm told him concerning the public's right to obtain copies of police accident reports or autopsies. They had none. The Fairfax County website offered procedure one could use to justify the need to see a report, but that discovery was rendered useless given the time it would take for such a request to be processed.

More bad news came from Sharon. She heard from Randy Dodd that the Garvins had filed a motion to suppress the accident report and autopsy.

"On what grounds?" Daniels asked.

"Dodd said he'd forward me their filing."

Then he got even worse news. Channel 5 reporter Cynthia Renfro let Sharon know that her editors had decided against airing the interview and also vetoed her spending any time investigating Sharon's claims.

"She said to contact me if we came up with some hard evidence," Sharon said sheepishly as if it had been her fault.

"This is beginning to piss me off," Daniels mumbled.

"There's got to be some way we can find out what's in those reports," Sharon said between munches on a salad she'd brought to the apartment.

He shook his head. "I'm afraid that's a dead-end."

"Can't you ask the President to help?"

"As I said once or twice before, he can't risk it unless we can show him some hard evidence that it would be worth chancing being called on the carpet by Henry Garvin."

She moaned. "They all want us to produce evidence, but won't help us get it."

"I know it seems that way, but we still have options. I'm going to go through my lists. Why don't you continue to try to drum up some additional media interest?"

He spent the next hour going over his notes looking for any angle he might have overlooked. "The car," he said banging his fist on the desk. "Has Dodd tried to see the car?" he called to Sharon.

"What good would that do?" Sharon answered from the kitchen where she was doing her media research.

He got up and walked into the kitchen.

"You never know when some detail will change an understanding of a situation." The day before the Fairfax County Police had issued a brief statement attributing Ethan's death to 'driver error.' "We have no idea what caused them to conclude the accident was caused by driver error. Perhaps looking at the car will give us some clues."

"Do you think he was being chased?"

"Possibly. We won't know what a close examination of the car might reveal unless someone takes a look."

"Okay. I'll email him that he should do that."

"The car was probably declared a total loss. That means it will eventually be taken to some junkyard and sold as scrap. Dodd should be able to find it."

Sharon typed away on the laptop he had purchased for her use while at the apartment. "I'm sending him a note."

Daniels got up and went into the kitchen. "That brings up another possibility. In order for the insurance company to declare the car a loss, someone had to have looked at it."

"The insurance company?"

"Yes, they employ accident investigators to determine how much the company should pay out. We need to talk to whoever looked at Ethan's car, but I've no idea how we find the right person."

"Another dead-end?"

"Not necessarily. I'll call your lawyer. Maybe he can help us."

Daniels' call to Aaron Baker, the lawyer who helped Sharon get her belongings back, went to voice mail. When Baker called back late that afternoon he denied any knowledge about how to find which insurance investigator had inspected Ethan's car.

"I'll have to ask Mr. Worthington to find someone else who can help us," Daniels told Baker, "because the only reason I can figure for the family to have taken extra steps to prevent public access to those documents is they're trying to hide something."

That got a quick reaction. "That's preposterous," Baker said. "Preventing the public from getting the accident report and autopsy is designed to protect the family's privacy--not to cover up something politically damaging."

"Then help us prove that," Daniels stated.

Baker relented. He promised not only to find out which company insured Ethan's car, but also whether an investigation had been conducted and if so, by whom.

They didn't hear back from Baker until Wednesday. "The company that insured Ethan Garvin's car hired an independent investigator to confirm the car was totaled. I can give you the man's name and contact information if you insist on pursuing this wild goose chase. It's my judgment that you'll discover there was nothing to hide other than a tragic death at too young an age."

Sharon should be the one to call the investigator, Daniels decided. Hearing from the fiancé of the deceased would raise fewer questions than getting a call from a "private investigator"--the job title he attached to his Joe Johnson alias. "Ask him if we can get a copy of his report?"

Sharon wrote that down on her notepad.

"And ask him if he has any photos from the scene. I'd like to see them if he does."

She cringed. "I don't have to look at them, do I?"

"No, of course not. Let's see if he has any first."

"What about the autopsy?" Sharon asked.

"Good point. Perhaps he saw it before it was sealed."

"What if he has a copy?"

Daniels shrugged his shoulders. "I doubt it, but who knows. Good question."

He realized he might have been selling her short. She'd been a mess when he first met her, but she was holding up pretty well.

It took several calls before she was able to get Ralph Anderson, private insurance investigator, on the phone. He was only willing to talk in person off-the-record and for a fee of $500. Daniels mouthed that she should accept his terms.

Anderson agreed to meet her the next day at his office in Southeast D.C. On the drive over, Daniels stopped at Alexander Worthington's office to pick up a copy of his "private investigator's license," in case Anderson demanded to see it.

The look on Anderson's face showed he was surprised to see a man standing in the doorway to his office with the young woman he was expecting.

"My name is Joe Johnson. I'm a licensed private investigator," Daniels said, flashing his license. "I want to make it clear that you'll only get your money when we've seen the information you told Ms. Washburn you possessed."

Anderson, a squat man in his mid-fifties with bushy eyebrows, who was wearing a brown suit that looked like it hadn't been dry-cleaned in ages, didn't look happy, but he motioned them into his office.

The second floor office, which was above a tattoo parlor, consisted of one large room with a desk backed up to windows which looked like they hadn't been washed in years. Two large bookshelves were filled with stacks of files. Anderson led them to a round table.

"I'm not pulling a fast one on you, Miss Washburn," the investigator said, addressing Sharon. "You didn't need to bring this Mr. private investigator."

"I'm glad to hear that," she answered, "but there are a lot of dishonest people in this world. I didn't want to give you five hundred dollars and find out you don't have any of the things you said you had."

Anderson looked disappointed. "I hope I'm not the one who's being tricked."

Daniels pulled an envelope out of his jacket and displayed its contents. "Five hundred dollars in fifty's."

The man looked like he wanted to examine the bills, but decided against it. "Okay. I'll show you."

Anderson placed on the table a photocopy of an insurance company report form along with reprints of a series of photos he had taken of the vehicle.

Sharon turned aside when Anderson turned over the first photo of Ethan's car. She told Daniels on the drive over that Ethan owned a Chevy because his father insisted everyone in the family drive cars made in the U.S. According to Sharon, he'd purchased the car with money earned at his prior job before he started working fulltime on his father's campaign.

Daniels read Anderson's conclusion that the car met the insurance company's definition of "totaled," in that the cost to repair it would exceed sixty percent of the car's market value at the time of the accident.

"Are you expected to make any statements as to the cause of the accident?"

"Yes and no," Anderson replied. "If it seems that the driver damaged the car purposely, I must say why I believe that might be the case. In this instance, since the driver was killed, I could not reach that conclusion."

Daniels kept probing. "What in your opinion caused the driver to leave the road?"

Anderson hesitated. "That is a difficult question and one thank goodness I am not required to express an opinion on."

"I understand the insurance company may not require it," Daniels said, scanning through the report pages, "but did you personally form an opinion?"

The investigator looked over at Sharon who was dabbing her eyes with a tissue. "The police ruled it driver error."

"On what basis?"

"Speeding, I recall."

"Based on what evidence?"

"I don't know. You'll have to ask them," Anderson replied.

"I will do so, but consider the circumstances. Mr. Garvin was the son of the man just elected president of the United States. As far as we know, he was in good health and had everything to look forward to. He also knew the road he was driving on since he lived less than five miles from the accident scene. It was daytime and it's unlikely that weather conditions were a factor. Although it was cloudy, it was not snowing or raining at the time, and the temperature was above freezing. Yet his car left the road and plummeted down the embankment turning over twice before being stopped by boulders in deep water."

Anderson nodded as Daniels outlined each point.

"I'm afraid I cannot help you, Mr. Johnson. I don't have a better answer than the one the police came up with."

"What about mechanical problems? Could it have been caused by a blown tire or break line failure?"

"Tires? No. The tires on this car will not explode even if he ran over many nails."

"Did you inspect the tires?"

Anderson took the report away from Daniels and searched until he found a page showing closed-up photos of the tires. All four seemed to be intact.

"Where was that photo taken?" Daniels asked.

"Police impound."

"Is the car still there?"

"Another question I cannot answer. Now, I believe I have earned my payment."

"I still have a few more questions," Daniels stated. He was getting annoyed that Anderson was unwilling to offer his opinion outside the scope of what the insurance company required. "Did you see the police report?"

"I did," the investigator replied.

"Do you have a copy?"

Anderson shook his head. "I was given a copy which was sent to the insurance company. I am not allowed to keep one for my own records."

"The autopsy?"

"The same."

"Was a toxicology report done?"

Anderson thought for a moment. "I believe so."

"What did it show?" Daniels asked.

Anderson shrugged. "Nothing. He was not a drug user, nor was he high on alcohol."

"Was he wearing his seat belt?"

"That model will not start if the driver does not engage the seat belt."

Daniels thought for a moment. "Back to the vehicle. Any evidence of mechanical failure-- steering or brakes?"

"No, no, no."

Daniels didn't care that the investigator was getting annoyed. He was not giving up until all his questions were answered. "I assume the car was not in auto drive."

"If it had been, it would not have gone off the road."

"What about the windshield? Perhaps a rock was thrown up by a car in front of Mr. Garvin--"

Anderson took the report out of Daniels' hands and opened it to an inside page. "Look at this section--no mechanical failure. The windshield was broken, yes, but by a tree branch. Here's the picture."

The photo showed a large branch penetrating the front windshield.

Anderson stood there defiantly prepared for more questions. Daniels turned to Sharon to see if she wanted to ask anything.

She dabbed her eyes. "What about his iPhone?"

Anderson looked surprised and asked her to repeat the question.

"As I recall, no cell phone was retrieved from the vehicle," he said after Sharon complied.

Daniels still wasn't satisfied. He took the envelope with the cash out of his jacket pocket. "I'll double this amount if you can tell us anything of relevance about the cause of this accident that is not in the report or that you have not already told us."

Anderson looked like he'd been insulted. "I haven't withheld any information. You asked to see the report. I made a copy for you. Take it. It's identical to what I sent to the insurance company."

"What about in your notes?" Daniels asked. "Could you look them over to see if there's something you've forgotten?"

Anderson's face darkened. He seemed about to argue, but then walked over to a file cabinet behind his desk, searched through the top drawer and pulled out a folder. Daniels noted that it was pretty thick. Anderson looked through the folder with his back to them.

"May I?" Daniels asked.

Anderson turned around and opened the file. "You asked to see the report. I complied. Now you want to see my notes too? You will not be able to read them, Mr. Johnson, unless you can read my shorthand."

Daniels scanned the writing. It was illegible. He knew he was beaten. He handed over the envelope with the money. "If you think of anything, no matter how insignificant it seems, please contact Miss Washburn. We'll make it worth your while."

The investigator took the envelope, but didn't say anything until he had escorted them to the front door of his office. "Good day," he said in a tone that conveyed that he was happy to see the last of them.

The next morning on his drive into the District, Daniels felt glum as it dawned on him that Henry Garvin would be sworn in as President of the United States in a little over six weeks. December 1st--the original deadline had come and gone and he was no closer to coming up with the answers President Palmer had charged him with finding.

He had spent the prior night at Maureen's apartment and while things seemed good between them on the surface, he felt underlying tension when they parted that morning. When he asked about it, she blamed being distracted on the fact her cleaning woman was due shortly, and she had things to do before the woman arrived. He gave her a quick kiss and instead of heading to Secret Service headquarters, which is where he implied he was going, he drove into D.C. to Charlotte Palmer's P Street apartment. His goal that morning was to find a lead that he had not explored sufficiently or some piece of information that would point to where he should go next.

The meeting with the insurance investigator had not yielded the wealth of information he hoped it would. In fact, they learned almost nothing new, as the man was unwilling to venture beyond what he'd been required to do for his employer--namely, confirm that Ethan's Chevy Malibu exceeded the sixty percent damage threshold, thereby earning the 'totaled' designation.

What irked Daniels the most as he sorted through the folders he'd created to store notes on each aspect of the investigation was his dependence on reporters for concrete information about the accident and subsequent investigation. Further, they'd only been able to interest two reporters, and neither seemed particularly gung-ho. According to Sharon, no one in the national media would touch the topic, even when she called reporters she knew from her job.

"One reporter told me I'm unlikely to convince anyone to investigate."

"Why's that?" Daniels asked.

"The Garvins have put out the word that I was stalking Ethan and am now trying to do anything to get my name in the media at his expense."

"That's b.s."

"That's Mrs. Garvin," Sharon said. "Mr. Garvin would never say something like that."

"I guess we'll just have to prove them wrong," Daniels said.

Sharon flashed a brief smile and raised her arm half-heartedly. "Yeah."

Adding to his discomfort that morning was the fact he'd not heard from his son. He was beginning to doubt that his ex had contacted Trey.

Sharon left the apartment at noon. She was planning on spending the weekend in Philadelphia with her college roommate and rather than fight the weekend traffic on I-95, she was taking the train. Daniels headed to the local branch of a gym he belonged to in Alexandria. He felt flabby having missed too many workout sessions due to the investigation.

When he returned to his apartment late in the afternoon, he put in a call to Randy Dodd. Perhaps letting him know someone else was digging for answers might spur him to work harder.

Dodd didn't answer his cell and when it went into answer mode, Daniels had to make a quick decision about whether to leave a message.

"Randy, My name is Joe Johnson. I'm a private investigator and have been hired to assist Sharon Washburn in determining the cause of Ethan

Garvin's accident. I'd like to talk to you as soon as possible."

With little else to do, Daniels spent several fruitless hours surfing the Web for information on court cases relating to providing media access to police reports.

He was back in his apartment after stopping by his favorite diner for their meatloaf special when his cell rang. It was Randy Dodd.

"How can I help you, Mr. Johnson?"

"I wanted to introduce myself and explain that I'm investigating the Garvin matter for Ms. Washburn. I thought we might meet and compare notes. You won't have to worry about my spilling the beans to some other journalist. You probably want to be the first to go to press."

"With regard to publishing, Mr. Johnson, I've talked to a couple of editors, and so far no one thinks there's a real story here. It's natural for Ms. Washburn to want some kind of explanation other than her fiancé drove himself into that ditch, but so far she hasn't come up with any real evidence contradicting that conclusion. So, I'm inclined to agree with the editors that there's no real story and I've stopped wasting my time looking into it."

"What about the fact that he knew that patch of road was unsafe and even called the highway department to complain about it?"

"I looked into that, Mr. Johnson. The highway people wouldn't confirm or deny over the phone that Ethan Garvin had registered a complaint about that section of the road and they told me I needed to file a Freedom of Information request in order for them to search their records."

"Did you?"

"I did, but as you probably know, they have thirty days to respond."

"What about the car? Have you seen it?"

"It's been demolished."

"That happened pretty fast, wouldn't you say?"

"It did, and no doubt the Garvins pushed for a quick conclusion to the police investigation so that they could dispose of the car, but that by itself doesn't prove anything."

"Have you been able to look at the police department photos?" Daniels asked.

"No. As I told Ms. Washburn, everything to do with the case has been suppressed from public access under the pretext that someone might use the information to harass or embarrass the president-elect or members of his family."

"Did Ms. Washburn mention one of the TV reporters stated on the day of the accident that an investigator told her the accident was 'suspicious'?"

"Yes, and I asked the Fairfax County Police about that. They said that's standard procedure when there is no obvious initial reason for an accident. Later they determined it was caused by driver error--namely excessive speed. End of story."

"So you're giving up?"

"At this point I've nothing to go on. Even if Ethan Garvin had reported that the road was dangerous, it doesn't mean he wasn't distracted and hence missed the curve."

"Distracted how?"

"He could have been looking at some papers in his car or answering his cell phone or a dozen other things."

"But no papers or cellphone were found in the car. I know that much."

"How do you know that, Mr. Johnson?"

"Ms. Washburn said she tried to find out if Ethan had the briefcase she'd given him for his birthday in the car or the iPhone, which he'd just purchased, but was told neither was recovered."

"Sorry. I just don't think there's a story here. Tell Ms. Washburn for me, will you?'

Daniels sat staring out the window reviewing the conversation with Randy Dodd trying to see if there was something else he could have said that would have altered the free-lancer's decision. He had to admit that Dodd's response was reasonable. Even if he told the reporter his underlying interest, he didn't think he could criticize Dodd if he reached the same conclusion. There just wasn't any hard evidence to suggest someone had killed Ethan Garvin.

Monday, December 11

Monday felt like a wasted day. Nothing but dead-ends. Daniels texted Sharon mid afternoon to let her know he was leaving Mrs. Palmer's apartment. He hadn't heard from her all day. Perhaps she decided to spend an extra day with her friend in Philly. His phone buzzed as he was getting into his car. It was Sharon.

"Mr. Daniels. The train just got in. I'm in a cab on the way to my apartment. I hope you don't want me to come there now. I'm exhausted."

"No, I've already left. I'll be back tomorrow by ten."

"Okay. I'll see you then."

He tuned in a jazz station on the way to the gym where he planned a strenuous workout in hopes of taking his mind off the investigation. He had just pulled into the gym's parking lot and opened the car door when his phone buzzed.

"Thank goodness, I got you, Mr. Daniels," Sharon said, sounding out of breath. "You won't believe this. Someone smashed the taillights on my car. What a mess! Wait! There's a piece of paper stuck . . . I've got to put the phone down."

Daniels closed the car door.

"Oh, my God. They're going to kill me. Oh, my god."

"Sharon! What is it?"

"It's a note. They did it on purpose. They--"

"Sharon!"

"Oh, my god!"

"Sharon, read me the note."

"Okay. Okay. Just a . . .It . . . It says 'Stop messing where you don't belong or else.' What should I do? They're going to kill me."

"Give me your address; then go into your apartment and lock your doors. Don't answer the door until I get there. Got it?"

"But what if they're waiting for me--"

"Okay. Stay by your car. I'll be there in less than thirty minutes."

Daniels allowed his phone's GPS to find the shortest route to her Arlington address. As he reached the apartment complex, he noted that the gated entry system had never been activated. That made it easy for whoever had vandalized Sharon's car to do so without detection.

When he spotted her, Sharon was pacing back and forth beside her white Camry.

She ran towards him as he pulled into a vacant spot.

"Here it is. See what--"

"I can't touch it. Hold it up so I can read it."

Her hand was shaking. She unfolded the note, tearing it slightly on the fold.

The note had been constructed from words cut out of a newspaper, and pasted on a standard sheet of typing paper. He had her turn it over, but there was nothing on the other side.

"Okay. Fold it back up and let me take a look at your car."

Daniels took a couple of photos of the damage and then suggested they go inside. Sharon made him enter the apartment first. "No one here."

She didn't seem satisfied. "What should I do? They're going to kill me--"

"Sharon. I'm not going to let anyone hurt you."

"But--"

"They're amateurs," Daniels said.

"Why?"

"Professionals don't send notes made up of newspaper clippings. A good lab can often pick up prints from the newspaper ink."

"Why would they break my taillights? Do you think it's a hoax?"

He wished he could tell her it was. "No, I just think whoever's behind this may not have done this kind of thing before. In any case, it's time to call the police."

"The police? But what can--"

"Sharon, I know you're scared, but this may turn out to be the break we've been looking for."

She ran her hands through her hair. "I don't understand."

"Clearly someone doesn't want us investigating Ethan's death. It means you were right all along and now we've something to give to those reporters to get them to dig deeper."

She seemed to take that in, but still seemed pretty shaken.

"Make yourself some tea, why don't you?"

She sighed and went to put some water on her stove.

"You need to notify the police so there's a record of the threat," he told her, after came back over and sat down, "but I won't be able to stick around." He doubted the phony ID Alexander Worthington gave him would stand up to scrutiny.

"But what if they come back tonight?"

"Do you have a friend you can stay with a few nights?"

She didn't look reassured, but made the call to the local police and then called a girlfriend who agreed to put her up for the night.

"When the police ask you about the note, tell them you've been talking to reporters about Ethan's death, and that whoever killed him must have found out and is now threatening you."

"Okay."

"I'll call Randy Dodd to alert him to this latest development. Can you call Cynthia Renfro? She's probably gone for the day, so leave a message and ask her to call you."

"Sure."

"Good, and whatever you do, when the police come, don't mention my name."

He tried Dodd's number on his way back to his apartment, but the call went to voice mail. He left a message. "There's been a new development in the Ethan Garvin case. Someone vandalized Sharon Washburn's car and left her a threatening note. Call me for details."

Dodd called back an hour later.

"I think that confirms what Ms. Washburn has been saying all along," Daniels told him after he reported what had happened. "Wouldn't you agree?"

Dodd answered after a long pause. "I find it strange, Mr. Johnson, that you call to tell me about this threat soon after I tell you I'm not interested in pursuing the investigation any further."

Daniels realized what Dodd was driving at. "Are you implying that I broke her tail lights and wrote the note?"

"I've been around the block a few times, Mr. Johnson. I've seen some pretty shady things done to get publicity."

"Does Sharon Washburn strike you as the type to pull a stunt like that?"

"I'm not questioning her, Mr. Johnson. I find your arrival on the scene and this sudden turn strange. That's all."

"I'd be pretty dumb to do such a thing right after we talked, don't you think?"

"I have no idea how smart or dumb you are, Mr. Johnson, but until you or Ms. Washburn come up with some real evidence that Ethan Garvin's death was other than an unfortunate accident, don't call me again."

The phone line went dead. It took all of Daniels' willpower not to throw his phone at something. "Damn," he shouted at the top of his voice. He took a deep breath, recalling his training for how to handle setbacks.

He resisted the urge to shout again, but instead focused on coming to terms with Dodd's unwillingness to pursue the investigation. Perhaps Cynthia Renfro will be less suspicious. Dodd's reaction also reminded him how badly they needed to get other reporters involved. He'd talk to Sharon about that the next day.

Sharon seemed the worse for wear when she arrived at Charlotte Palmer's apartment the next morning. She was wearing jeans instead of her normal business attire and it was clear from her blotched face and red eyes that she hadn't gotten much sleep. "I forgot to call Renfro," she said while fixing a cup of tea. "I'll do it right now."

Daniels raised his hand. "Before you call, think about what message you want to convey. What about this: after you tell her about the threat, say something like, 'if whoever murdered Ethan Garvin thinks they can scare me off, they're wrong,'––but only if you mean it."

She nodded. "I'm really scared. Doesn't this prove that Ethan was murdered?"

"It certainly looks that way."

Her face showed her fighting with her emotions, holding back tears. "I don't know if I can sound that brave."

"Do it for Ethan, and just as importantly do it for yourself."

She sighed, and then nodded.

Daniels hoped the crisis was over, but suddenly Sharon's eyes opened wide.

"But whoever did this . . . won't they–– "

"Hear about it? Yes. That's what we want. We want to smoke them out into the open."

Sharon wrapped her arms around herself. "By using me as bait?"

"Sharon, I said I'm not going to let anything happen to you, and I mean it. Call Renfro; then we'll talk about keeping you safe."

She had to leave a message for Cynthia Renfro, and then disappeared into the bathroom. Daniels was deep in thought about how he was going to protect her. Maybe it was time to tell her the real reason President Palmer had asked him to investigate Ethan's death. If someone were willing to murder the son of the president-elect, they'd not hesitate terminating her as well. On the other hand, telling her would likely make her even more afraid than she already was. Instead, he needed to concentrate on how he was going to fulfill his promise to protect her.

Having her stay at a friend's wasn't safe enough. He had to find someplace else. He slapped his forehead. The answer was obvious. If she moved into the P Street apartment, he could hire retired Secret Service agents to protect her when he wasn't there.

He was in the middle of making a list of retired agents who might be available when Sharon whispered that Cynthia Renfro was on the line. He motioned for her to put the call on speaker.

"Ms. Washburn, I only have a minute. So make it quick."

Sharon stumbled over her words as she explained about the taillights and the note.

"You filed a police report with Arlington Police?"

"I did."

"Okay, I'll check with them and get back to you."

Renfro hung up.

Sharon looked exasperated. "I'm sorry--"

"Don't worry, you did fine. If she says she'll check out your story, she will."

"I don't know if I can do this anymore, Mr. Daniels."

"Sure you can. Sit. I've got a plan to make sure nothing happens to you."

She sat in the big easy chair, pulling her knees up to her chest.

"I want you to move in here for a while. I'll give you twenty-four hour protection."

Her eyes got big.

"I was about to call a few of my retired Secret Service friends. I'll work it out that someone is here with you all the time--even when you leave the building. How does that sound?"

"Doesn't this belong to the first lady?"

"It does, but she won't be needing it for a while."

"And you're sure they won't find me here?"

"Secret Service agents are trained to protect the President of the United States, members of his family, and other dignitaries with our lives. No one is going to lay a finger on you."

It took most of the rest of the day, but Daniels secured the services of three retired agents and worked out a schedule so that either he or one of them would be with Sharon at all times. None wanted to be paid to help out, but he insisted.

"Where'd you get the scratch?" asked Ricardo "Ricky" Alvarez, the first one he called because they'd come up together.

"I'd have to kill you if I told you," Daniels said, trying not to laugh as he said it.

"All right, Daniels," Alvarez said. "I won't ask too many questions, but at least you got to tell me who wants to hurt this girl."

"That's what I'm trying to figure out. I'll tell you more when you get here."

"Okay. I'll be there around midnight so I can get the lay of the land."

Alvarez was taking the two a.m. to ten a.m. shift. He was a widower and was used to being up nights because he'd been substituting overnights for a security service. Sam Freeman, another retired agent who continued to live in the region, would come in at six p.m. and work until two a.m. while Daniels would be with Sharon from ten to six. Nate Parenti, a third retired agent, agreed to do twelve-hour shifts on weekends, but wasn't available during the week. That meant Daniels needed a fourth agent to alternate with Parenti since he couldn't tell Maureen what he was up to and had to be available to her on weekends.

He left messages with a couple of retired agents he thought might be willing, then accompanied Sharon to her apartment in Silver Spring so she could pack some clothes and necessities to bring back to the apartment.

Ricardo Alvarez arrived shortly after midnight for his two a.m. shift to reconnect with his old running mate and learn the lay of the land.

"That's some story," Alvarez said, a coffee in hand, when Daniels finished telling him how President Palmer had asked him to conduct the investigation and how things had gone thus far. "It seems whenever there's a big mess that needs to be cleaned up, they call on a person of color."

Daniels shrugged. "I don't think Palmer thought about it that way."

"Maybe not," Alvarez said, "but you about to retire having done twenty years. Shouldn't he have thought about giving you a break and asking some younger guy?"

Daniels laughed. "You've got a point there."

"I'm just surprised you stuck it out with the service this long."

Although they'd become agents the same year, Alvarez had retired early. "Can't take them playing with my life no more," was what he told Daniels at the time. Alvarez had three kids and a wife just diagnosed with stage-three breast cancer. Plus, he was supporting his parents. He couldn't put up with having to move to a new city every two years.

Daniels had considered retiring at the time. Had he already met Maureen Thornberry he might have done so. As it was he had no personal life and couldn't see leaving a good paying job with the agency to work private security. Most high paying private security jobs were overseas and many were in places like Afghanistan, which meant putting one's life on the line for someone else's pleasure.

"At least they finally settled the suit," Alvarez said after draining his beer.

Daniels remembered learning shortly after he was hired about a discrimination suit filed by a group of black agents. He couldn't believe it took more than twenty years to adjudicate, but a federal court finally ruled in favor of the complainants, requiring the agency to undertake in a series of steps to prevent future discrimination.

"You never joined the suit?" Alvarez asked.

Daniels shook his head. He had been given an opportunity to add his name when hired, but declined. "If a judge was going to ask me in a court of law whether I'd been discriminated against, I needed to have a damn good answer. At that point I didn't have one."

"But you told me later on you felt you were being given assignments other guys didn't want."

"True, but I didn't have any proof it was because I'm black, and plenty of white guys complained too."

"It certainly seemed to me whenever there was someplace no one wanted to go, some boss would say, 'What about Alvarez?' and I'd be told to pack my bags because I was going to North Dakota."

Daniels laughed. "I know what you're saying. One time when I asked to stay on the East Coast they sent me to Phoenix. Alysia was furious. She wanted me to claim discrimination, but again, it seemed it was happening to everyone. I didn't feel justified."

"You're a better man than I, Daniels," Alvarez said. "In any case, you probably want to get going. I'm all set here."

"Great. I knew I could count on you."

"Absolutely, and I meant it about not needing to be paid."

"Don't look a gift horse in the mouth," Daniels said. "I've been given the money to pay you guys and you're going to get paid."

Alvarez put his coffee container in the trash. "I suppose, with Christmas around the corner."

"You've got grandkids now, right?" Daniels asked putting his empty on the counter.

"Two and one on the way. You?"

"Sore subject. I know my boy got married, but we don't talk."

Alvarez shook his head. "That ain't right, amigo."

"You're telling me. It's mostly my fault."

"So what. Fix it."

Daniels nodded. "I'm trying. I'm trying."

Sharon was arranging her belongings in the master bedroom the next morning when Cynthia Renfro called back. She put the call on speaker so Daniels could listen in. "Who do you think did this?" Renfro asked.

"It must be the people who killed Ethan," Sharon replied, not sounding as sure of herself as Daniels would have liked.

"Remind me again why you think someone wanted to kill the son of the president-elect of the United States?"

"I don't know, Miss Renfro. He must have found out something about somebody they didn't want him to know."

"That's pretty vague, Miss Washburn. Unfortunately, this taillight incident isn't enough for my assignment editor to run with it. Isn't there anything else you can tell me?"

"Let me talk to her," Daniels said reaching for the phone.

"Ms. Renfro. This is Joe Johnson. I'm a private investigator. I've been hired to protect Miss Washburn as a result of this threat."

"I'm listening," Renfro said after a moment of silence.

"It seems to me that the investigation into Ethan's death was shortchanged. They are calling it driver error, but is that because they didn't look for a different explanation?"

"That's possible, but I need evidence," Renfro said.

He knew he had to make his best case. "It comes down to how closely they examined the vehicle. Have you seen it?"

"Look, I'm having a hard time convincing my assignment editor to let me spend any time on this much less go chasing after car wrecks, not knowing what I'm supposed to be looking for."

"Look for something that explains why he drove into that ditch."

"That's a big ask, Mr. Johnson."

"I understand, but I'd think the fact that someone threatened Ms. Washburn would change your editor's mind."

"I'll try again, but I can't promise anything."

"Won't she discover the car's already been demolished?" Sharon asked when Renfro ended the call.

"That's what Randy Dodd told us, but maybe he never checked or the fact that another reporter is asking might shake loose some more details. Let's see what she finds out."

Sharon nodded. "Then what?"

"If the car was demolished, we can suggest that Renfro contact the Garvins to ask them why it was done so quickly!"

Daniels phone rang. It was Chaz Nelson, one of the retired agents he'd tried to call. Nelson agreed to back Parenti on weekends. Daniels scheduled a time for him to come by to get briefed.

A while later Sharon called him into the living room. She had an all-news station on the TV. "Remember that story about Henry Garvin's not meeting with reporters? It seems the press is starting to pay more attention to his never being available."

"What now?" Daniels asked.

"Their press secretary is trying to deflect rumors by repeating the story that Ethan's dad is busy putting together his cabinet. Today he's supposedly busy meeting with candidates for Secretary of Defense."

The screen showed a limo driving up in front of the Garvin compound in Bethesda.

"That's not Henry Garvin," Sharon said.

"Say what?"

"The man greeting General Kimball and waving to the cameras. That's not Ethan's dad."

"Who is it?"

Sharon shrugged. "I think it's his twin brother. The first time I met him I couldn't tell them apart."

"So you think this brother is pretending to be Henry Garvin?"

"Sounds weird, I'll admit."

"Wouldn't other people catch on?"

She shrugged her shoulders.

"Are you sure it was the brother?"

"Robert is heavier and his face is a little fuller, but he was only on camera for a few seconds."

"Mention that to Cynthia Renfro the next time we talk to her. Maybe she'll contact the Garvin campaign and see what they say."

Thursday, December 14

"Ethan Garvin's car has been demolished," Cynthia Renfro informed Sharon two days later. "I tracked down the salvage lot where it was taken and spoke to the owner. He was paid extra to crush the car immediately without recovering any parts except the tires."

"Is that unusual?" Sharon asked.

"It is and get this. The Garvins had two men accompany the tow truck from the police impound to the salvage yard. The salvage owner called them goons in suits."

"Probably the same two who prevented me from entering the Garvins' farmhouse to retrieve my belongings."

"They told the owner they were there to make sure nothing was removed from the car before it was crushed."

"They must have been hiding something," Sharon ventured.

"That's one way to interpret it, Ms. Washburn, but we don't have any hard evidence to back that up. There's a logical answer to everything you've told me. The family was probably afraid someone would salvage parts of Ethan's car to sell them on E-bay or something disgusting like that."

"Ms. Renfro, it's me, Joe Johnson."

"I didn't realize I was talking to both of you."

"Sorry. We have you on speaker. You make a valid point about the possible justification for demolishing the car the way they did. So, why not ask the Garvins to see what they say?"

"Mr. Johnson, I can't just pick up the phone and talk to Henry Garvin. Best I'll get is some lawyer who will tell me he doesn't have the authority to answer my questions."

Daniels knew she was probably right. "Give it a try? See what kind of response you get. You might be surprised."

"I'll think about it, Mr. Johnson."

"There's a second reason I want her to call the Garvins," Daniels said to Sharon once they'd hung up. "It should alert whoever sent you that note that we have not given up."

Sharon hugged herself. "Did you have to tell me that?"

Daniels started to slap his forehead, but made himself stop. "Sorry. Don't you feel safe with my guys protecting you?"

"What if they send four or five guys up here?"

"You've been watching too much TV. With security cameras recording who comes into this building, security downstairs and one of my guys in the apartment at all times, no one is going to get anywhere close to you."

Sharon didn't look convinced. She gave him a weak smile and went into the kitchen presumably to make herself another cup of tea.

That evening, he arrived at Maureen's apartment past seven thirty, having waited for Sam Freeman to show up for his shift before leaving

Sharon for the evening. They hadn't heard anything further from Renfro and Sharon was not making any progress getting other reporters interested in her claims.

Daniels hoped an evening relaxing with Maureen would take his mind off the investigation. He read someplace your brain keeps working even while you're asleep. Maybe his brain would come up with some avenue to take the investigation that would prove more promising than what they'd accomplished thus far.

After he helped with cleanup after dinner, Daniels said he needed to call his ex to see if she'd contacted his son. "It's been over a week since I talked to her and nothing has happened."

"Be polite," Maureen reminded him.

"You mean yelling and carrying on won't convince her?" he replied, trying to keep a straight face.

Maureen put up her dukes. He ducked her soft jab and went into the living room, sat on the couch and dialed his ex-wife's number.

Alysia's second husband, George Thompson, answered the phone. "She don't want to talk to you, Daniels."

"I don't mean to be a bother, George," Daniels said, trying to follow Maureen's advice, "but I need to get in touch with my son."

"Hold on."

Daniels waited, but it was George, not Alysia, who came back on the phone. "She said she told him."

"And?"

"And what, Daniels? She told him. Now leave us alone."

The line went dead.

"Bastard," Daniels said, wishing the guy was standing in front of him.

"No luck?" Maureen inquired.

"There has to be some other way to reach him."

"Might your mother know?"

"Good idea. I owe her a call anyway." He checked the time. It was past nine. "Mom's usually in bed by now."

"What about your sister?"

"I asked her once. She said she didn't have Trey's phone number, but she may have his address. That would be a start."

"Call her."

Daniels had detected a little resentment a few weeks ago when he called his sister to say that he wouldn't be coming for Thanksgiving. "Unless there's a national emergency, I'll definitely have Christmas off," he told her. "I'll bring Maureen and we'll stay at least two nights."

His sister Alice answered after several rings, but told him she'd have to call him back because she was putting her daughter Rachelle's kids to sleep.

"Where's their mother?" Daniels asked.

"I can't go into that now, Eugene," she replied. "I'll call you back."

When Alice returned his call, she divulged that she had his son's mailing address, but no phone number. "He calls Mother on the appropriate holidays, unlike some other people I know."

"Do we have to go into this again? I'm retiring in a few weeks and then I won't have any excuses."

"Yeah. You retire when Mother has one foot in the grave--"

"Could you just give me the address?"

It turned out his son lived in Millersville, which was about twenty minutes away from NSA headquarters in Fort Meade.

"Can I come with you?" Maureen asked, when Daniels announced he was going there in person.

Daniels frowned. "I'm not so sure that's a good idea."

"Seeing me he might want to listen to what you have to say."

Daniels couldn't tell Maureen the real reason he couldn't take her. "I don't want to give him some excuse like 'you abandoned Mom for a white woman.'"

Maureen's eyes opened wide. "Oh."

"Not saying he'd say that, but he might think it."

"Okay, but just remember, he doesn't have to give you the time of day."

That's what he was afraid of.

Sunday would be the best day to knock on Trey's front door, but he knew he wouldn't be home before three. Knowing Alysia, she probably insisted her son and his family join her every Sunday for church. She would also feed them afterwards.

It was mid afternoon when Daniels reached his son's Tremont Street house in Millersville. It was a nice looking single-level suburban house with a two-car garage on a corner lot. It had to cost at least half a million being so close to Fort Meade.

Daniels had rehearsed different opening lines on the drive from Alexandria, but now that he was there, he feared he'd stumble over his words and the reception would be a door slammed in his face. Buck up, he told himself a few times. He got out of the car, walked up the driveway to the front door, and hit the buzzer.

A young woman opened the door. She was holding a baby as if she'd been burping it. Daniels could see why his son had been attracted to her. She had large expressive eyes, a pretty face and hadn't straightened her naturally curly hair. Best of all, she didn't look suspicious at seeing a stranger on her front steps.

"Is Trey home?" Daniels mumbled.

"Who may I say is calling?"

"His father."

That got her attention. "Oh. I'd forgotten he had a father--other than George, of course. Come on in. I'll get him." She left Daniels in the hallway. An open floor plan exposed a small dining room to the left. On the right a family room opened into the kitchen. Trey's wife disappeared in the back of the house where her husband most likely housed his computers.

Daniels could hear their voices, but couldn't make out what was being said. It sounded like an argument. Finally, Trey came out by himself, stopping a good distance from where Daniels was standing. "What do you want?"

Daniels hardly recognized him. It had been seven years. His body had filled in and his face had hard edges that hadn't been there before. "Trey, please hear me out."

"If this is about putting my child on your life insurance, forget it. We don't want any blood money."

Daniels ignored the retort. "That's not the reason I wanted to talk to you--"

"I can't wait to hear what the real reason is."

"I'm your father, Trey. I want to have a relationship with you and your family."

Trey scowled.

"I'm not an ogre or whatever your mother has painted me."

"You weren't a father to me when I needed one. What makes you think I want one now?"

"You're right. I wasn't there when I should have been."

Just then Trey's wife came out of the back without the baby. "Trey, don't make your father stand there with his coat on. Come in, Mr. Daniels. Would you like a cup of coffee?"

"It's nice of you to offer, but I'm not sure Trey wants me to stay."

"Sure he does. He's just too proud to say it."

Trey looked like a fox trapped in a snare.

Daniels gave Trey's wife his best smile. "I appreciate what you're saying . . . Sorry, I don't even know your name."

"I'm Brianna. Trey, take his coat. Come in and sit down. The baby's napping. I was going to make some coffee for us anyway."

Trey turned his hands up, as if defeated. Daniels took off his coat and offered to remove his shoes.

"That's not necessary," Brianna said. "We're going to replace this carpeting as soon as we save a little money. Isn't that right, Trey?"

Trey shrugged.

Daniels handed Trey his coat and followed Brianna towards the kitchen. "How long have you lived here?"

"Not even a year, but we love it. It's the perfect size for us right now and it's close to Trey's work."

"You're still at NSA?" Daniels asked Trey who had plopped himself down in an easy chair in the family room.

"He's been there five years now," Brianna said when Trey ignored the question.

Daniels picked out a chair facing Trey. It was time for his pitch. *Make it short,* he told himself.

"Trey, hear me out. I need your help on a project. It's highly classified so if you don't mind, Brianna, I don't want to put you at risk by disclosing information you can't know about."

"Trey?" Brianna asked from the kitchen where she was measuring coffee into a black automatic.

Trey shook his head. "If this was official business, you'd be contacting me through work."

Daniels expected his response. "It's an off-the-books investigation––official, but I'm unable to go through standard channels."

"Why me?" Trey asked.

"Because you're the only person I know who is qualified to do what I need."

"Maybe you should hear him out," Brianna said.

"No," Trey said.

"Trey. That's not nice," Brianna said.

Daniels ignored Trey's response. "You're looking good, son. Married life suits you."

"Just tell me what you want so I can say 'no.'"

"Can we go in the back?"

Trey got up and headed to the back of the house.

"Sorry, Brianna," Daniels said as he followed, not knowing what else to say.

Trey left the door open to his study. Daniels found him sitting in a swivel chair in front of a bank of computer monitors. With no place to sit, he pulled the door closed and remained standing.

"What I'm working on was assigned to me by President Palmer in person. He asked me to investigate the death of Henry Garvin's son Ethan, but I'm having problems accessing certain kinds of data. That's why I'm here."

Trey looked puzzled. "Why you?"

"Good question. The short answer is that he couldn't go through regular channels because Ethan came to him the day before he died promising to bring him some highly classified information. If true, that would put Palmer in conflict with the president-elect, which in turn could create a constitutional crisis. That information, however, was not in Ethan's car. President Palmer asked me to find out if Ethan was deluded or whether someone had him killed in order to prevent him from delivering that information."

"You can't be serious!"

"Deadly."

"Okay. Let's assume you're telling the truth. You still haven't said what you want from me."

Daniels nodded. He hadn't been confident he'd even get to this part of his mission, but Trey was listening. It was time to get down to steel tacks.

Monday, December 18

Sharon knocked on the closed study door. "It's Renfro."

Daniels had been constructing a list of Henry Garvin's top staffers in hopes of identifying the person called "Z" who Ethan complained hung around the campaign but lacked a defined role. "Put her on speaker."

"Go ahead," Sharon told the TV reporter after setting her phone down on the desk. "We're listening."

"I wanted to let you know I contacted the Garvins. It didn't go well. The bottom line is that I won't be pursuing this story any further."

"Why's that?" Daniels asked.

"I don't have time to go into details, but let me warn you the person I spoke with said the Garvins will sue if Ms. Washburn continues to smear their son's memory."

Sharon jumped out of her seat. "WHAT?"

"That's ridiculous," Daniels said waving his arm towards Sharon in an effort to calm her down. "Since when does the media back down from threats?"

"We're not backing down," Renfro said. "We haven't found any facts that support the theory that

Ethan Garvin's death was anything but an unfortunate accident."

"What did they say that changed your mind?"

"They confirmed my skepticism as to whether there's anything to this story."

"How? What did they say?"

"Are you sure you want to hear this, Mr. Johnson?"

"Yes, I'm sure."

"They suggested Ms. Washburn is under the illusion that she was engaged to Ethan Garvin, when the more accurate description of their relationship is that she was stalking him."

Sharon sat down like she'd been struck. "Oh my god. How can they--"

Daniels motioned for her to calm down. She leaned back into the chair her hands on the top of her head.

"Ms. Renfro. Are you aware a court found Ms. Washburn's claim credible and awarded her an engagement ring and other items that were at the family's farmhouse in Fairfax County?"

"I am, Mr. Johnson, but that's circumstantial. It doesn't prove that they were engaged or that Ms. Washburn is not living under some sort of illusion."

"That's a slander designed to stop you from asking questions," Daniels said.

"It may be, but it fits with the notion she invented the story that he was murdered so she can have from his death what she couldn't have from his life."

"What about the threat on her life?"

"The police found no witnesses to that incident. The Garvins' representative asked me if I had considered the possibility that she damaged her own car when people weren't buying her story."

Sharon jumped out of the chair. "I can't take any more of this. She ran from the study slamming the French doors on her way out.

"I didn't want to go into all that, Mr. Johnson, because I knew it would upset Ms. Washburn, but you have to consider the possibility that she made it all up."

"Not a chance," Daniels said. "Ms. Washburn did not break her car lights or compose that note."

"Bottom line? My editor told me not to pursue this story any further. Frankly, I agree with him."

"Could you tell me just one more thing, Ms. Renfro? Who did you speak to?"

"Gary Knowlton, a long-time aide to Mr. Garvin who said he knew Ethan from birth. He said Ethan broke up with Ms. Washburn after college, but she kept pursuing him and he took pity on her and took her out a few times."

"How did he explain the engagement ring?"

"I didn't ask him about that, but what you're calling an engagement ring, might have been something else. It's also possible he purchased it for someone else he was dating."

"And she came to possess it how?"

"You'll have to ask her. I'm sorry, Mr. Johnson. I'm late for a meeting. Good luck and be careful. Pay attention to the facts, not just the theories."

Daniels stood by the desk for a few seconds before going to look for Sharon. He found her in the bedroom, curled up on the bed with the covers over her.

"Sharon."

"Go away. I don't want to talk."

"I know you're upset, but you can't let these things get to you. It's how these people play the game."

"How could she believe those lies?"

"Don't worry about her. We'll find someone else to help us."

Sharon blew her nose into the wad of tissues she'd been clutching. "I don't know if I can keep doing this, Mr. Daniels."

Daniels, who had been standing in the doorway, stepped into the room and sat down on a chair near the bed. "Sharon, don't let them beat you. If you give up, you'll never learn the truth."

She remained still for thirty seconds, then sighed, slowly threw off the blanket and pushed herself up to a sitting position.

"That's the girl."

"It hurt," she mumbled, as she stood up.

"I know." He held her by both shoulders. "Straight back. Chin up." She obeyed. "That's better. Ready?" She nodded. "Say it."

"I'm ready."

"Louder."

"I'M READY."

"Ready to do what?"

Sharon took a deep breath. "Ready to fight back."

He smiled. "Okay. Let's get back to work."

After the disastrous phone call from Cynthia Renfro, Daniels suggested they not call any more reporters until they came up with evidence so convincing it couldn't be ignored. "We need a motive and some likely suspects."

"I've racked my brain," Sharon pleaded, "but I can't think of anyone who would want to kill him."

Daniels paced the room. "Let's start with the campaign. What about the campaign itself could have disturbed him?"

"That they were doing something illegal like spying on the Republicans."

"That's one possibility. Can you think of any others?"

Sharon got up and stood behind her chair. "Maybe it had something to do with money. Perhaps his father promised something to one of his contributors that would be illegal."

"Those are good suggestions, but why wait until after the election to report it?"

"Loyalty to his father. Maybe he thought there was a good explanation, but his father never came up with one."

Daniels nodded. "Then once the election is over . . ."

"Say. Do you think that's the information he was bringing to the White House?"

"Possibly."

"It would have to be something pretty serious."

"Exactly. You said he didn't get along with a few people on the campaign. Let's focus on them."

"Okay, but it seems pretty unlikely that we'll find something. Aren't they vetted or something?"

"I assume that's the case, but we need to start looking anyway."

An hour later he was still researching Henry Garvin's campaign team when he received a text message from a numbered account. "Does tomorrow work?" It had to be from Trey. His son promised one day's help after Daniels outlined the task President Palmer had dumped on him.

He went into the kitchen to tell Sharon.

"Do you know what today is?" she asked before he would tell her about Trey.

"What?"

She held up the newspaper she'd been reading. "The Monday after the second Wednesday of December."

"What's the punch line?" Daniels asked thinking she was being humorous.

"It's the day the electors meet in each of the fifty states and vote for president and vice president."

Daniels had to consider that for a moment. "So that means nothing can stop Henry Garvin from becoming the President of the United States."

Sharon nodded. "I guess not."

"But that doesn't mean we should stop trying to get the truth about what happened to Ethan, right?"

"Of course not. The truth needs to come out."

"Good. I've got good news to share--"

"But it says here that it's not official until January 6th."

"How's that?" Daniels asked.

"That's when Congress meets to certify the results."

"Interesting."

President Palmer must be aware of that fact, Daniels thought, but he hadn't given him January 6th as the deadline for their investigation. It had been December first. Was there some other procedure that could prevent Henry Garvin from becoming president after Congress certified the Electoral

College vote? It was unlikely. Sweat broke out on Daniels' forehead. The clock was ticking and he felt like he was in quicksand.

"So what were you going to tell me?" Sharon asked.

"Oh, sorry. My son, who is a crackerjack computer programmer, is going to help us out for one day."

"Doing what?"

"I've got a long list in the other room. Come take a look."

When he knew Trey would be there the next day, Daniels began to organize the list of things he needed help with. While he was doing that, he asked Sharon to construct biographies of Henry Garvin's top campaign officials. On the surface none stood out as a likely suspect in Ethan's death, but they had to start somewhere.

"What about the guy they called 'Z'?" Sharon asked.

"I haven't been able to find anyone that fits. Tell me what you know about him."

"Not much. Ethan said this 'Z' showed up at odd times, but didn't seem to have an official title."

That was going to make it difficult unless he could convince one of the campaign staffers to help out, but which one would even speak to him? Without much confidence he added the task of identifying "Z" to the bottom of the list he was readying for Trey's visit.

Same Day

When he was shown into Katherine Garvin's office, Gary Knowlton tried not to show his frustration. She had been on his case about one thing or another since early that morning, but he had no idea what the topic was going to be this time and therefore couldn't prepare while waiting outside her office. He was pissed about having to wait for her to see him having been summoned more than half an hour ago.

"She hasn't stopped her nonsense," Mrs. Garvin informed him after her secretary left them.

"Who?"

"Who do you think?"

"The Washburn girl?"

She gave him a look that told him she thought he was being dense.

"What has she done now?"

"She's calling up all kinds of reporters demanding they look into Ethan's death."

That's unlikely to work, he wanted to tell her, but kept his mouth shut.

"That little warning your guys gave her obviously didn't scare her one bit."

Knowlton couldn't let that comment go by without a response. "She moved out of her apartment."

"And have you found where she's staying?"

Knowlton swallowed. "We're working on it."

"This Agent Agnew must be related to Spiro," Mrs. Garvin said, daring Knowlton to disagree.

Agnew was the lead agent Knowlton had working for him. He knew he'd better smile at her joke. "What do you want me to do?"

"Try harder. Do something that makes her run home to Mommy and Daddy."

Knowlton nodded.

"You picked him."

"Agnew?"

"Who do you think I'm talking about?"

"Got it."

"So much for Secret Service training if they can't scare a flighty wisp of a girl enough to stop her nonsense."

"They can and they will."

"What about using our other friends?" Katherine Garvin asked.

"I'm keeping them informed."

"Use them. They'll do things your Mr. Agnew seems reluctant to do."

Knowlton nodded. He hated when she was right.

Tuesday, December 12:

Daniels was pleased to find his son waiting in the building lobby to Mrs. Palmer's apartment when he arrived. He messaged Ricardo Alvarez, the overnight guard, they were on their way up.

Although Daniels had told Trey about the threat on Sharon's life, about moving her into Mrs. Palmer's apartment, and about hiring retired agents to guard her, he could hardly object if Trey didn't buy the entire story. He hoped meeting Sharon in person would convince his son not only that he was sane, but in real need of his search and programming expertise.

After being introduced to Sharon and before starting on the list of things his father gave him to research, Trey insisted on checking out the security on their digital devices.

"Your computers are not set up properly if you want to prevent someone from monitoring your online activity. It will only take me a few minutes to fix that. Then I'll be ready to hear how you think I can help."

When Trey finished his task, Daniels went over what they knew about Ethan's death and what they hoped Trey could discover. It didn't take long for Trey to garner one important fact they weren't aware of--i.e., the name of three people who'd seen Ethan's car leave the road and called 911.

"Great start," Daniels told him.

"Thanks. Got any coffee around here?"

"There's a coffee shop down the street," Daniels answered. "I'll join you."

Outside it was a chilly, but sunny day with promise of snow over the weekend. Days like this made Daniels forget how hot and muggy D.C. could be in the summer. He was glad he'd worn a hat.

"I must admit I didn't believe a word of what you were saying," Trey told his father as they walked over to 21st Street. "I thought it was some weird way you came up with to get into my good graces."

"More than anything, Trey, I want a relationship with you and your family. I know the timing is suspicious, but you are the only person I know with the skills I need and someone I knew I could trust if you were willing to help."

Trey nodded. "But that doesn't mean I don't think you're nuts for accepting this assignment as you call it."

Daniels raised his hands in surrender.

"I suppose it is impossible to say 'no' to a president," Trey said, as they reached their destination, "but this is a job for the FBI or some agency that could put dozens of people on it."

Daniels held the door for someone hurrying out with coffees in both hands. "I told the President that, but he explained why that wasn't an option. I even tried to tell him I wasn't the man for the job, but he disagreed."

They resumed the discussion after they'd purchased their coffees and then remained outside under Charlotte Palmer's apartment building awning.

"The bottom line, Trey, is that I've got a job to do and like every other job I've been asked to do, I'm going to give it my all."

"Except for parenting," Trey said, looking his father in the face.

Daniels had gone over that accusation a thousand times when it was first leveled at him by his ex. He still couldn't see how he could have done better given the demands of life as a Marine and then a Secret Service agent, but saying so wouldn't win the argument. It was time to throw in the towel. "You're right. I failed there. Can you ever forgive me?"

Trey who had been standing rigid took a deep breath. "I forgive you, Dad."

Daniels reached out his arms. Their hug was brief and awkward, but to Daniels it was a start.

"I'll do what I can the rest of the day," Trey said, "but I can't guarantee I'll be able to come up what you need."

Daniels nodded. "I understand."

"What's your plan B?"

"You're my plan B and I don't have a plan C."

Trey retreated towards the building entrance. "You'd better start working on one."

Upstairs they found Sharon in a panic. "I tried calling you," she said to Daniels. "You left your phone here."

Daniels threw his coat on a chair. "What's the matter?"

"They found me. You said you'd protect me, but they found me."

"Slow down. Did someone call you?"

"They messaged me." She handed him her cell phone.

Daniels read the message out loud, "You thought we wouldn't find you? Stop the interfering or else."

"Let me see if I can trace it," Trey suggested, taking the phone and heading into the study.

Sharon looked like she was down to her last thread. "You said--"

"I understand. You're upset, but I meant it when I said I won't let anyone touch you."

"You keep saying that, Mr. Daniels, and I want to believe you, but they know where I am. They know where I am."

She turned and buried herself under a blanket on the living room couch.

Daniels followed. "Let Trey work his magic. Then we'll decide whether to contact the police."

Getting no response, Daniels went into the study. His son's fingers were flying across the keyboard. He sat in the easy chair in the corner and waited. Finally, Trey turned to him. "I traced it to Indonesia, but from there, it's a black hole."

"Indonesia!"

"That doesn't mean that's where it originated, but someone has routed the message through a number of servers to make it hard to track. I might have gotten further from my office, of course, but with the tools available to me here, that's the best I can do."

"How did they find her phone?"

"That's the easy part. She has the vanilla security offered by her provider, which in this case was no barrier for whoever wanted to find her."

"Can you do something to stop them from contacting her again?"

"I can tell you what to ask for when you call the provider. It's going to cost her a few bucks more each month, but it's worth it."

"I need to add it to my phone as well," Daniels told him.

"Not a problem. Show me your phone."

Less than an hour later the security level of both phones had been upgraded to the most expensive package offered, although Trey confessed no perfect security system existed for ordinary consumers.

Daniels' telling Sharon she wouldn't be receiving any more texts from that sender did little to allay her fears, but the incident had served one benefit. It convinced Trey someone wanted the investigation stopped.

"Are you sure you can protect her?" Trey asked his father when Sharon was out of earshot.

"You fixed it so they won't be able to trace her location from her phone, right?"

Trey nodded.

"And I've got someone here with her twenty-four seven."

"I guess your guys know what they're doing."

"Damn straight."

"On another subject, you said you haven't told Sharon everything. Don't you think it's time to let her know what's really going on?"

Daniels still felt hesitant to do so. "I thought I was protecting her by not getting into the whole China thing, but that seems to have backfired."

"Apparently so. Anyway, what else can I do for you today?" Trey asked.

Daniels gave Trey his list, and then went into the living room to have a conversation with Sharon.

"I've decided against reporting this latest threat to the police," he said.

Sharon pushed herself to a seated position. "Why not?"

"We'd have to let them come here and that would raise a whole lot of questions I'd rather not answer. If the people who threatened you don't know about this place, calling the police might lead them here."

"Why are you saying they don't know where I am? How could they--"

"Sharon, listen to me. They found your cell number, but that doesn't mean they know where you are. Trey has made it unlikely they can in the future either."

"Are you sure?"

"Look, if they knew, wouldn't they have said so to increase your fear level?"

"Yeah. That would raise it to a twenty from a nineteen on a scale of one to ten." She allowed a smile to creep over her face.

"That's the spirit."

She frowned and turned away. "Everything keeps getting worse."

"I hear you, but think of it this way, these threats tell us we're on the right track. We may be a lot closer than we think."

She offered a thin smile. "Whoopee."

He sat down opposite Sharon. It was time to tell her the full story. "While we're clearing the air, I need to--."

"Hey guys, listen up," Trey said, coming into the room. "Some guy named Randy Dodd just texted you that he's got some information you'll want to see. He wants to meet you tomorrow morning at the American City Diner on Connecticut. I texted back that you'd be there. I hope that was okay."

There was no question Daniels wanted to hear what Dodd had to say. "This could be our big break."

"Let's hope so," Sharon replied. "Can I come also?"

"Better not," Daniels said. "You'd better stay out of sight."

Wednesday, December 20

Hopeful that the investigation had finally gotten a break, Daniels got to the diner a half hour early to choose a booth in the back where he and Dodd would be able to talk without worrying about being overheard.

To pass the time, he brought the *Washington Post* and *Washington Times* to catch up on news on Henry Garvin. Ever since Sharon had suggested the man who waved to the media was not the president-elect, he made it a point to look for any reports where Garvin had been seen in public. His failure to hold any press conferences or to make any personal appearances since Ethan's death had resulted in increased questioning by the press. Garvin's press secretary tried to suppress the questions by arguing Garvin chose to spend his time putting together his cabinet rather than worrying about satisfying the press's need for photo ops.

When the waitress appeared with more coffee, Daniels checked the time. It was five after ten. He had no idea where Dodd lived, but assumed he'd chosen the location for convenience. He once read that people who live far away from a meeting place often show up early while those who live nearby are often late. He hoped that was the case here.

He turned to the Post's crossword puzzle, which kept him occupied despite a growing feeling in the pit of his stomach that something was amiss. When his cell showed 10:30, he tried Dodd's phone, but the call was thrown into voice mail. "Dodd. I'm here at the diner . . . in the back."

He wondered if Dodd was sitting elsewhere or waiting outside. Deciding to check, he strolled through the diner without seeing a male younger than forty sitting by himself. He went up front and told the hostess he was checking to see if his friend was waiting outside, but stepping out the front door, no one fit his preconceived notion of what Dodd would look like.

Another thought occurred to him as he walked back to his table. Was the message real? Given that someone had found Sharon Washburn's phone number and sent her a threatening message, perhaps they'd uncovered his number as well and had sent him on a wild goose chase.

He called the apartment. His sub for that morning, Nate Parenti, answered the phone. "Everything okay there?"

"Yup. Should I be worried?"

"Not sure. Is Ms. Washburn up and about?"

"She's right here. Want to talk to her?"

"I do."

"What did he have to say?" Sharon asked when she came on the line. "Is it the break we've been looking for?"

He hated to answer. "He hasn't shown."

"Oh, no! Did he call you?"

"No. I tried to call him, but he didn't answer. I'll wait another half hour. If he doesn't show, I'll have to assume something prevented him from coming."

"Do you think something bad--"

"Let's not speculate. He may just be late."

"Are you coming here today?"

"Of course. Do you need something?"

"No. I just need to do something other than sit around waiting for the next bad thing to happen."

"Go out. Go shopping or eat lunch out. Nate will go with you."

Daniels waited another thirty minutes, but when Dodd didn't show or call he left the waitress a huge tip and headed to Mrs. Palmer's P Street apartment. Sharon must have taken his advice, as she was not there when Daniels arrived. He'd just sat down, intending to go back to the crossword puzzle while eating the sandwich he'd picked up on his way when headline in the Metro section caught his eye.

> *D.C. Resident's Body Found Near Home.*
> *The body of an adult male was found in an alley off 12th Street in Columbia Heights shortly after midnight. D.C. Police report the man apparently was a robbery victim, as his empty billfold was found a few feet from the body. The victim's name is being withheld pending notification of next of kin.*

It was Randy Dodd. Daniels didn't know how he knew, but he did. He couldn't call the D.C. police without raising questions about who he was and why he was calling. The story lacked a byline, but he called the *Post* to see if the name of the victim had been released. The person who answered the phone wasn't helpful. He didn't bother leaving a message when she transferred Daniels to someone who wasn't there. Maybe there'd be more information in the next day's edition.

When Sharon returned to the apartment, her smile turned into a frown as soon as she saw Daniels' face. She dropped the shopping bags she'd been carrying. "Now what?"

Daniels showed her the newspaper article.

"Oh, my god," she said. "Is it . . .?"

"I don't know for sure, but I have a bad feeling about this."

"I'm going to be sick," Sharon mumbled before running into the bathroom. When she appeared fifteen minutes later, her face was white, and her hands were shaking. "What are we going to do?"

"Not panic."

"Not panic! What does that mean? Everything keeps going wrong and all you can tell me is not to panic?"

Daniels couldn't dispute Sharon's charge. "We don't know for certain that it's him and if it is, it could just be that he was in the wrong place at the wrong time."

She sat down in the living room easy chair staring at him. "You don't believe that, do you?"

Daniels didn't have a good answer. If Dodd were dead, if someone had killed him to prevent him from disclosing some information vital to their investigation, his entire conception of what they were up against would have to change. It would mean Sharon's belief that Ethan was killed had a foundation in reality. It would also imply whatever information Ethan had been about to disclose justified his decision to turn on his own father. Until

Daniels found out what it was all about, he was playing rugby with a blindfold.

Sharon stood up and pulled her cell out of her pants pocket. "We have to tell someone--the police, the FBI--someone."

Daniels jumped up. "Not yet, Sharon. First, we need to find out if it was Dodd."

It was hours before Daniels felt he could leave the P Street apartment without worrying Sharon would call the police or do something equally disruptive of the investigation.

Daniels had another worry. What if the people who had threatened Sharon were on to him? They might not know where he was keeping Sharon, but if his efforts to remain in the background failed, Trey and his family would be at risk as well. He couldn't take that chance and resolved to hire a couple more retired agents to watch Trey's house, but first he had to contact Alexander Worthington for a cash infusion as the Joe Johnson bank account was close to zero.

That evening, Daniels wasn't surprised when Maureen kept asking him what was wrong, claiming he was quieter than usual. He didn't have a good answer, so he pleaded pre-retirement anxiety.

"Less than five weeks, Eugene," she told him while clearing the dinner plates.

When had she started calling him by his middle name he wondered? She must have picked it up from his sister. "I know. The other day I realized I've no idea what I'm going to do to fill my days."

"You'll be surprised how busy you'll be."

"I'm not like you, Mo. You've got so many interests and friends to talk to constantly, and--"

"Maybe you need to make some friends."

Daniels turned around to see if she was serious. "I do have friends. Lots of them."

"Do you see any of them more than twice a year?"

"I see my golfing buddies once a week all summer."

She shook her head. She remarked more than once that most of his friends were single men and that the few who were married didn't seem to want to socialize with their wives.

Is that the difference between men and women, Daniels wondered? Women are always making new friends. Men have the friends they have and don't feel they need more.

"Are you sure that's all that's on your mind?"

Daniels hadn't been paying attention. "Say it again."

"I said are you sure retirement is what's bothering you?"

He shrugged, lacking an answer that might satisfy her.

"There's nothing you want to tell me?"

He looked at her again. She was dead serious.

"Can't think of anything."

"Don't wait too long," she said.

What's that supposed to mean? "Okay," he said, not knowing what else to say.

Later, as they sat watching a TV show, he wondered if some part of the story about how he was spending his time had come unraveled. Maureen was obviously suspicious about his comings and goings, most of which he blamed on work, but he wasn't ready to tell her the truth--not when people who knew too much were dying.

"Did you and your son get together yet?" she asked when the show finished.

"Actually, we did--yesterday. He came into D.C. and we had lunch together."

"Nice. What did you talk about?"

"My retiring. I told him about you."

"How did that go?"

"He's anxious to meet you."

She smiled. "I'm ready."

"We haven't set a date yet. Probably wait until after the inauguration."

The next morning Daniels went out for a *Post* while his coffee was brewing. He found what he was looking for in the obits.

Randall Martin Dodd, 27, Crime Victim

The police were treating Dodd's death as if it was a robbery, but Daniels knew better. He was killed because of what he knew. He had to find out what Dodd wanted to tell them. His one hope was that his son could help him. Otherwise, he'd no idea where to turn.

He'd left things vague with Trey, thanking him for the help he'd provided without pressing his son in terms of any future assistance. He didn't want Trey to think his interest in him was solely related to the case. As a result, he failed to ask him if he could call on him another time. Now he needed him desperately.

"Let me call Trey and see if they have plans Saturday," he suggested to Maureen over breakfast. The two of them were flying to Atlanta Sunday morning to spend Christmas with his mother and his sister's family.

"Okay," she said. "I was planning on shopping while you watched your football games, but I can probably finish what I need to do before Saturday."

Brianna answered the phone. "Hi, Mr. Daniels. Trey is getting dressed for work."

"I wondered if it would be okay if I came by Saturday afternoon to introduce both of you to my fiancé. Also, I didn't get much of a chance to meet LeBron last time."

"Let me check with Trey."

A couple of minutes later, she said she'd like to have them come for dinner Saturday night. That way they'd get to meet LeBron who was usually awake in the late afternoon.

Daniels agreed and asked what they could bring.

"Neither Trey nor I drink wine," she answered. "So don't waste your money. Just come with your appetites."

"How about dessert?" Daniels offered. "The bakery down the street makes a mean double-layer chocolate cake."

When he answered the front door, Trey was only slightly more relaxed than he'd been the previous week. "Don't worry, I don't plan on visiting every week, son," Daniels said after introducing Maureen.

"Don't say that, Mr. Daniels," Brianna called from the kitchen. "You're welcome here as often as you like, right, Trey?"

Trey managed a half-hearted shrug.

"You picked a winner, when you proposed to that young lady," Daniels said.

Trey cracked a smile. "You don't have to tell me."

Daniels accepted the beer Brianna offered, which she said she'd purchased just for him, and when everyone had a beverage, he proposed a toast. "To Trey, Brianna, and LeBron. Health, security, and above all happiness."

"To your happiness as well Mr. Daniels and Ms. Thornberry," Brianna replied.

Maureen lifted her water glass. "I wish you'd call me Maureen."

Daniels raised his glass as well. "And it would make my day if both of you would call me Dad."

"To Maureen and Dad, then," Brianna said.

Trey clinked glasses with everyone. His smile was the most genuine Daniels had seen since he'd showed up on his doorstep the prior Sunday.

Later, Daniels pulled Trey aside while Maureen was helping Brianna put the baby to sleep. "The man I was supposed to meet was killed Tuesday night."

"You're kidding me."

"Unfortunately, no. The police are treating it as a murder-robbery, but I'm convinced it was because he found out something that incriminated the people behind Ethan Garvin's accident."

"The more you tell me about this investigation of yours, the more I think you need to go to President Palmer and tell him you're in over your head."

Daniels gave that a moment's consideration. "Perhaps you're right, but I've never been a quitter--"

"I'm not saying quit; I'm just saying you can't do this on your own, and need I point out that the next person to show up dead could be you or the young woman in that apartment."

"I'm aware of that, Trey, and I appreciate your concern, but--"

"But nothing, and don't forget I've got a wife and child to look out for."

"Absolutely. You're right. I'm sorry I involved you as deeply as I have. If it helps you sleep sounder at night, I've got two agents taking turns watching your house starting tomorrow."

Trey shook his head in dismay. "Great. Does that mean you think they're on to you?"

"I don't think so, but I'm not taking any chances."

Trey walked around the room for a minute muttering to himself. "Given I've already stuck my neck out I might as well put it in the noose. Tell me more about this Dodd fellow."

Sunday, December 24

Daniels didn't mind that his sister Alice wasn't able to pick them up at the Atlanta airport. He preferred renting a car and, although his mother would be joining them Christmas day, he knew he needed to head directly to the nursing home before doing anything else.

Three hours later on the drive to his sister's house, Maureen kept telling Daniels to stop apologizing for his mother's behavior. When they arrived she cursed her son for neglecting her, then wouldn't let go of his hand the entire time they were there.

"She liked you," Daniels said.

"I hope so," Maureen replied. "I wouldn't want her as an enemy."

Christmas eve at his sister's was enhanced by the flowers and chocolates Maureen had delivered to Alice King's house. After dinner, they retired to the living room where the discussion ranged from childhood memories to the nursing home aides to Tucker's and Maureen's wedding plans. Alice's youngest daughter made a brief appearance, then disappeared into the night, promising to arrive the next day with presents.

Normally Daniels didn't mind if the TV was on as long as it was tuned to a music channel, but when he heard the president-elect would be making a statement that evening, he let the others know he wanted to listen.

"Why do you care?" Alice asked when he turned up the volume to hear what the president-elect had to say. "Aren't you retiring in a few weeks?"

"Four weeks from today actually," Daniels answered. "I'm just curious what he's about to say."

When introduced, Garvin came forward from the back of the platform and waved to the small crowd that had gathered outside the family home while they applauded wildly for a minute or more.

Daniels wished Sharon were there so she could tell him if the man on the podium was actually Henry Garvin or his twin Richard. If pressed, he'd guess this time it was actually Henry. The cameras would provide close-ups and too many people who knew the brothers could tell them apart.

"It's a bit chilly out here," were Garvin's first words, "so I'm not going to make this a long speech."

The crowd cheered again.

"From myself and my family I wish everyone in America and every peace loving person worldwide a merry Christmas."

Mrs. Garvin, who was standing close to her husband, whispered something to him when he paused to let the crowd cheer.

Garvin gave a slight nod, and then continued. "As some of you know, I have not made a lot of personal appearances lately. I have been hard at work with my advisors selecting members of my cabinet, considering legislation, and preparing a budget, which I must present to Congress in January. In the coming days, my press office will be releasing more names of nominees, and given the state of the country's economy, we are preparing to undertake a number of measures to increase world trade. To that end, we look forward to the upcoming talks with the Chinese government on trade and climate change. We'll have more to say about that in the weeks ahead."

Mild applause.

"I won't bore you with the details tonight. I'll end by saying 'God bless all of you and God bless America.'"

"Good for him," Alice said. "Short and sweet."

A little too short, Daniels thought. He'd said the right things, but didn't seem to project the kind of energy Daniels remembered him displaying during the campaign. Maybe it was just the cold weather.

"I hope he has some answers to the country's economic problems," Maureen stated. "We certainly can't borrow any more money from China without expecting them to dictate domestic policies--like asking us to balance our budget when they don't balance theirs."

Daniels was glad to hear Maureen's remarks. She was coming around to his point of view, which reflected what he'd learned by paying attention to Edwin Palmer's speeches and policy statements.

"Isn't China an ally?" Alice asked.

"Sometimes," Daniels replied. "They tried to bully President Palmer when he first took office."

"Didn't Palmer campaign against adjusting the terms of the 2014 agreement on carbon emissions that was signed by President Obama and China's Premier Xi Jinping?" Maureen asked.

Daniels nodded his agreement. "He did. When the two leaders met in person, the Chinese Premier demanded the U.S. lower our CO2 emission targets without offering to lower theirs. Experts praised Palmer for battling the current premier to a draw."

"So what's this upcoming conference about?" Alice asked.

"Good question," Maureen said. "I'll bet Eugene knows."

Daniels laughed. "From what I've read, China wants to be allowed to increase its CO2 ceiling given that the dire predictions of rising sea levels have not materialized, and they want the U.S. to impose even stricter limits. In other words they want us to produce less while they are allowed to produce more."

"How can they justify that?" Alice asked.

"They claim the U.S. was responsible for much of the pollution during the last century and thus needs to pay back the rest of the world."

"And what do you think Henry Garvin will do?" Maureen asked.

"Good question. Time will tell."

The next day, during the flight back to D.C., Daniels scanned the Atlanta and Washington papers on his tablet for commentaries on the president-elect's brief speech. He was also interested in the upcoming talks with China. He wondered if the mysterious campaign official they'd been unable to identify would be attending. If so, Henry Garvin would be president by then and the investigation into Ethan's charges would have been for naught.

Although Sharon wasn't expected back from visiting her parents in Indiana until later in the week,

Daniels planned to ask her to research the China talks using some of the advanced search techniques Trey had taught her. If Trey was willing to come into the District, Daniels would have to decide which was the more important task--looking into Randy Dodd's murder or identifying the mysterious consultant.

The name Cynthia Renfro kept popping up as he mulled over the state of the investigation. How could he get her interested in doing more for them? Perhaps she could be persuaded to try to find out details not reported in the papers about Randy Dodd's death?

With less than four weeks to go, Daniels also knew he had to talk to President Palmer. He hated the thought of letting the man down, but he had to tell him the investigation was at a near stand-still.

In terms of making progress, the Secret Service wasn't being helpful when they informed him he'd maxed out on the number of personal days he would be allowed to use until his retirement. They instructed him to report back to work on Thursday. Daniels didn't know how he could work five days a week and still have enough time or energy to work on the president's assignment.

Daniels decided to let Palmer know where things stood in case he wanted to take Daniels off the case.

When he arrived at the P Street apartment Wednesday morning, he was surprised to learn that Sharon was flying back that day.

"I was tired of family asking me what I'm going to do now that I've left my job," she confessed when she showed up at the apartment shortly after two. "It seems their lives are incomplete unless everyone around them has a plan."

Daniels laughed. "I'm glad you're back. Given what Mr. Garvin said the other night, I'd like you to research that upcoming China conference. Try to find out who they are sending as delegates."

He also had to re-schedule Sharon's bodyguards. That had to be done right away because he had given time off to the guys who had not accompanied Sharon to Indiana. Once he'd informed his crew of their new hours, he started working on a statement to send to the President. He was in the midst of trying to condense all that had happened since they'd talked to two pages with room for his conclusions when Sharon interrupted him.

"Get this," she said, coming into the study with her tablet in hand.

"What's that?"

"Henry Garvin spent a year in China when he was at Brown."

"That's interesting. Tell me more."

"It says in his campaign biography that he went to China through an exchange program operated by Oberlin College."

"I wonder," Daniels said. "Could something have happened while he was in China that might shed some light on Ethan's accident?"

She shrugged her shoulders. "How can we find out?"

He shook his head. "No idea."

"It seems every time we find a promising avenue, we hit a road block before we get anywhere," Sharon said.

"It seems that way, but there are still some avenues you can explore. Check on all the committees Henry Garvin served on during his tenure in Congress. Do any have anything to do with China? I'd like to see a list. Also, have you read all of Garvin's comments on China, gone through all of his speeches, read through the debate transcripts and media interviews?"

She shook her head. "That's probably a ton of stuff."

"Then you'd better get started."

"And what am I looking for exactly?"

"To start, I want to know how he plans to respond to China's latest demands."

Sharon looked puzzled. "What does that have to do with Ethan?"

Was this the moment to tell her what Ethan told the President? To do so might elevate her fear level off the scale. "If the man they called 'Z' is Chinese, perhaps that's the connection, but to tell the truth, Sharon, I'm in the dark. That's why we need to get up to speed on Henry Garvin's views on these issues."

Near the end of the afternoon, Sharon asked him if she could read his report to the President. "I like it," she said after perusing the document, "but I think you ought to deliver it orally."

Daniels was taken aback for a moment, but then remembered communications was her specialty. "Okay, why?"

"I think it will have more impact that way. Second, don't you want an answer right away?"

"True."

"If you give it to him in writing it takes away the sense of urgency. He's probably going to spend New Year's with his family, which means it might be days before you hear from him."

"You're right," Daniels said. "I want him to know my feelings won't be hurt if he tells me to stop so he can turn it over to someone else."

"At this late date?"

"I can't make that decision."

"And, if he says it's you or no one?"

"I want him to know working five days a week at the agency will interfere with making progress in this investigation."

"Make it that simple. Like this: 'Mr. President, if you want me to continue, I'll never get to the bottom of it if I have to work my regular job too.'"

Daniels nodded. She was right.

Soon after he got to his office at Secret Service headquarters Thursday morning, Daniels submitted a request for a few minutes of the President's time using the procedure Palmer outlined at their first meeting back in November. He got a response a few hours later. Palmer had made time for him at the residence at 10:00 p.m. that evening.

When he arrived at the White House, Daniels was escorted to the residence wing of the building where he found the President at the bar in the living room pouring himself a Scotch. "You won't tell anyone, will you?"

Daniels laughed. "Not if you pour me one, too."

Palmer found another glass. "How much?"

"An inch will do. Thank you, sir."

"I assume this is not a social visit, Agent Daniels."

"Unfortunately, no. I wanted to brief you on my progress and offer to step aside if you want to assign the project to someone else."

"Now why would I do that?"

"There are less than four weeks before the inauguration and I'm moving forward at a crawl. I'm confident Ethan Garvin was the victim of foul play, but have yet to discover who was responsible or why they did it."

"And the material he promised me?"

Daniels shook his head.

Palmer took a sip from his drink and wandered over to an easy chair. Daniels remained standing, knowing he could not sit unless invited.

"That's disappointing, but I still have confidence in you."

"What do you make of Henry Garvin's refusal to make public appearances?" Daniels asked when Palmer didn't continue.

Palmer seemed surprised at the question. "It's a little unusual, but he's not obligated to do so."

"What if it's related to Ethan's accusation and demise?"

The President motioned for Daniels to sit. "In what way?"

"Ethan's fiancé says she says Henry may hold himself responsible for his son's death."

Palmer nodded. "That would fit with what Ethan told me that morning, although I still find it hard to believe what he said had an ounce of truth to it."

"That's what I thought when I started on this," Daniels admitted, "but I can't find any evidence Ethan was mentally ill. Maybe he misjudged a piece of information that made it look like his father was doing someone else's bidding."

"That's why we need to see what Ethan thought was so incriminating."

"Have you talked to Henry lately?" Daniels asked.

"No, only to some of his staffers."

"What if you called to speak to him?"

"What would that accomplish?"

Daniels sat on the edge of a chair opposite Palmer. "If you can get the president-elect on the phone, tell him Ethan came to you with a strange story and you'd like to discuss it with him in person. Ask him to come to the White House."

"I'll have to think about that."

"If he agrees to come, make sure I'm in the room or at least where I can watch and listen."

"I'll give you an answer tomorrow evening. I'll send you a memo when I'm available to talk. Meanwhile, is there anything else I can do to help?"

"Yes, a couple of things. First, can you get me a copy of Ethan's sealed accident report and autopsy?"

"Have you asked Worthington to do it?"

"He said he'd try, but so far has come up empty."

"Okay. I'll see what I can do. Any thing else?"

"Secret Service Personnel is denying me use of any more of my unused personal time until I retire. They say they're short-staffed."

"I'll take care of it."

"Thank you, Sir."

"Thank you, Agent Daniels." He raised his glass and drained it. 'Onward."

Friday, December 29

Tired and anxious, Daniels arrived at the P Street apartment in the late afternoon Friday, having put in a full day's work at Secret Service headquarters going over details with the man chosen to replace him. He was at his desk looking over what Sharon had come up with on the China trade talks when he was interrupted by a call from the building's security desk. "We have a visitor for a Mr. Daniels."

Who could it be?

"There's no one here by that name," Daniels replied, hoping the doorman was mistaken, since the building staff only knew him as Joe Johnson.

"That's what I told the lady, but she insists she saw a Mr. Daniels and a young lady enter the building fifteen minutes ago. You fit the description she gave me."

Daniels and Sharon had returned about that time from a quick dinner at a nearby restaurant. Could someone he knew have spotted them?

"Okay. I'll be right down," he said.

"What's up?" Sharon inquired as Daniels headed for the apartment front door.

"Someone is downstairs asking for me by my real name. It might be a friend or colleague who saw us on the street a few minutes ago. I'll figure out some excuse why I'm here. I'll be right back."

When the elevator doors opened on the ground floor, Daniels panicked. He recognized the person standing with her back to him by her tan winter coat and brown leather hat. The person looking out to the street where a light wispy snow had been falling most of the afternoon was none other than Maureen Thornberry.

Daniels reached for the button to close the elevator door, but she turned and saw him. *Caught.* He stepped off the elevator and walked past her to the security desk. "Sorry for the misunderstanding, Mr. Cho. I'll escort Ms. Thornberry upstairs."

He turned and took Maureen by the elbow, directing her towards the elevator.

She pulled her arm out of his grasp. "What are you doing? Where are you taking me?"

"Please don't make a fuss. Come with me, and all your questions will be answered."

"They'd better be," she said, her face bright red as she stepped into the elevator.

Daniels pushed the button for the ninth floor and turned to face his fiancé. Maureen's her jaw locked in anger. Her anger surely reflected her discovering that he was spending time in a luxury apartment building with a pretty young woman. *This is bad*, Daniels said to himself over and over as the elevator ascended. Neither spoke. When they reached the ninth floor, Daniels motioned for Maureen to get off. She hesitated, but exited the elevator as he was about to take her arm.

"This way," he said, heading down the hall toward Mrs. Palmer's apartment. He stopped outside the apartment door. "This is not what you think."

She simply glared at him.

"This apartment belongs to Charlotte Palmer--the President's wife."

Maureen looked at him like he'd lost his mind.

"I've made a terrible mistake," she said, starting to back away. "I'll just leave now and mail you your ring and other possessions."

"Maureen," Daniels said, "give me a chance to explain."

"What explanation can there possibly be? You're telling me this apartment belongs to the President's wife. Yet I saw you come into the building with some little hottie. I hope the two of you have a happy life together."

"Maureen. It's Mrs. Palmer's apartment and I'm here on official business."

"What kind of cockamamie story is that?"

"Let me--"

"And what about the young lady who seems to be living here? I suppose that's the Palmers' daughter and you're protecting her?"

Daniels punched in the code to open the door. "No. I mean-- Please, come inside and let me . . ."

Maureen started back to the elevator. He had to act fast. "The young woman who is staying here was Ethan Garvin's fiancé, and I am protecting her."

Maureen stopped and turned back. "This gets more and more outlandish. You're a nice man, Tucker Daniels, but you need to brush up on your lying skills."

"What's going on?" Sharon Washburn had stuck her head out of the doorway. She took one look at Maureen and seemed to assess the situation. "You must be Mr. Daniels' fiancé. He's told me how lucky he is and how he's looking forward to spending the rest of his life with you. I'm Sharon Washburn," she said stepping out in the hall, sticking out her hand. "I was engaged to Ethan Garvin."

Maureen was clearly caught off guard. She hesitated, but then shook Sharon's hand briefly.

"Will you come inside?" Sharon asked. "You're probably wondering what your fiancé is doing here."

"That's an understatement," Maureen said, her face still red with anger. She followed Sharon into the apartment, but not until Daniels stepped aside to give them wide berth.

"He probably hasn't told you anything," Sharon said, motioning for Maureen to follow her into the living room. "I'm not sure even I know the whole story."

"So, I'm not the only one he's kept in the dark?" Maureen said, glancing daggers at Daniels.

"I understand why he--," Sharon said, stopping in mid-sentence. She turned to Daniels. "Oh no, now she's at risk, too!"

Daniels turned his hands up to the ceiling and shook his head slowly.

"What do you mean?" Maureen asked.

Sharon turned back to their visitor. "Two people have been killed Miss. . . ."

"Maureen. You can call me Maureen."

"Two people have been killed, Maureen--my fiancé and a reporter who was helping us investigate his death."

"That's terrible, but why . . ."

"Why am I here? They threatened to harm me. Mr. Daniels has retired Secret Service agents here twenty-four hours a day, but I'm still afraid they're going to break in here and kill me."

Maureen looked around as if searching for the Secret Service agents.

"Mr. Alvarez leaves when Mr. Daniels arrives," Sharon said, seeing Maureen's confusion, "and Mr. Freeman comes at six when Mr. Daniels leaves."

Maureen sat down on the couch in the living room after Sharon plunked herself on one of the uncomfortable, artsy chairs opposite the couch. Daniels remained standing at the entrance to the room. He sensed the tide was slowly turning in his favor. He didn't want to do or say anything that would reverse its direction.

"I'm still angry," Maureen informed Daniels half an hour later, after he supplemented those parts of the story that Sharon omitted or got wrong. "At least you could have warned me you were involved in some classified work for the President, so that I didn't come over here and embarrass myself."

"You're right. I--"

"I'm not sure where this leaves us," Maureen said. He could see her start to tear up. "I don't know if I can be married to someone who keeps deep secrets," she said getting up as if to leave.

Daniels' mouth was open, but words failed to come out.

Maureen headed towards the apartment door. She stopped before opening it. "I'll leave you two to your investigation. Nice to meet you, Ms. Washburn."

"Please, call me Sharon."

"That's nice of you, Sharon, but I'm not sure we'll ever meet again. As for you Mr. Daniels, I'll let you know when I've decided where this leaves us."

Daniels collapsed on the living room couch as Maureen left. Sharon was wise enough to leave him alone.

Earlier that day, Daniels had received word he was told to report to the President's private study in the residence at ten p.m. He spent the rest of the day mulling over in his mind what to do to salvage his relationship without coming up with an answer. Having to go to the White House got him back on course as he reviewed what he needed to tell the President.

Edward Palmer was sitting in an easy chair watching a college women's basketball game on a 70 inch TV screen. He motioned for Daniels to sit and didn't say anything until there was a commercial time out.

"Nebraska is not known for women's basketball. In fact, they're not known for their women's sports period, but this year they have a chance to make it to the tournament."

Daniels surmised the President was referring to the NCAA tournament. "I didn't know you were a basketball fan, Mr. President."

"I'm a Nebraska fan, Agent--my alma mater. Anyway, I've got some good news. First, you've been re-assigned to me to be used in any capacity I choose. That means you're free to devote twenty-four hours a day to solving this mystery, assuming you solve problems in your sleep, which I've heard some people can do."

"I wish I could," Daniels murmured.

"The point is you don't have to show up at headquarters any more. However, you'd better pop in once or twice a week to tell me how you're doing."

"Will do."

Palmer switched sound back on to the game as the commercial was over, but he lowered it to a dull roar.

"Also, Transportation decided to do a study of solo car accidents in Fairfax County. They're gathering data today. You'll have your accident report by Monday."

"Great."

"Now, as the radio newscaster Paul Harvey used to say, 'here's the rest of the story.' Earlier today, I tried calling Henry Garvin, to whom I haven't spoken since I offered him condolences for his son's death seven weeks ago. Mrs. Garvin came on the line and said Henry was under the weather. She asked if he could call me back tomorrow or the next day. I said it was crucial that I speak to him. She said she'd be glad to convey the message. I said what I had to say was for Henry's ears only. She asked if it could wait twenty-four hours. I said I didn't want to go public with the fact that I was prevented from talking to her husband. She quickly backtracked and asked if it could wait until the morning. When she made it clear that was the best she could do, I agreed. That's where things stand. I expect to hear from him tomorrow morning."

"Interesting, don't you think?"

"I do. Something is amiss there. I'm glad you brought it up. I should have been paying more attention, but as you can imagine, there's a lot to do around here to wrap things up."

On his drive home, Daniels decided he shouldn't give Maureen too much time to think things over before he approached her. Even though she'd said she'd contact him, Daniels showed up at her apartment at seven a.m. the next morning with chocolates, flowers, and a steaming large coffee.

"I don't know if I'm ready to talk to you, Mr. Daniels," she said maintaining the safety chain on the door. Her face was puffy and her eyes red.

"I hear you, Ms. Thornberry . . . err, Maureen. I know you're upset, but let's sit down and talk this through before one of us does something we'll both regret."

She didn't respond.

"Can I come in? This coffee is burning my hand."

She gave him a disapproving headshake, but opened the door.

"I already have mine," she said when he set the coffee, chocolates, and flowers on the kitchen island counter.

"The coffee is for me," Daniels said. "The rest is for you."

"You think that's all it's going to take-- flowers and chocolates?"

Daniels sighed. "I hoped it would get me in the door."

She retrieved her coffee mug and sat on a stool across from him. "Say your piece."

"Okay. The reason I didn't tell you anything after the President asked me to investigate Ethan's death was to protect you. If Ethan Garvin was telling the truth, anyone associated with the investigation was potentially in danger. As it turned out, we may indirectly be responsible for the death of a free-lance reporter."

She nodded. "That's awful, but--"

Daniels raised his hand. "I know I should have warned you, but once you tell someone you're involved in something like that it becomes a barrier that seems to grow bigger and bigger. That's what happened between Alysia and me."

Maureen nodded sympathetically.

"I could tell she started to have doubts when I had to go away for days at a time without being able to tell her where I was going or when I'd be back. She was stuck at home with a baby. I hated to do that, but I had to follow policy. People's lives were at stake then too."

"I don't dispute any of that, Tucker," Maureen said. "I made a fool of myself yesterday and I am as mad at myself as I am at you."

Daniels gave her a sympathetic smile. "I understand, but you had every reason to question what I was up to."

"I'm glad you agree."

"I do, but I wonder if something else is involved?"

"What's that?"

Daniels took a paper napkin out of the holder, folded it, and then wiped his mouth. "I'm almost afraid to say it."

"Tucker, if we're going to make this work, we have to be open--"

"That's a nice theory, Maureen, but sometimes it's better to leave things unsaid."

"Now you're upsetting me again."

"Okay. Here goes. I wondered if maybe subconsciously you wanted something like this to happen."

"What kind of nonsense--"

"Maybe you're having second thoughts about marrying a black man. There--I said it."

"Oh, Tucker."

She got up, came around the island, and wrapped her arms around him. "Tucker Eugene Daniels. Get that idea out of your head. I do love you and we are going to get married in four weeks and live happily ever after!"

Daniels rode on air on his way to the Dupont Circle apartment. He had worried about whether Maureen had any regrets agreeing to marry him, although she'd never given him any reason to think so. Now he was sure about their relationship and doubted anything could come between them.

Soon after he arrived at Mrs. Palmer's apartment, Daniels received an encrypted email from the federal Department of Transportation telling him he could pick up the report he was expecting at the their New Jersey Avenue location.

He took Sharon with him, giving her a chance to get out of the apartment and him a chance to assess how she was doing. She seemed more worried about him and Maureen than herself. That was good.

When they got back to Dupont Circle, he opened the autopsy report first. It showed what he expected. The cause of Ethan Garvin's death was due to drowning in the water-filled gulley. They weren't able to say whether he'd been conscious, but were unable to document any attempt on his part to escape the vehicle. Toxicology showed no traces of alcohol or any illegal drugs. The report mentioned that he'd been taking an over-the-counter stress-relieving compound--the kind that you can find in supermarkets these days. It contained some strange ingredients, including Ashwagandha, described in Ayurvedic publications--as calmness inducing. The report made it clear the compound did not contribute to the cause of death.

The accident report was bound to be much more interesting, but as he was opening the envelope the house phone rang, which could only mean a wrong number or building security.

"Mr. Johnson. A Mr. Sharp is here to see you. Shall I send him up?"

Trey! Great. "Yes, please do."

"My son's here," he told Sharon.

Trey got off the elevator carrying two large computer cases.

"What's all this?" Daniels said, greeting his son with an awkward hug.

"Briana told me to come in to see what I could do to help."

"Great. Come in. What's all that stuff?"

"I brought my own gear. Yours is too slow, and this way you won't have to look over my shoulder while I work."

Daniels laughed. He didn't mind the dig. It was so much better than silence. "I was just about to delve into Ethan Garvin's accident report when you showed up, but I'm sure I can find something for you to work on while I do that."

Trey was setting up his hardware when the house phone rang again.

Who could it be now, Daniels wondered.

"Mr. Johnson. You have another visitor."

"Okay."

Peter G. Pollak

"It's Ms. Thornberry. Should I--"

Daniels wasn't expecting her either. Why was she there? "Yes, please send her up."

"Maureen's here," he told the others. She hadn't said anything about coming into the city when he left her that morning.

Daniels greeted her as she got off the elevator. She'd done her best to cover up evidence that she'd spent most of the night crying.

"I decided I wasn't doing anything valuable to the world sitting at home wondering if you were making any progress. Maybe I can help. Is that okay?"

Daniels held the door for her. "You're joining the team?"

"If you'll have me."

"Of course, of course. Come in." He escorted Maureen into the apartment. "Guess who's here?"

"Hello, Ms. Thornberry," Trey said looking up from behind the desk in the study where he'd been plugging in his power cords.

"Hello, Trey. Please, call me Maureen."

"The only problem is where to put you," Daniels said.

"She can sit with me," Sharon piped up. "I need another pair of eyes to look through all this stuff about Henry Garvin's China policies."

"Done," Daniels said. He'd tried to handle the investigation on his own and had resisted when Sharon wanted to sign on fulltime, and he'd only gotten Trey involved when he couldn't think of any other way to get the information he needed. Now Maureen was joining up. It wasn't how he was used to working, but circumstances demanded change. "Okay, guys. This may turn out to be an impossible assignment, but things could be worse. I could be here trying to do this by myself. Let's see if we can crack this thing open."

Sharon raised her mug and said, "Amen to that."

Maureen, who had poured herself and Trey glasses of water, raised hers. "I second."

Trey raised his glass. "Mission impossible without Tom Cruise."

Daniels lofted his coffee mug. "I'd rather have you three."

Saturday, December 30

Before he could dissect the accident report, Daniels had to put Trey to work. One question that totally stymied him was the identity of the Asian who had been described by Ethan as a campaign consultant with no portfolio or official duty.

"That's all you have to go on?" Trey asked when Daniels told him the problem.

"Some of the campaign people apparently called him 'Mr. Z' because his name was too difficult for them to remember."

"Now that helps," Trey said, giving his father a *what's next* look.

"Whoever he is, he didn't have an official role," Daniels stated. "At least we haven't been able to find any. I know it sounds impossible, but see what you can do."

"Lovely," Daniels heard Trey say as he closed the door to the spare bedroom where he exiled himself to read the accident report.

Daniels had one more task to do before he could get to the Fairfax County Police Department's accident report--finding two agents to shadow Maureen. Now that she had joined the team, he'd feel a lot better if he could call on someone to keep an eye on her during the hours they were not in each other's company.

His first choice was Sandra Burke––one of the first minority women hired by the Agency. Daniels knew she stayed in the region after she retired because she had come to a number of recent Agency get-togethers. He didn't have her contact information but he suspected Nate Parenti would. He left a message for Nate asking him to find Burke for him.

He felt better about reaching Mary Broussard, another retired female agent. Broussard had worked in his division and they'd stayed in touch when a knee injury forced her to retire on disability. She answered her phone right away and he was happy to learn she was looking for part-time work.

"When do I start?" she asked him after stating confidently her injury was healed to the point where it shouldn't prevent her from doing what Daniels described he needed her to do.

That done, he dove into the accident report. Because the past 96 hours of speedometer readings could be retrieved and analyzed on all recently-manufactured passenger vehicles he learned Ethan's car was travelling fourteen miles per hour above the 40 MPH speed limit for that section of the road. Daniels was surprised to read that speed was thus determined to be the primary factor in causing the accident. It didn't seem excessive, but the road conditions would have to be taken into account.

The report's author addressed whether some factor other than speed had caused the car to leave the road. They pointed out that the tires were guaranteed against blowouts, and when they examined the tires, none had suffered damage consistent with a blowout.

The report supported the insurance investigator's conclusion concerning mechanical issues. "All indicators show the car was running as intended," the report's author wrote.

Morning fog was the only other possible cause they could attach to the accident based on interviews with school bus drivers who had been on that road that morning.

Daniels turned to the beginning of the report. The first part covered environmental conditions. The accident occurred at 7:31:26 a.m. In terms of the road's general condition, the report stated the road was dry and the sky, overcast. Bright sun was ruled out as a contributing factor. In the next section they wrote lack of a barrier rail on that curve and the fact that the gully was full of water contributed to the severity of the accident. Recent rains and the road repairs created what was not a normal condition.

After several read-throughs, Daniel concluded the report raised more questions than it answered. They didn't know why Ethan had been speeding when he knew that section of the road was hilly and curvy. Daniels recalled they hadn't interviewed Sharon Washburn, but they did interview Ethan's mother. She claimed to lack any knowledge as to where he was going that morning or why he might have been speeding.

The one positive was the report included notes from an interview police had conducted with one of the people who called in the accident. A nearby resident, seventy-eight year old Christopher Chesswood was apparently the first person on the scene. Chesswood told the police he didn't see the accident, but from the amount of smoke coming out of the ditch he guessed it must have occurred only a few minutes before he got there. Chesswood admitted being unable to go into the ditch due to the severity of the slope. Instead, he called 911 and waited for the police and ambulance to arrive.

The report catalogued the car's contents or lack thereof. It seemed Ethan had a set of spare clothes in the back including dress shoes in a valise, but they did not recover any electronics--no cellphone, tablet, or computer. Nor did they find Ethan's briefcase. Since Sharon had been prevented from entering the family farmhouse, Daniels had no way of knowing whether Ethan had left it behind, but given the estimated time lapse between the accident and its discovery, it seemed unlikely that someone could have removed anything without being seen.

Given the assumption Ethan was heading to the White House with "evidence" of his father's perfidy, why would he have left those items behind? Of course, the authors of the report didn't touch on that subject or provide any clues.

Daniels knew Sharon would not want to read the report since it described Ethan's physical condition when the ambulance crew arrived, but he hoped Maureen would. Perhaps she would see something he'd overlooked.

"I think I've got something," Trey told Daniels as he came out of the spare bedroom. "I think the guy you're looking for works for the Chinese government."

"Really. Tell me what you found."

"Two trade representatives assigned to the Chinese embassy showed up at a number of campaign stops," Trey stated, "particularly to those with a large number of Asians in attendance."

"Interesting. Did you discover their names? I'd like to talk to them."

"Yes. Both begin with Z. One is named Zhai Qi; then other is a Zhang Heijing, but you can't talk to either unless you want to call China. Both are currently back in Beijing."

"Damn," Daniels said. "Just our luck. How'd you figure it out?"

Trey pointed to an array of photos on his large monitor. "Pattern recognition. I set up a search on every photo taken of each of Henry Garvin's campaign stops and events. I discovered more than three dozen people whose facial elements might have qualified as your person of interest, but I was able to narrow down the list by matching each person with the location the photo was taken."

"I'm not sure I'm following," Daniels said.

"Misters Zhai and Zhang were the only ones who appeared in more than one location. The others were just local people attending one event. Those two participated in a number of events including Garvin's appearances in the Chinatown sections of San Francisco and New York."

"Sharon, come out here," Daniels called to Sharon who was in the kitchen working with Maureen. "Do you recognize either of these men?" he asked when she came into the study. "There's a good chance one of them is your mysterious "Z.""

She shook her head. "I don't think so, but after Ethan announced our engagement I was told quite bluntly by Mrs. Garvin to stay away from campaign events."

"The problem is neither is still in the states, right Trey?"

Trey nodded. "The latest information is that both left the country on November 10th--two days after the election."

Daniels studied the photo on Trey's monitor. "One of them may be the guy who has been pulling the strings in the Garvin campaign, but how do we prove that?"

"Given that you can't use official channels, I can't see any way you can reach out to him," Trey said, "and since I don't read Chinese, I'm not going to be able to learn much more about either of them."

"Another dead end?" Sharon asked.

Daniels hated to admit this was happening all too often. "It appears that way. On the other hand, we won't be wasting our time trying to track down Mr. Z."

"What's left to work on?" asked Maureen.

"I've got an assignment, hon. Thanks to having a copy of the accident report, we now have the name and address of the man who discovered the wreck. I'd like you to see if he'll talk to us."

"On what basis--friend of Ethan's fiancé?"

"That might not fly. Let me think. Have you ever done any reporting?"

She laughed. "Me?"

"You. I hereby appoint you a reporter for the *Fairfax County Inquirer*."

"Is there such a publication?" Sharon asked.

"There is now," Daniels said. "Trey, do you know how to set up an online publication? I'd like to start posting information about Ethan's accident."

"To what end, Tucker?" Maureen asked.

"To stir things up and who knows maybe someone out there has some information that can help us. Can you do it, Trey?"

Trey smiled and turned his hands to the ceiling. "Piece of sweet potato pie! I'll set up an account for you with blogging software that will enable you to post new items whenever you like. I can tie it into social media, including Facebook, Twitter, Google+, and a few others, so anytime you post something it will show up on those sites as well."

"Perfect," Daniels said. "Now who around here can write?"

Sharon raised her hand. "That would be me, but I don't like that 'stir things up' bit. Every time we do that I get targeted."

"We'll make everything anonymous," Daniels said, "and I'll remind your watchers to be on their toes. So, will you write the copy for us?"

Sharon gave him a brief nod to show she wasn't enthused. "Okay. Tell me what you want to say and I'll put it in a newsy format."

"Excellent," Daniels said. "I need a couple of minutes to think this through."

Daniels retreated to his temporary office in the spare bedroom. A few hours later the *Fairfax County Inquirer* was launched with its first story, the title of which was "Unanswered Questions About Ethan Garvin's Fatal Accident." Questions were bullet-pointed after an introductory paragraph encouraging anyone with information to contact them through the website or using the email address, editor@fairfaxinquirer.com. Trey set it up so that all four of them would receive anything sent to the website or email.

"We'll add a new post every other day detailing one question at a time," Daniels said as they gathered around Trey's monitor to admire their work.

"Good plan," Trey said. "To maximize exposure you need to add new information on a regular pattern."

At the end of the afternoon Daniels pulled Trey aside to thank him again for his help.

"I talked to the President as you suggested," he told his son, "and he repeated that it's me or it won't get done. Your help today was invaluable."

Trey was packing his computers. "I don't know how many more days I can give you, Dad."

Tucker couldn't answer for a few seconds. That was the second time Trey called him Dad. When he told Maureen how that made him feel at the restaurant they'd stopped at for dinner, she put her hand on his. "You're a good man, Tucker Daniels."

While he didn't feel particularly good, he felt very fortunate at that moment. Now all they needed was a break.

Daniels worked with Sharon Sunday morning to prepare a second news post for the *Fairfax County Inquirer*, which they titled "What caused Ethan Garvin's fatal accident?" They drafted two more articles that they planned on posting after the New Year.

Daniels drove Sharon and the two agents who'd be guarding her to the airport for her flight to Indianapolis where she'd be spending the next five days with her family.

"Don't go anyplace by yourself," he instructed in the car. "Don't go anyplace where there are not a lot of people around, and don't accept any candy canes from strangers."

Daniels was glad to see that Sharon laughed at the last 'don't.' There had been no more threats since the text message--probably thanks to Trey's having added several layers of security to her personal phone as well as the cell Daniels had given her to use to contact him directly.

After promising to try to set up a meeting with the accident witness, Maureen begged Daniels for Sunday off in order to catch up on some shopping. As a result, Daniels was the only person working that afternoon from the P Street apartment. He was anxious to learn whether their publication had gotten any attention. Trey had showed him how to check on how many people had opened the link to the initial *Fairfax County Inquirer.*

He was surprised to see dozens of comments--most were from people selling things or asking for money, except one. Cynthia Renfro, the local Fox reporter who had dropped the investigation, posted a two-word comment. "Call me."

Daniels left a message when Renfro's phone went into voice mail. He was deep into reviewing the materials Sharon had compiled on the upcoming China mission when Maureen called.

"I just talked to Christopher Chesswood."

"Who?"

"The man who called 911."

"Oh, right."

"Except he said the police told him he wouldn't have to talk to reporters. I promised not to mention him by name in our story or provide any other information that could be used to identify him."

"Good. Did he agree?"

"Eventually. I had to make up a story about how we found his name since I didn't want to admit that we had a copy of the accident report."

"Smart thinking."

"He said I could come by Tuesday morning after 10 am."

"I'll go with you," Daniels said.

"I was counting on it."

Tuesday, January 2

The Tuesday after New Year's Day, Daniels picked up Maureen and punched Christopher Chesswood's address into his car's GPS. Chesswood lived on a rural road in western Fairfax County. An elderly woman Daniels assumed to be his wife answered the door. Maureen introduced herself by showing the woman the press pass they had made for the occasion.

Mrs. Chesswood didn't give them a chance to state their names. "He changed his mind. He doesn't want to talk to you." She would have closed the door in their faces had Daniels not stuck out his hand.

"Why is that?" he demanded.

"He doesn't want to go to jail."

"Go to jail!" Maureen said. "Why would he think that?"

"He got a call telling him it would be a violation of the oath he signed when he gave his statement."

"Nonsense," Daniels said. "There's no such law. Someone's trying to scare him."

"Well, they did a good job of it. Kept both of us up most of the night."

"Did the person who called give his name or the name of his agency?"

"Can't say for sure. Chris, did they say where they were calling from?"

"Said it too fast," came the answer from somewhere inside the house.

"Mr. Chesswood. We're not asking you to violate any law. The Constitution protects your right to talk to us."

"Leave him alone," Mrs. Chesswood said, "or I'll call the cops."

"We'd better go," Maureen said.

Daniels wasn't ready to give up. "We're leaving, Mr. Chesswood, but it means the truth about what happened to Ethan Garvin may never be known."

"What happened is that he drove into a ditch and got himself killed," Mrs. Chesswood said.

"We think there's more to the story than that, Ma'am. He knew that road and had even called the county about putting up guard rails."

"Young people drive like maniacs around here. I've seen it plenty."

"I'm not denying that, Mrs. Chesswood," Daniels said. "I'm just saying that Ethan knew not to speed around that curve. Something caused him to speed. We're trying to find out what it was."

"And how is my husband supposed to help you figure that out?"

"Maybe he can; maybe he can't. We won't know unless he's willing to tell us what he saw."

"I'm not going to let you put words in his mouth."

"Of course not," Daniels said. "As Ms. Thornberry here told him yesterday, we won't use his name, your address, or anything else that someone could use to bother you folks."

"Well . . . you seem like nice enough folks. Let me go talk to him."

She left the door ajar as she disappeared into the house.

Daniels showed Maureen he had his fingers crossed.

"Silly," she said punching him in the arm.

A minute later Mrs. Chesswood returned. "I guess you can come in, but only for a minute."

She led them into a dark, but homey living room where Mr. Chesswood was sitting in a large easy chair with a blanket covering the lower half of his body. He had stringy white hair, wore a plaid flannel shirt, and was unshaved. He put on his wire-rim glasses as they approached and started to pull the blanket aside.

"No need to get up," Daniels told him.

"He's been napping since breakfast," said Mrs. Chesswood. "Too tired to do anything else."

"We won't stay long," Daniels assured her. He stepped forward and shook the elderly man's arthritic hand.

"I'm not this way usually," he said in a thin voice, covering himself up again.

"No need to apologize," Maureen said. Having asked permission to record the conversation, she placed her iPhone on the coffee table.

"Please tell us what you saw that morning," Daniels said.

Chesswood cleared his throat. "That weren't the first car I seen in a ditch on that road, but it were the worst."

"What did you see?" Daniels asked.

The old man tugged on the blanket and sat up a little straighter. "All I could see at first was smoke coming from around the curve. Naturally, I slowed down. When I turned the corner, I could see the wheels of a car up in the air. I pulled up ahead about fifty yards onto the shoulder where I wouldn't get rear-ended and got out. When I came back, the tires on the car were still spinning. I couldn't go down there, it being too steep, so I went back to my car and hit the emergency button. I've got that service, you know, where you hit that button if you need help."

"Did you see anything else? Any other cars, for example?"

"Funny you should ask. The police never did."

"Never asked what?"

"Whether I saw any other cars."

"Did you?"

"Yep. When I started to pull over I noticed a SUV up ahead. I wondered why he hadn't stopped. He must have seen the car go in the ditch. If he'd stopped they might have got to that poor boy in time."

"Can you describe the SUV?"

Chesswood rubbed his chin. "It was too far to see the license plate or anything like that, but I recognized the tail lights. It was a Mercedes. My son-in-law has one just like it."

"How far away was it would you say?"

"Pretty far. There's a straight stretch along Al Weiss' corn patch after that curve."

"And the Fairfax Police never asked you about seeing any other cars?"

"Nope. Seemed like they were just interested in whether I saw the car leave the road, and I told them I didn't."

"What year is your son's Mercedes?" Maureen asked.

"He's my son-in-law. Got it last year when he got promoted. He works for the IRS. Good kid. Does our taxes for us each year."

"That's nice," Daniels said. "How long did it take before the ambulance got there?"

"Too damn long, if you ask me. I know we're out here a ways, but I was just hoping they'd get there in time to save that boy's life."

"You stayed there the whole time?"

"When the police got there, they asked me a few questions, and said I could go. Eventually I did, not wanting to be nosey."

"And they never followed up?"

"They came here with a typed-out version of what I told them to sign, but they didn't ask me anything else. So, I figured they had everything they needed."

"Could you tell what color the Mercedes was?"

"Black or maybe dark blue."

"Had you ever seen that particular Mercedes before?" Maureen asked.

"I seen my son-in-law's, but he lives in Chevy Chase."

"What color is his Mercedes?"

"Dark red, right hon?" Chesswood said looking over to his wife.

"Do you know what model your son-in-law drives?"

"They use numbers, not names. Martha, do you recall which one Ronnie drives?"

Mrs. Chesswood had brought out a pot of coffee with a dish of home-made cookies. "Four hundred something, I think."

"Do you know anyone who lives out this way who owns one like the one you saw?" Daniels asked.

"Can't say I ever seen anyone else with one like it. You, Martha?"

"Can't say that I have."

Daniels reached for a cookie. "This is good coffee, Mrs. Chesswood."

"Thank you, sir. I'm not used to closing the door on folks. I felt I owed you that much."

"What do you think?" Maureen asked Daniels after they'd thanked the Chesswoods and were driving back to Alexandria.

"It's critical that we find the driver of that Mercedes," Daniels answered.

"I agree, but how?"

"Trey might be able to find it."

"That would be great."

"There are cameras all over the place, including major intersections. If he can access the ones along that road . . ."

"Tucker, do you think the Mercedes pushed Ethan's car off the road?"

"It might have. The Fairfax Police never checked that angle, and now that Ethan's sedan has been demolished there's little chance of our proving it happened that way, if indeed it did."

"But it isn't likely a camera recorded the accident, is it?"

"Probably. Trey and his computers can do a lot of powerful stuff and it doesn't hurt to ask."

"You'd better be careful about asking him to do too much," Maureen stated.

"I know. I know."

"He's already given us two days. I wonder how Brianna feels about that."

"She's good . . . or at least I think she is."

"You'd better ask her."

"You're right, but we're so damn close to breaking this thing open."

"Not necessarily. What if the driver of that car was in front of Ethan?"

Daniels sped into the far left lane to pass a slow car hogging the middle lane. "I suppose that's possible."

"Maybe they were taking a child to the emergency room," Maureen said. "There could be an explanation other than they were somehow responsible for the accident or they couldn't be bothered to stop to help."

Daniels knew he was beat. Maureen was right. He couldn't jump to conclusions not supported by the evidence, and if he put all his money on this being the key, he could not only waste time but also miss something else that led to the answer. They'd just have to see what Trey could come up with.

The next day Maureen rode with Daniels to Dupont Circle. After a quick meeting to go over what everyone was working on, Daniels texted Trey that he would like to talk to him. Trey had set up a number of phony online accounts so he and his father could text each other without being traced.

Next Daniels checked the comments section of the website. Their latest post asked why the Garvins were in such a hurry to demolish Ethan's car. Yet, other than posts from people wanting to share their millions or find him a wife from the

Philippines, nothing popped up related to their quest.

An hour later Trey called him on a burner phone. "I'm off tomorrow," Trey said after Daniels explained what he needed, "but the kind of searches you're talking about, I'd have to do that from my office and there's no way that's going to happen."

"I see," Daniels said. He couldn't stop thinking that Henry Garvin's inauguration was less than three weeks away and Congress would be voting to accept the election results on Saturday.

"Even then it would be a long shot that I'd find the vehicle you're looking for. Perhaps the President can help."

"He might," Daniels admitted. "That's how we were able to put our hands on the accident report even knowing he'll probably get hell for it once Henry Garvin's people find out."

"Maybe you'd be better off pursuing some other angle," Trey said.

"I just wish there was some other angle to pursue," Daniels replied. He had yet to connect with Cynthia Renfro, but other than that, he couldn't think of any pebbles, much less stones, he'd left unturned.

"What kind of responses are you getting from the articles you're posting?" Trey asked.

Daniels laughed. "Mostly junk. We put a new one up today. It says we're looking for the late model Mercedes SUV that was on Route 616 the morning of November 8 between 7:15 and 7:45 a.m. Maybe that will yield something and you won't have to try to find the car for me."

"I hope so," Trey said, "because this is not a job I can do at home. You need official status to access those cameras."

Wondering what he could accomplish, Daniels nevertheless drove himself into the city Wednesday morning to Mrs. Palmer's apartment. Sharon wasn't due back until that evening from her holiday trip home and Maureen told him she would come in the next day unless he couldn't function without her. Daniels wasn't sure what he would have asked her to do if she had joined him.

Trey was off work, but he said he wouldn't come into D.C. unless Daniels had a task he couldn't manage on his own. "I can't think of any reason to drag you down here," his father texted him.

Daniels let himself into the apartment wondering why he had even bothered showing up. Henry Garvin's inauguration was around the corner, and if Ethan's accusation was something other than the product of a misunderstanding, Daniels only had a few days left to prove it before it would be too late. Congress was scheduled to ratify the Electoral College vote Saturday morning.

"Don't show up the morning of the inauguration and expect me to be able to stop it," Palmer had told Daniels on the day he gave him this crazy assignment.

Daniels had never quit anything in his life. He'd learned that lesson as a child. His father wanted him to learn to defend himself and enrolled him in a karate class at the local Y in Richmond. He was eight or nine years old at the time and the memory of what happened still embarrassed him forty-five years later.

The third or fourth class, his father had dropped him off telling him he had to run an errand, but he'd be back to pick him up. An older kid the previous class had roughed him up. He didn't want to experience a repeat and tried to hide in the coatroom, but was found out by the parent of another pupil.

When his father learned what he'd done, he told Tucker he had to go back the next Saturday and apologize to the sensei in front of the entire group. What had been worse than having to do that was the knowledge his father was disappointed in him.

Quitting now was not an option no matter how slim the chances of his succeeding. He wasn't going to let down the President, or his father.

Daniels' first task that morning was to try to reach Cynthia Renfro. He was in luck on his first try.

"Ms. Renfro. This is Joe Johnson. You asked us to call you."

"I've been reading your posts. I see you're still at it."

"We're not giving up."

"Good for you. I feel bad that I wasn't able to stick it out. I wanted to tell you if you do come up with some hard evidence, come to me first and I'll get you on the air."

"I appreciate that, Ms. Renfro. I'll do that."

After concluding that phone call, Daniels decided he needed some coffee. He walked his usual twelve blocks indirect route, which made him feel like he was getting some exercise, and ended up at the neighborhood coffee shop. The weather was unseasonably warm. It looked like it was about to rain, which to Daniels was a heck of a lot better than snow.

When he got back to the apartment, he remembered to check the *Fairfax County Inquirer's* emails and the comments on the website. Going through them was a pain, but he wouldn't have seen the one from Renfro if he hadn't been diligent. When he got tired of deleting sales pitches and illogical rants, he worked on the previous day's *Washington Post* crossword puzzle even though the Tuesday puzzle was typically one of the hardest of the week. When he tired of that, he got to work cleaning up the *Inquirer's* emails and comments. He was almost done when one caught his eye.

Gary Knowlton owns a dark blue Mercedes SUV, it read.

It took Daniels a minute to remember where he knew that name. He pawed through the folder he'd created on the campaign committee staffers to make sure he was right. Sure enough, Gary Knowlton was near the top of the list. He was Henry Garvin's long-time personal aide.

Thursday, January 4

Patience he kept telling himself. It was nearly eleven before Daniels had a chance to tell Sharon and Maureen about the message that claimed Henry Garvin's top aide Gary Knowlton possessed a dark blue Mercedes SUV. Before he could get down to business, Sharon needed to be escorted to her apartment to pick up some clothes and Maureen said she could use some extra time that morning as well. He tried not to bark orders for the women to fall in line while they heated up water for Sharon's tea and Maureen washed the few dishes Daniels had left in the sink from the day before––despite his protesting that she didn't have to do so.

"I talked to Trey late yesterday and asked him if he could find the license plate number to Gary Knowlton's Mercedes," Daniels told the two women when they finally sat down at the kitchen island and he was able to tell them about the anonymous message.

"Trey said he couldn't promise results, but he'll try. He's using another half vacation day and will be here with his computers around one-thirty."

"What about the person who sent the message?" Maureen asked.

"I asked Trey to try to see if he could trace that, but he warned me that the chances of succeeding are slim. Meanwhile we have a decision to make, which is what should we do with this information?"

"What are our options?" Sharon asked.

Daniels consulted his yellow pad where he'd written down a number of possible approaches. "I've narrowed it down to three options. One of us-- probably Sharon--tries to contact Knowlton directly. Two, we can give the information to Cynthia Renfro and let her pose that question to him, or three, we can post the information on our *Fairfax County Inquirer* website and see what that scares up."

"I vote for number two," Maureen said.

Daniels nodded. "Ask Renfro to do it?"

"Yes. Didn't she talk to him once before?"

"She did."

"He's more likely to take her call than ours."

"That makes sense," Daniels admitted. "What do you think, Sharon?"

"I agree. Let's see what she can find out."

"Keep in mind," Daniels said, "just by asking the question, we're practically accusing Knowlton of having some involvement in Ethan's accident. If he was there, at minimum, he failed to stop to help. That's a felony which means prison time if he's found guilty. That alone would be big news."

"Why wouldn't he have stopped?" Sharon asked, "and what was he doing there in the first place?"

Maureen raised her hand. "Not so fast. We're assuming it was his Mercedes SUV that Mr. Chesswood saw. What if Knowlton has an iron-clad alibi? We could damage our case and get into trouble if we accuse him of something he's innocent of doing."

"That's why we should let Renfro talk to him," Daniels said. "Let's see what he says."

Sharon nodded.

"Okay," Daniels said. "We're in agreement. I'll try Renfro, and we'll see what Trey can come up with. Meanwhile why don't you ladies do some background research on Gary Knowlton? I'd like to know who this guy is."

When Daniels tried Cynthia Renfro, her voice mail said she was on vacation until the following Monday.

"Now what?" Maureen asked when Daniels told them. "Wait for her to get back or choose one of the other options?"

"I vote to wait," Sharon said. "A few days won't hurt."

"That's cutting things too close," Daniels said. "We're less than three weeks from the inauguration."

"What does that have to do with it?" Sharon asked.

Daniels turned to Maureen who gave him a 'don't look at me' response. "I guess it's time I told you the full story," he said turning back to Sharon.

Sharon stood up and went around to the back of her chair. Her eyes were as large as doughnuts and her face was bright red. "What do you mean, the full story?"

"I did it for your protection, but it's time I told you why the White House is so interested in Ethan's death. This investigation is not just about Ethan's accident. It's about something he told President Palmer the day before he died."

"And you knew this?" Sharon asked Maureen.

Maureen shook her head. "Not moi."

"So, tell me," Sharon said, turning to face Daniels, her hands on her hips. "What did Ethan tell the President?"

"He said he had proof that his father was beholden to someone in the Chinese government and was planning to help China at our expense."

Sharon looked stunned.

"We believe he was on his way to the White House with his evidence the day he died."

Sharon pointed her finger at him. "You knew all along that he was murdered!"

"Not true, and we still don't have hard proof."

Sharon stood there, looking as if she was going to spit.

"Listen to me," Daniels said. "Ethan may have thought he had proof to back his accusation, but his information might have been false––something planted by someone who wanted to undermine his father's presidency."

Sharon walked back and forth digesting what Daniels had told her. "So that's why you were so interested in whether the briefcase was in the car," she said coming back to stand behind her chair.

Daniels couldn't deny it.

"Why didn't you tell me?" she demanded.

"The simple truth is I thought it would put you in danger."

She started pacing again. "But you did put me in danger, didn't you? I've been stuck here in someone else's apartment for weeks without any idea who's after me or why."

"No," Daniels said. "I did not put you in danger. It was your desire to learn the truth of what happened to your fiancé. They would have left you alone if you had gone off into the sunset."

"Then why didn't you tell me when they threatened me?" Sharon demanded.

"I probably should have," Daniels admitted.

"When are you going to learn, Eugene?" Maureen chimed in.

"Eugene?" Sharon said. "You mean Tucker Daniels isn't his real name!"

Maureen laughed. "Sorry. That's his middle name. I call him that when he's sailing against the current and needs to correct his course."

Sharon rubbed her face and gave Daniels an if-looks-could-kill stare.

Maureen went over to her and gave her a hug.

"It's all beginning to make sense," Sharon said more to herself than the others. "He felt he was in danger, but probably had no idea he was in danger from his own father."

"Which still may not be the case," Daniels pointed out.

"Then who?"

"My bet is that it's someone on his father's staff."

Sharon slammed her fist on the island counter. "Oh my god! Gary Knowlton! Gary Knowlton must be the one who killed Ethan. We've got to tell someone. The FBI. Someone."

She reached for her phone.

Daniels jumped up and put his hand over hers. "Hold on a minute. We still don't have any real proof, but when we do, I'll go to President Palmer."

"So, that's the reason for the urgency," Sharon said sitting back down. "Once Henry Garvin is president it'll be too late to stop him!"

"That's the reason," he confessed, glad the truth had finally come out.

Sharon faced him with her hands on her hips. "I'm still pissed at you, Mr. Tucker Eugene Daniels, but I guess that doesn't matter now. For Ethan's sake, we've got to finish the job. We have to find out what evidence he had and expose whoever is behind this."

"Does that mean you agree we can't wait for Cynthia Renfro to get back from her vacation?" Daniels asked.

"Definitely," Sharon answered.

"Maureen?" Daniels asked turning to his fiancé.

She nodded her agreement. "But if we do go public, we need to think about how to word it so that we protect ourselves."

"You're right," Daniels said. "How we word it is important. Let's take a few minutes and write out how each of us think we ought to word the post."

It took over an hour with a short break for lunch before they reached an agreement about the wording. They were just about to post the information on the *Fairfax County Inquirer* website when Trey showed up.

Daniels proposed a break while he got his son working on the data searches to identify Gary Knowlton's license plate number and see if they could find evidence that his car was in the neighborhood of Ethan's accident on the day in question.

"Okay," Daniels said, coming back into the kitchen. "Which version do you want to go with?"

In the end, Maureen's version won out. She read it out loud:

"Was Henry Garvin's long-time aide, Gary Knowlton, the driver of the dark-colored Mercedes SUV seen leaving the scene of the accident in which Ethan Garvin was killed on November 10 of last year? If so, what was he doing there and why did he flee the scene of the accident without calling for help? If you have any information pertaining to this question, please contact us by email, text message, comment, or phone."

"I'll make sure Cynthia Renfro sees this," Daniels said. "Maybe she'll cut short her vacation to try to reach Knowlton for a comment."

"I would be surprised if other reporters don't start asking him as well," Maureen said.

"Good point," Daniels said. "Sharon's got a list of reporters she tried to contact earlier. Why don't the two of you send out emails to each of them with a link to our post?"

At the end of the afternoon, Trey had to report not only hadn't he been able to find the license plate for Gary Knowlton's Mercedes SUV, but he couldn't access any of the highway cameras on I-95 or I-66. "I'll see if I can come up with some excuse at work tomorrow to probe for both, but don't count on it," he told them before leaving.

Late in the afternoon they heard from Cynthia Renfro. "I got your email. Where did this come from?"

"The man who called in the accident saw a black Mercedes leaving the scene," Daniels replied.

"And you connected this to Mr. Knowlton, how?" Renfro wanted to know.

"An anonymous tip."

"Which you believed?"

"Not necessarily," Daniels replied, "but I thought it credible enough to post a question about it. If he tells us we're wrong; he was elsewhere, fine."

"Why didn't you call me?"

"I did try to reach you, but since you weren't going to be in the office until Monday––"

"You gave up too easily," she said. "I always check my voice messages. Now it's going to be difficult for me to get through because he'll know why I'm calling."

"Will you try anyway?"

"Already did. Left a message, but as I say, chances of his returning my call are slim."

"Doesn't that suggest guilt?" Daniels asked.

"It could also mean he's going to use one of his buddies at the networks to respond."

"Damn!" They'd blown it.

"I'll let you know if I hear from him. Meanwhile keep an eye out for some kind of response from the Garvin team."

They didn't have to wait long. A CNN anchor announced the Garvin press office had issued a statement that the Garvins were extremely disappointed that one of Ethan's former girlfriends, who they did not identify by name, was intent on smearing the President-elect and his campaign team by her delusional theories concerning Ethan's death.

The press secretary warned the media not to be taken in by idle accusations of someone who had already been reprimanded for falsely claiming that she was Ethan's fiancé.

"Those bastards," was Sharon's response. "Those f-ing bastards."

"Notice that they don't mention Gary Knowlton by name," Maureen said.

"Exactly," Daniels said. "They hope the media will ignore everything we do, attributing it to Sharon's supposed delusions."

Sharon balled up her fists. "Oh, what I'd like to do to those bastards."

"Think of it this way," Daniels said, "you've gotten under their skin. That means we must be getting close to the truth."

Maureen motioned for them to look at her monitor. "Look here. Our question is being fed all over the Internet. It's popping up on Facebook and people are re-Tweeting it."

"Great," Daniels said. "Maybe someone who knows the truth will come forward."

The next day Trey reported that he had Knowlton's license plate number, but couldn't run any checks on local traffic cameras without violating all kinds of regulations and getting himself into trouble."

"Not a problem, Trey," Daniels told him. "I'll try to reach President Palmer to see if DOT can do that for us."

"When are you going to see the president?" Maureen asked when he told the women about Trey's success finding Knowlton's license plate number.

"Tonight hopefully. Meanwhile you guys keep working on the China-USA Trade Conference. See if you can find out if either Mr. Zhai or Mr. Zhang is part of their delegation."

It seemed they were making progress––slowly, but with so little time left, would it matter?

Friday, January 5

Gary Knowlton entered the Georgetown mansion's alcove, sat down, and picked up one of the news magazines that lay on the table that separated sections of the cushioned seating area. He tried to read, but was unable to concentrate even though he was interested in the column by an academic expert assessing the incoming administration's chances of revitalizing the economy.

"Okay. I'm here," Katherine Garvin said, closing the door behind her. "What's so urgent?"

Knowlton handed her the printout of the latest post on the *Fairfax County Inquirer* website. The lines around her mouth grew taut as she read the document. He wanted to ask her if she was getting any sleep.

"Wild speculation," she concluded. She handed it back.

"The press has already started calling," he said, folding the paper and returning it to his jacket pocket.

"Stall them."

"That will only work for so long."

"Who's behind this?" she asked.

"It's got to be the Washburn girl."

"The little bitch. I warned Ethan about her. She can't be doing this by herself. Who's helping her?"

"Someone with juice apparently," he replied. "It took a while, but we found out where she's moved to. It's an apartment on P Street off Dupont Circle, and she has a bodyguard with her wherever she goes."

"She can't afford that neighborhood or the bodyguards. Get me the names of all of the owners."

"I'll get right on it."

"See that you do." She turned and left the room.

Knowlton let out a sigh and took his cell out of his pocket.

Same Day

Daniels was worried; instead of using one of the untraceable cellphones he'd purchased expressly for Sharon to use when calling the media, she'd been using the one that was registered to his personal account. She was urging reporters to ask Gary Knowlton, Henry Garvin's long-time personal aide, whether it was his Mercedes SUV that had been seen leaving the scene of Ethan Garvin's car accident. Daniels didn't want to think about the negative consequences that could result if those who were trying to stop the investigation were able to trace those calls.

On the plus side, the volume of activity in response to their *Fairfax County Inquirer* post was phenomenal. People were sharing the item and supporting the demand that Knowlton answer the question.

Daniels resisted speaking to any of the reporters himself, as he didn't want to use his Joe Johnson alias lest someone discover he was not who he said he was. Of course, he couldn't use his real name either.

They'd rehearsed the most likely questions Sharon would be asked, starting with 'how did you obtain that information?' She was handling the reporters like the pro she was. They might not like her response that she couldn't reveal her source, but they should understand. They too had a practice of protecting their sources.

Daniels was anxious to see whether either Knowlton or the Garvins would respond. Nothing happened for half a day, but, as major media outlets joined the chorus, they could no longer ignore the question. Shortly before noon Saturday--an ideal time to issue a press release--the Garvin press office put out a brief statement in which they said the post was yet another product from Sharon Washburn's "fertile imagination."

Daniels was not surprised. "Don't fret about it," he told Sharon. "We're getting under their skin."

Yet, as the day wore on, Daniels was concerned the story would fall apart given that they lacked hard evidence Knowlton's Mercedes had been in Fairfax County the morning of November 10. He had been counting on Trey, but thus far: no smoking camera. Trey couldn't work on it at home because he couldn't access the data and so far had not found a rationale to ask for permission to do so at work.

If they did find an image of Knowlton's car entering either I-95 or I-66 heading back into D.C., he would have to explain what he was doing in Fairfax County at that time of the morning so far from his Bethesda home. That would invoke a ton of questions that would be difficult to answer without implicating himself in Ethan's death.

Putting aside his concern about Sharon's use of the traceable phone, Daniels wandered into the kitchen in Charlotte Palmer's apartment at two p.m.--the time Sharon and Maureen said they'd be ready with their report on the upcoming Chinese trade conference. "All set?"

"We are," Maureen answered. "I'm just printing out some charts. Need more coffee? You have time to go out."

Daniels shook his head. He was trying to limit his coffee intake in response to recent bouts of heartburn. "I'm trying your suggestion of drinking hot water with lemon."

"Good man," Maureen said. "I'll be right back."

Daniels was looking forward to seeing what they'd learned. Having Sharon and Maureen's help was turning out to be extremely useful and not just because it saved him time. As he should have known right from the start, three heads were better than one.

When she returned with her printouts, Maureen began. "You asked us to put the upcoming China trade conference into perspective in hopes it would shed some light on Ethan's accusation. Sharon is going to talk about the upcoming conference after I present a brief history of the two seminal climate and trade agreements--the one signed by Barack Obama in 2014 and the one negotiated by President Palmer during his first term."

"I'm all ears," Daniels said, sipping on his lemon hot water.

Maureen took a deep breath and began. "Experts suggest the U.S. and China both recognize while they compete with each other there are areas where they benefit by cooperating. In 2014, the U.S. was negotiating trade agreements with Japan, Australia, and other Far East nations, which provided an incentive for China to come to the table on controlling CO_2 emissions. That resulted in the first climate deal."

"Refresh my memory. What did they agree at that point?"

"Both parties set goals for the year 2030. The U.S. was to reduce its CO_2 emissions by twenty-five percent. China on the other hand was to stop increasing its output."

Daniels scowled. "That seems a bit unequal."

"Critics made the same point, but President Obama claimed it was a victory because up until then China hadn't signified any willingness to control CO_2 emissions."

Daniels nodded. "Okay. What came next?"

Maureen showed him a piece of paper with charts showing the terms of the 2014 and subsequent deal. "Shortly thereafter China wanted to renegotiate that agreement since a slowdown in their economy had brought them closer to that target than they foresaw and they thought they could use the opportunity to pressure the U.S. on several issues."

"I remember following it at the time," Daniels said, "but give me a refresher."

Maureen nodded. "The key takeaway is that China said they would curtail CO_2 growth five years sooner if the U.S. agreed to further reductions in its targets. They also wanted the U.S. to back down on some key issues relating to the South China Sea. President Palmer went against elements in his own party who favored that deal because he feared it would slow the U.S. economy, which was still recovering from the long recessionary decade that began in 2008. He was also unwilling to concede to China control over any portion of that strategic waterway."

"Got it," Daniels said.

"My turn," Sharon said. "The push for a new round of discussions, which will take place this coming February, experts believe is due to a long-standing division among the leaders of the Chinese Communist Party over a number of issues, including CO_2 emissions and the South China Sea."

"Lay it out for me," Daniels asked.

"The group we call the hardliners responded to unrest in their country by ramping up controls over the Chinese people. They clamped down on the private sector and they increased censoring private individuals' Internet activity. That led to several high profile arrests, disappearances, and imprisonments. They also resisted calls for political and economic reforms from the U.S."

"Reforms such as what?" Daniels asked.

Maureen jumped in. "Such as greater transparency into the financials reported by their publicly-held companies. There is strong evidence that some of those companies have issued phony financials."

"But the big issues as far as the U.S. has been concerned," Sharon added, "are transparency into measurement of CO_2 emissions and China's aggressive posture toward the South China Sea."

"Go on," Daniels requested.

Sharon pointed to the printout. "One of the reasons President Palmer said no to renegotiating the 2014 agreement was there was credible evidence China was fudging its CO_2 numbers."

"Bottom line?" Daniels asked.

Maureen raised her hand. "We can't allow China to get away with phony data while we have to comply with strict emission standards."

"And with regard to the South China Sea."

"China claims it's theirs. The Philippines and other countries have their own claims, which the U.S. has backed. Remember China tried to build some artificial islands in the region to advance their zone of influence?"

"I do, but I have a question," Daniels said. "Since there's a hardline group, are there also 'softliners'?"

"I wouldn't call them that," Maureen replied, "but from what we can tell, there is a group headed by the current premier who is willing to implement political reforms and allow the U.S. greater access to their pollution data in return for granting China trade terms similar to those we've granted to Japan and other Asian countries."

"The current premier is a reformer?" Daniels asked.

"Not exactly a reformer," Maureen answered. "You have to remember it's all relative. The key question is not how great a gap exists between the positions of the two groups, but what are the hardliners willing to do in order to control the process?"

"I know there's more to this than what you've presented and we could spend the rest of the week discussing it," Daniels said, "but can you bring it back to Henry Garvin?"

"Absolutely," Maureen replied. "Here's a list of committees Henry Garvin has served on during his twenty-four years as a member of Congress. Several deal directly with China on trade matters, but one stands out--Senate Foreign Relations. He'd served on that committee over the past ten years including the subcommittee on Near East, South Asia, Central Asia and Counterterrorism."

"Interesting," Daniels said. "Another question: who's China sending to D.C. next month?"

Sharon raised her hand. "As far as we can tell, the leader of the delegation is a hardliner. One expert wrote how that happened in a blog I read just yesterday. Apparently the leader of the hardliners, a man named Shen Wei, convinced the inner circle of the Communist Party that it would be counter-productive to send Premier Wan since his positions are well known and as a result they would have hardly any bargaining room."

"What do you think Henry Garvin will do when confronted with a hardliner?"

"That's my topic," Sharon said. "During the campaign, he said he would stick with President Palmer's agreement which demands that China give us freer access to their pollution data, but when you look at the people he's relying on for advice, you get a different picture. For example, Harris Neumann of Harvard is known for arguing that our taking a hardline with China will alienate them and as a result will harm the global effort to reduce CO_2 emissions."

"In other words," Daniels said, "he recommends giving in to China's hardliners."

"Exactly," Sharon and Maureen said simultaneously.

"And he's got Henry Garvin's ear?"

"He does and he's not the only person on the transition team who thinks we've been too hard on China," Sharon said, handing Daniels a sheet of paper. "Here's a list of a few others."

After Daniels scanned the list and set it aside, Maureen handed him another sheet of paper. "Here's a chart that shows what China says they're doing versus what climate experts claim they can detect coming out of China's factories and power plants. Estimates range from a ten to a forty percent discrepancy."

"Very interesting," Daniels said. "Good job, you guys. Let me study this stuff and then we'll talk later about where we go from here."

When they reconvened, Daniels asked if they'd learned whether either of the Chinese nationals who had been informal consultants to the Garvin team, was a hardliner or a reformer and whether either was scheduled to be part of the delegation being sent to the U.S. for the trade conference.

"Unfortunately," Maureen reported, "we've not been able to learn anything about either man other than their titles. Both appear to be mid-level officials in the commerce ministry."

Daniels sighed. "Keep trying, but without access to someone who knows the ins and outs of Chinese politics, we're at a huge disadvantage."

Another potential monkey wrench was thrown on top of the pile that afternoon when U.S. Secret Service notified Daniels that he was to report to headquarters 10 a.m. Monday. The person making the call wasn't able to say what the meeting was about. Most likely it had something to do with his retirement, but he knew he'd lose sleep wondering.

Late that evening, Trey texted him that he still hadn't been able to access the data files that had toll records, but he'd go into his office over the weekend. He might be able to convince one of the people in charge he had a legitimate reason to look at the highway camera data.

Saturday morning January 6, Daniels watched on CNN Congress ratify the election results. It seemed everything he'd done the past two months had been in vain, but he wasn't going to stop trying to get to the bottom of Ethan Garvin's claim. It didn't look like they would be able to stop Henry Garvin from being inaugurated, but the truth had to come out eventually.

To pass the time Saturday and Sunday afternoons, Daniels tried to get into the spirit of the NFL playoffs by watching parts of the four games scheduled for that weekend. His mind kept returning to the piles of folders he'd brought with him back to his apartment. As he paged through the folders, each of which represented one potential avenue they had investigated, he kept coming up with the same conclusion. They had to find evidence that showed whether Gary Knowlton had seen Ethan drive off the road. If so, perhaps they'd have enough leverage to find out what happened to Ethan's briefcase and what he intended to show President Palmer.

At 10 a.m. sharp Monday morning Daniels was shown into the office of Josephine Morrison, in the personnel section at the U.S. Secret Service. Morrison was Daniels' junior by at least twenty years, but she treated Daniels like she treated everyone else--as if he was an Army private. Morrison remained seated at her desk looking over some papers, making Daniels wait. Finally, she closed the file she'd been studying, looked up, and handed Daniels a thin file.

"I know you're retiring in a couple of weeks, Agent Daniels, but regs say you need to report to Rowley on Wednesday for firearms qualifying certification."

Daniels opened the file, but none of the words on the page, nor what Morrison told him made any sense. "Firearms certification?"

"Like I said, Agent, regs are regs."

Daniels started to complain, but he knew Morrison was not going to fight this on his behalf. Why should she?

"At least it gets you out of the White House for a couple of days," Morrison said, winking at Daniels.

Daniels closed the folder. Apparently Morrison thought Daniels was unhappy about his special assignment. Little did she know!

Morrison picked up the next item off the pile on her desk. "Next."

On the drive over to Dupont Circle Daniels argued with himself about how to respond to the latest in agency bureaucratic nonsense. It was possible that President Palmer could intervene, but he'd already gone outside normal protocol to get his assignment changed once. Would he do it again?

When he got to the apartment, he informed Maureen and Sharon that it looked like he'd be tied up Wednesday and Thursday. That dampened the mood when they did what they'd gotten in the habit of doing each morning--i.e., go over what each of them was working on.

"I've crossed off everything on my list," Maureen announced.

"Me, too," Sharon stated.

Daniels rubbed his forehead to try to dampen the headache that had been building since he'd woken up that morning. "We're not going to quit."

Sharon looked at him wide-eyed.

"Damn straight," Maureen said. "Don't worry about us. We'll find something to research. Just do what you need to work on."

The problem was Daniels couldn't come up with a single thing he could work on that he hadn't beaten like a dusty rug hung over a clothesline. He took the large coffee he'd picked up from around the corner and went into the spare bedroom to check his email, hoping for help from people who were reading their posts on the Fairfax County Inquirer.

Halfway through that job, a text appeared from Trey. "Got something."

"Great. What?" Daniels typed.

"Not what you think. Watch your inbox."

Half an hour later an email appeared with an attachment from one of Trey's anonymous email accounts. Daniels eagerly printed it out, and then called the women into the room.

"What is it?" Maureen asked. "Find something?"

"Trey sent me something. I hope it's what we've been looking for."

It wasn't. As Daniels read through the two-page printout, he realized he'd forgotten all about having asked Trey to check into the disappearance of Ethan's cellphone. Sharon had made a big deal about how Ethan practically slept with his brand-new iPhone. She didn't think he would have left the house that morning without it. If so, why hadn't the accident investigation team found it?

Trey's cover note explained that the last model didn't need to be on to be traceable. "If you have the right software, an i-10 can be traced if the battery is completely dead. It can even be found in some cases if the unit has been damaged."

"Trey has traced Ethan's cellphone to a salvage yard in Southwest D.C.," Daniels announced. "It's time for a road trip."

"Looks like there's more," Maureen pointed out as paper continued to pour off the printer.

Daniels studied the printout. "Ah ha. It explains what we need to do in order to find the phone once we reach the salvage yard." He read for another minute. "He says we need to download an app before we go. Can we use your iPhone, Hon?"

Maureen nodded. "Of course. Let me see the instructions."

Two hours later, they were arguing with the owner of M&M Auto Salvage on First Street in Southwest D.C. about whether he was going to let the three of them wander around his yard searching for a missing cellphone.

Fortunately, Daniels had stopped at an ATM on the way and had downloaded five thousand dollars out of his Joe Johnson account.

"You need a search warrant," the owner, who called himself Sarge, repeated for the third or fourth time. He puffed out his chest daring Daniels to try to step around him.

"We're not cops," Daniels repeated in response. He knew a black man with two white women looked suspicious, and was not surprised that Sarge wasn't buying their story that the phone had been stolen and they just learned how to search for it.

"Everyone knows that's what you do when you lose one of them things," said the Salvage guy, blowing his cigar smoke directly in Daniels' face.

"What's the harm in letting us try to find it?" Maureen asked.

"First, it's gonna be buried in several tons of metal and second it ain't gonna be in any shape to use once you find it," Sarge replied. He spit some tobacco juice on the ground and looked up at Maureen. "So, what's your real game, lady?"

"We can pay," Daniels said, interrupting whatever Maureen intended to say.

"Not enough to make it worthwhile," Sarge said turning his back to them.

"How much would that take?"

Sarge stopped and turned towards them. He blew smoke directly at Maureen, who had to turn away.

"How much?" Daniels repeated.

"First, find the damn phone. Then come get me." He moved away from the gate, and retreated to his office shed.

"Bastard," Maureen muttered.

Daniels removed the chain that kept the gate closed and held it open for the women to walk into the yard.

"This way," Maureen said pointing in the direction the app on her phone indicated.

Half an hour later they narrowed the location down to a large pile of crushed vehicles. Daniels went to retrieve the salvage man.

"I want two grand to move the junk on top of the sedan and another two to open 'er up. In cash."

"It's a deal," Daniels said.

Sarge held his hand out. "It's your funeral."

Monday, January 8

Before the salvage company owner was willing to unpack the stack of crushed vehicles, he tried to jack up the price yet another time.

"Keep the damn phone, then," Daniels told him. He didn't look at either of the women knowing doing so would give away the fact that he was bluffing.

The salvage man snarled, and in the end, they reached a total price of forty-five hundred—half upfront; half when the phone had been recovered. Only then did the salvage owner drive a massive crane to the spot, and unpack the stack of crushed vehicles one by one until Ethan's sedan was exposed. The owner lit another cigar while two muscular associates, wielding five-foot-long crowbars, cracked open the rear passenger side of the car, and retrieved the remains of an iPhone 10.

Sharon had stuck it out until the program running on Maureen's phone narrowed down the stacks of cars to the one that held the remains of Ethan's sedan. At that point, she mumbled an apology, turned, and hastily retreated to Daniels car.

"You okay?" Daniels asked after the recovery job was finished. He could tell she'd been crying.

Sharon nodded. "I just couldn't--"

"There's no need to apologize," Maureen said, getting into the car.

"The phone isn't in as bad a shape as I thought it would be," Daniels said, showing Sharon the contents of the plastic bag they used to deposit the crushed remains of the iPhone. "If Trey can't recover the data himself, maybe he knows people who can."

"That will take time, won't it?" Sharon asked as Daniels wheeled out of the parking lot.

"It will, but if he needs to farm it out, I'll offer them a ton of cash to get it done yesterday."

"Even so," Maureen interjected, "it could be days before we know if anything can be pulled off the phone and then who knows how long it will take to go through what they recover to learn if there's anything valuable to our investigation."

"All true," Daniels said, "but it's our best bet unless Trey can come up with video that proves Gary Knowlton's car was on Fairfax County Route 624 the morning of November 10. We just don't have any other avenues to pursue at the moment."

After Daniels dropped Sharon and Maureen off at Dupont Circle, he headed to Prince George's County to drop the cell off at Trey's house. "Urgent. Need to recover data off Ethan's phone ASAP," he wrote on a slip of paper that he inserted in the plastic bag holding the remains of the phone.

He'd barely gotten back to D.C. and was pulling into the parking lot at Maureen's apartment building when Trey called him.

"I'm not sure anyone can recover anything from this mess."

"Give it a try."

"This is not my area of expertise," Trey said.

"Can you find someone who knows this stuff? I can pay whatever they want to drop whatever they're working on and make this a priority. Oh, yeah. They have to sign a non-disclosure agreement."

"You're probably talking about extra for that," Trey said.

"As the saying goes, money is no object."

Daniels was in luck the next evening when he contacted the White House hoping President Palmer was available. Palmer had returned earlier that day from a weekend at his farm for the final days of his administration and was willing to give Daniels a few minutes at 10 p.m.

Daniels found the President in the library in the residence, dressed in a bathrobe with furry slippers, once again watching women's college basketball.

"How are they doing?" Daniels asked after Palmer motioned him to sit in one of the chairs facing the large screen TV.

"They stumbled last week against Notre Dame, but are looking good tonight. The Lady Hawkeyes aren't as good as they have been in the past," he said, muting the sound. "But, I don't imagine you came here to discuss women's basketball."

"True," Daniels replied. "I wanted to give you some good news. We may have caught a break."

"I'm all ears."

"We've recovered Ethan Garvin's cellphone and have turned it over to the best data recovery guys in the business."

"You locked them into some kind of non-disclosure, I hope."

"I did. Trey Sharp--that's my son--works for the National Security Agency. He modified one of the forms they use for contractors. No one who hasn't signed over their life and fortune will be allowed to touch the device or the data."

"Good, but in case you hadn't noticed we've run out of time, Agent Daniels. Congress ratified the electoral college vote on Saturday."

Daniels was about to say he was aware of that fact, but wisely kept his mouth closed.

The President pumped his fist. "That's how you do it," he yelled at the screen.

Daniels had missed whatever play elicited that outburst. He hoped for a time out or some kind of stoppage to bring up the other reason he'd come there that evening.

The President turned in his direction. "Do you really think Gary Knowlton had something to do with Ethan's death?"

"It looks that way. I suspect Knowlton was working with a Chinese national who served as consultant to the campaign."

"Have you got a name for this other fellow?"

"Not exactly. We have two suspects--both of whose names begin with the letter Z."

"What makes you suspect it's one of them?"

"Sharon--that's Ethan's fiancé--told me that Ethan was suspicious of one particular individual's presence during the campaign. All she remembers was they called him "Mr. Z." Given that Ethan says his father is about to betray us to China, it seems logical that China would have someone keeping an eye on Henry."

"I still have a hard time believing any of this. So, have you talked to either of these guys?"

"Unfortunately, we haven't. Both went back to China a few days after the election. That's another reason we feel one of them might be the person that China used to keep tabs on Henry Garvin."

"Write the names down for me. I'll see if I can find out anything about them from State."

"That'd be great."

"Anything else?"

"Yes. We're trying to prove that Knowlton was there when Ethan's car went off the road, but we need to search toll image data for that day and we haven't been able to access that on our own."

"Are you certain that data exists?"

"My son said toll data is kept now for twelve months."

"Okay, then. I'll see if I can get someone to trace that as well, but I have to be careful. I'm calling in a lot of chits on this investigation, and if someone leaks my requests to the press, the jig's up as they say."

When Daniels told President Palmer they had hired the best recovery firm in the business, he hadn't exactly told the truth. Trey explained that federal rules required companies engaged in retrieving data from computers and the like were required by law to fill out an online form each time they started a new project. The form required identification of the owner of the device being worked on as well as other information including the serial number of the device. The purpose of the legislation was to prevent criminal organizations from recovering data from stolen equipment. Consequently, if they took Ethan's phone to a legitimate recovery outfit, they would be alerting the entire world that Ethan's cell phone had been recovered. That would undoubtedly lead his parents to go to court to take possession of the device and quash the information. Even lying about whose phone was being probed wouldn't work because the phone's serial number was linked to Ethan.

To get around that obstacle, Trey contacted a colleague from work who once mentioned he did some recovery work on the side. Trey explained the project, telling his colleague that the owner of the devise would pay three times the man's normal fee to find out if there was any recoverable data if he could do it in less than forty-eight hours. The man picked up the phone from Trey's house and called in sick.

When got home from his talk with President Palmer, Daniels was excited to see a message from Trey from earlier that evening.

"We're in," Trey told him.

Daniels let out a huge sigh of relief. "Great news," he texted Trey, hoping his son was at his computer. "How long will it take for him to extract the data?"

Trey responded right back. "He's already started, but we need your help. Some of the data will be harder to recover than other data. It will take more time if you want him to go through various versions of each file to construct the most up-to-date version of each document. Bottom line, he needs to know how much time you want him to put into the recovery process?"

"Damn," Daniels said. "I don't know. As long as it takes, I suppose."

"That could be days or even weeks because he has no idea how long some of the routines he'll be running will take. You need to set a time limit."

"What would you do, Trey?"

"Depends what you're looking for. It would help if you came up with some key words we can search for."

"I can do that. I'm looking for anything that references China, CO2 emissions, trade, the name Zhang Heijing or Zhai Qi."

"What else?" Trey asked, after Daniels spelled out the two names.

Daniels thought. "Gary Knowlton, Henry Garvin, Edwin Palmer, cyber security—"

"Whoa. That's a good start. Let's see what we can come up with in the next twenty-four hours. Meanwhile be ready with some other terms if those come up empty."

Daniels explained that he was going to be tied up with an overnight stay at the Rowley Secret Service training center. "Send what you find to Maureen," he texted Trey. "She and Sharon will have to look through the material until I can get back to the apartment."

"Why do you have to do that now?" Trey asked about the firearms recertification.

"I've no choice. That's how things work. You do what you're told until the day they release you."

"It's almost as if someone doesn't want you to get to the bottom of this."

"I had that thought myself, but I can't imagine who would be able to pull that kind of string. I think it's just bad luck."

Daniels arrived at the Secret Service's 440-acre James T. Rowley Training Center located near Laurel, Maryland well before the time he was scheduled to report. He found himself waiting for the re-certification process to begin with twenty-three other agents--none of whom were about to retire.

Thanks to scandals involving the U.S. Secret Service during the Bush and Obama administrations, Congress had increased funding for the agency, some of which was used to hire more agents so that agents would be given time to engage in required physical and logistical training. The requirements for firearms certification varied based on the agent's responsibility. Given his management position within the Uniformed Division, Daniels was only required to go through the certification process at Rowley once a year. Other agents, including those on the counterassault teams, had to re-certify four times a year.

Even if he were not involved in the Ethan Garvin investigation, he would have found his having to attend firearm certification less than two weeks before he retired a ridiculous example of bureaucratic asininity, but there was nothing he could do about it. With time running out on the investigation, he found it difficult to concentrate on the certification process. As a result his initial scores were borderline passing.

What if I fail, he asked himself during the lunch break? Are they going to make me come back for remedial instruction? It occurred to him he ought not give the keyboard artists in headquarters an opportunity to exert their authority. Fearing that outcome, he concentrated on the tests and as a result his afternoon scores were more respectable.

Late Wednesday afternoon, he was required to sit through a presentation on the proper procedure for turning in his firearms, keys, and all other agency equipment that had been assigned to him in the course of his duties. He also had to sit through a video on how to structure his life in retirement to avoid depression and other symptoms related to being released from a high stress occupation where everything ran by the clock.

Daniels wasn't worried about how he'd use his time after January 22. He was just anxious to return to D.C. to see what kind of data had been recovered from Ethan's phone.

It wasn't until mid-afternoon Thursday that the re-certification process was officially over. The first thing he did when they gave him back his cell phone, which had been confiscated while on facility grounds, was to call Sharon at the apartment.

"Hear anything from Trey?"

"Nothing," she replied.

"Damn. I guess that means they're still trying to recover the data. He normally doesn't get home from work until after six. The guy who's working on this might not have wanted to contact him at work. I'll call him then."

"Okay," Sharon said. "Let me know if they found something."

"I will. What have you and Maureen been working on?"

"You didn't leave me anything special to work on, so I've just been monitoring the news."

"Anything interesting happen while I was out of touch?"

"Nope. Stories on the inauguration, like which groups are performing and what events require tickets. That kind of thing."

"Okay. Is Maureen there or did she go home?"

"She didn't come in today."

"No? Well, I can understand that given there was nothing that important for you guys to work on. I'll be in tomorrow."

"Okay, see you then."

Daniels called Maureen's cell. It went to voice mail. He left a message that he was done and was heading back to D.C. He asked her to call him when she got the message.

When he got back to Alexandria, he picked up his mail and scrounged around in his refrigerator hoping there was something he could eat for dinner. There wasn't. He ordered take out Chinese.

It was too early to call Trey, and he hadn't heard from Maureen. He tried her number again. It went to voice mail. "Call me," was all he said.

Battery's probably dead, he thought, or maybe she left her phone at Macy's while picking out another outfit for Hawaii. He ate dinner slowly then called Trey.

"Nope," Trey said when Daniels reached him. "I haven't heard from my guy. I'll give him a call and let you know where things stand."

Daniels waited by the phone for the next half hour watching the news and then Jeopardy. Finally his cell rang. It was his son.

"So far, all he's finding is a lot of partials," Trey reported. "He's using several software programs to try to recover the data and each takes a few hours to run. He said he'd keep going all night."

"Thanks, Trey. I'll try to be patient."

It was now past seven and Daniels still hadn't heard from Maureen. He called Sandra Burke, one of the retired agents he'd hired to shadow Maureen when he wasn't with her himself. That call also went into voice mail. Then he tried Mary Broussard, the second agent. She confirmed that Sandra had relieved her at 8 a.m. that morning.

"Why wouldn't she be answering her cell?" Daniels asked.

"She turns it off when on duty," Broussard explains. "That way she's able to stay in the background without the distraction of having to answer a call from one of her grandkids or neighbors."

"When are you supposed to take over?"

"I'm on my way there now. I'll ask her to call you when I see her."

"Do that. I have been trying to reach Ms. Thornberry for the past few hours. She's not answering her cell either."

Daniels tried unsuccessfully not to think the worst while he waited for Burke's call, but he couldn't keep the negative images out of his mind. Car accident. Hospital. He probably wasn't listed yet as the person to contact in an emergency. That would be her mother in California. He thought about calling her, but decided against it. He didn't want to alarm her if Maureen just had car trouble and was stuck in some garage with a dead cell phone or waiting by the side of the road for the car to be towed.

His phone buzzed. Finally, he said to himself, but it was Sharon Washburn.

"What's up?" he asked after hitting 'answer.'

All he heard on the other end was someone sobbing.

"Sharon, what's going on? What happened? Are you okay?"

He couldn't make out Sharon's response.

"Take a breath. Then say it again."

"They…They have her. They have Maureen."

Thursday, January 11

Daniels couldn't catch his breath. His heart was racing and his head felt like it was underwater. He looked at Sharon's image on the phone to make sure he was talking to the right person.

Maybe he misunderstood. "Say it again."

"They've taken Maureen, Mr. Daniels," she said between sobs.

How? Who? When? Why?

"Mr. Daniels, are you there? Did you hear me that time?"

"Yes, sorry, Sharon. I'm . . . I'm . . ."

"I know."

"Are you sure? How do you know?"

"They sent us an email."

"I didn't--," he started to say, but then remembered his cellphone had been confiscated while he was at Rowley and he hadn't checked his email when he got it back. He was almost afraid to look now, thinking had he done so earlier he might have done something to save her.

"I tried calling her a few times today," Sharon said, "but she didn't answer. Then I was looking at the emails from the website and there it was."

"Ouch." Daniels banged his leg on the coffee table throwing himself down on the couch.

"You okay?" Sharon asked.

"No, and I mean yes. Read the entire message to me."

"Okay, just a minute."

Daniels told himself to breathe. *They won't hurt her. They just want to scare him, to get them to stop the investigation. I'll--*

"Okay. Here's what they wrote,

We warned you to stop interfering. You didn't listen. Hear this. We have Maureen Thornberry. She will be released after Inauguration Day, but only if you stop all activity. No more web posts, no more help from the White House. Don't try to find her if you value her life. Don't doubt us if you want to see her alive."

Daniels couldn't take it all in. "Read it again."

She read it twice more, each time pausing between sentences and enunciating carefully.

"What are you going to do?" Sharon asked after a minute of silence followed the last reading.

"I don't know . . . Find her."

"But they said--"

"I know what they said, but I can't let them get away with this."

"You don't have to shout--"

"I'm sorry. I'm not angry at you. It's my fault. Somehow I wasn't careful enough. I didn't see they were getting close to us. I . . ."

"It's not your fault, Mr. Daniels."

"Let me think on this some more, Sharon. I'll call if I'm not coming in tomorrow."

"God damn mother fuckin' sons of fuckin' bitches!" he yelled at the top of his voice after disconnecting the call. He got off the couch looking for something to destroy. He pushed his mail onto the floor and banged his fist on the table until he feared he'd broken little finger. Then swore some more. That elicited a banging on the wall of his unfriendly neighbor.

"And fuck you, too," he yelled at the wall.

He sat down again and buried his face in his hands, unaware of the time that was passing, replaying over and over the events of the past couple of weeks, looking for answers to questions he could barely formulate. *Who is behind this? How did they find out he was the one helping Sharon Washburn? Was it the time Sharon used his phone to talk to reporters? When and how had they abducted Maureen?*

The message said no more help from the White House. *How did they know about that? They had to have someone on the inside. Who? Who is the traitor?*

"I'm going to get you, motherfucker," he said not quite as loud as before, knowing the neighbor was just waiting for an opportunity to call the apartment supervisor on him, and knowing if someone came to the door to complain about the noise he'd probably beat the living piss out of that person, no matter their age or gender. Getting arrested for assaulting the building superintendent wouldn't help him get Maureen back.

He had to find her. He had to rescue her. That's all he could think of. He went into the bathroom and washed his face with cold water. He stared at the image in the mirror wondering how he'd ever gotten into a situation that he'd put his beloved Maureen's life in jeopardy. *What kind of fool are you Tucker Eugene Daniels*, he asked the mirror.

His cell buzzed again. It was Mary Broussard.

"Are you sitting down?" she asked.

"Talk to me!"

"It's Burke. She's dead."

Daniels collapsed onto his couch. "Holy Chr-
-. Sorry, I promised my mother I wouldn't say that
anymore. What happened?"

"Someone knifed her and dumped her body
in a trash collector in the basement of Ms.
Thornberry's building. The police are there now."

"Fuck. Knifed her! I can't--"

"And there's no sign of your fiancé."

"I know, Mary. I heard from the people who
took her."

"Took her?"

"She's been kidnapped, and we've been told
to stop going after the Garvins if we want to see her
returned alive."

"Those are some serious people."

"You don't have to tell me. Look, I'm going to
need to talk to Sandra's family. Can you get me the
contact information?"

Broussard agreed to call back with that
information. Daniels remained on the couch his head
in his hands. He never expected one of the agents
he'd hired to be killed. *It's my fault. I should have told
her what to expect.* A small voice reminded him that
he did tell both women the people they were
investigating were likely behind the death of a
reporter who had gotten too close. Dodd's death had
been made to look like a robbery. That was not the
case for Sandra Burke. The police would question
how she happened to be in Maureen's building. It
was likely they'd find someone in her family who
Burke had told she was working on a job, and then
someone would discover one of the residents of that
building complex was missing. It might take a couple
of days, but they'd put two and two together, and his

name would come up, and he didn't have answers to the questions they'd be asking him.

More pressing at the moment, Daniels fought the fear eating at his innards when he considered what the people who'd taken Maureen might do to her. He had to do something, but lacked a plan. He took off his shoes, and got out a yellow pad and a pen. Several hours later, however, a pile of crunched up yellow sheets on the floor and a blank top page to the pad was the sum total of his efforts.

As soon as it was light enough to get moving, Daniels showered, got dressed, and drove into the District. He arrived at Mrs. Palmer's apartment three hours ahead of schedule and went right up stairs instead of stopping for a coffee and a breakfast sandwich. Ricky Alvarez opened the door. "So sorry, Tuck. Let me know what you want me to do."

"Thanks. I'm still not sure what I'm going to do."

"We'll help you find her. Me, Sam, Parenti-- we all got friends who can pitch in."

"I've got to think. I'll let you know."

"Okay, but don't hesitate. We know how to find people. We'll find her."

Daniels wished it were that easy. On the ride in, he thought of calling every retired Secret Service agent he could count on. He could give out assignments. Check this, check that, but until he knew how they knew what he was doing and whether someone on the inside was involved, all that would do would be to jeopardize Maureen's well being. He couldn't take a chance they'd hurt her.

Sharon appeared in her dressing gown. She looked drawn and haggard. Daniels doubted she'd gotten much sleep either. When Alvarez went to get his coat, she came forward and gave Daniels an awkward hug. "She's going to be all right. She's just got to be."

Daniels nodded, although he didn't know at all that would be the case. "Let me see the email."

She went to the computer in the study and brought up the message.

"Can you or Trey find out who sent it?" Sharon asked.

"I'll see what Trey can do, but first I'm going to put up a notice offering to trade myself for Maureen."

Sharon gasped.

"It's the right thing to do. Plus, we'll have a chance to take them out if they agree to a trade."

He wrote and posted the trade offer and then scanned through comments, texts, and emails on their site. Nothing of value stuck out. It was still too early to call his son's house. He allowed himself the luxury of walking to the deli for a coffee and a breakfast sandwich. When he got back to the apartment, he dialed the number of the special phone Trey asked him to use.

He was surprised when Brianna answered it.

"Brianna. It's me. Has Trey left for work?"

"He's in the shower."

"Will you tell him to call me? It's an emergency."

"Sure, Mr. Daniels, I mean Dad."

"Thanks, Brianna."

Daniels sat at the computer table checking news websites for stories on Sandra Burke's murder while waiting for Trey to call back. He remembered he still hadn't checked his personal emails, and opened the app on his cell phone. The one from the kidnappers had been sent just after five in the afternoon. He'd been on the road then. He noticed Trey had texted him around eleven last night. He clicked on the message.

"We've found something. My guy is cleaning it up. You should have it by tomorrow morning."

He'd completely forgotten about Ethan's cell phone. What if they found who was behind all this? That had been their biggest problem all along--they had no idea who their enemy was. How can you fight a war if you don't know who you're fighting! Worse, how can you fight if your enemy knows who you are, but you don't know who they are!

His phone buzzed. He prayed for a brief second that it was Maureen calling to tell him she'd escaped, but it was Trey.

"Thanks for calling me back, son. What do you have?"

"You said you were looking for any entries on the day of the accident. It seems Ethan recorded a conversation that morning of his death with someone who came to his apartment to take him to his mother. He doesn't say that person's name. Maybe you can identify him."

"Excellent. Is that all?"

"No, there's a second file which it seems he recorded while he was driving just before he went off the road."

"Really. That's great news. I can't thank you enough."

"I still think you're way over your pay grade, Dad, but it's the least I could do."

"How do I get the files?"

"My guy is still cleaning them up. He says he'll be done some time today. I'll send them to you from a secure, untraceable email address. Click on them. Your iTunes program should open and start playing them."

Daniels didn't move after disconnecting the call. He didn't know how to deal with the ray of hope Trey had just offered him. He feared being too optimistic, but if the recordings disclosed who was behind Ethan Garvin's death, he'd know who had kidnapped Maureen.

"You should have told him."

Daniels hadn't realized Sharon was in the room with him.

"I just can't get the words out of my mouth."

Sharon gave him an understanding smile.

Daniels turned away to hide the tear that snuck out of his eye. They--no, he--needed to rescue her, but he needed leverage, something the kidnappers would want. He'd offer himself, but they hadn't responded. The files Trey was sending over could be the answer.

He showed Sharon the notice he'd posted on the *Fairfax County Inquirer* website.

She read it out loud. "Attention: Those in possession of our misplaced item, we are willing to trade you for a more valuable version. Text a time and place for the exchange."

"What do you think?"

"I hope they understand what you mean."

"I think they'll get it. Hopefully, we'll hear back shortly."

But they didn't hear back. The day dragged as Daniels waited for a response and tried to control his emotions. When Sam Freeman showed up at 6 p.m., Sharon convinced Daniels to go home to get some sleep.

"Tomorrow will be better," she told him.

He didn't think the next day could be worse and had doubts about whether it would be better, but he followed her advice. The next morning Daniels arrived at the apartment two hours ahead of time. The files Trey promised were not there. He didn't want to nag, so he went out for coffee and then filled Ricardo in on where things stood in the investigation. Finally, around 10:00, his phone rang.

"I've just sent them," Trey told him. "I think you're going to be pleasantly surprised. The quality is excellent."

Daniels double clicked on the file. His heart was racing again and his stomach was complaining about too much black coffee. The recording started to play.

I'll come over right after my meeting at the White House.

"That's Ethan," Sharon said.

Your mother wants to see you now.

It was a man's voice. "Who's that?" Daniels asked.

Sharon shook her head. "Don't know."

The White House wants me at nine.

"That's Ethan again," Sharon whispered.

Call them. Say you have to change to another day. What's so important that it can't wait—

You'll have to ask your mother. I'm just the messenger.

Daniels recognized the beeps of someone punching a phone number into a cell phone. It rang--three, four, five times, then picked up.

I can't come to the phone.

"That's Ethan's mother," Sharon whispered.

If you think you've reached the correct number, leave a message.

She's not answering. I'm sure it will be okay with her.

"That's--"

Daniels raised his hand. He recognized Ethan's voice by now.

My instructions are to bring you to the compound now, not when you feel like it, not later. Now! Get your things and let's go.

There was a brief pause.

I'll have to follow you.

No, I'll follow you. Get your stuff.

They heard footsteps, then the sound of the snaps on a briefcase being shut.

I'll carry that for you.

That's not necessary.

It's to make sure you actually show up at your mother's.

I said, I'm coming. You don't have to treat me like a child.

The recording stopped.

"He took Ethan's briefcase," Sharon said. "That's why it wasn't in his car."

Daniels nodded. "That has to be Gary Knowlton."

"So he was there!"

"We've got the bastard," Daniels said. "We've got him and that's how we're going to get Maureen back unharmed."

"How?"

"We threaten to release that tape to the public. He was behind Ethan, not in front of him. Knowlton saw Ethan's car go into the ditch and didn't stop. That's a felony."

"The bastard. That fucking bastard."

"Let's listen to the second tape," Daniels said. "It may give us more ammunition."

Daniels double-clicked on the second audio file. When it started Daniels knew Ethan was recording it while driving because of the background sound of the tires on the pavement and the sound of the engine. Ethan began to speak.

My mother sent Gary Knowlton to my apartment this morning, insisting I come to the family compound and not go to the White House like I promised President Palmer. They must know that I was going to spill the beans about how they're planning to betray our country.

Knowlton has my briefcase. It contains the documents I was planning on turning over to the President, including evidence my mother falsified campaign contributions from the Chinese Communist Party to make it look like they were from American citizens. The folder also includes copies of emails that confirm that my father will do what China wants at the upcoming trade and climate conference. It seems he's going to do that in order to keep them from revealing something that would destroy him, although I don't know what that is.

I don't know what they know about him that would make my father betray our country or why my mother and Gary Knowlton are going along with the Chinese government, but that's the sad truth.

The one time I tried to confront my father, even before I knew the full extent of it, he brushed me off, saying that I'd only hurt myself by pursuing the matter. Then, I asked him why he was not telling the American people the truth about his intentions vis-à-vis China's CO_2 emissions, which I'd learned about when I got a copy of an email exchange with a Harvard professor.

He told me he'd explain everything one day. I told him I needed to know now. He wasn't happy, but he told me he'd write . . .

There followed a period of silence when all they heard was background noise. Then Ethan started talking again.

Shit! I thought I'd lost Knowlton, but there's a school bus in front of me stopping to pick up some kids. I can't go around it. Damn! Knowlton's caught up to me. There are only two cars between us. Maybe I can lose him when I get on the highway. I'll pretend I'm going to take the exit to 495, but then at the last second stay on 395. Besides, what can he do--run me off the road?

The school bus is moving. I'm going to try to pass it. Maybe I can lose him before I get to the highway.

They heard nothing but car noises for almost a minute.

There. I've done it. Hopefully, the school bus will stop soon.

Ethan didn't say anything again for half a minute. Daniels wondered if it was the end of the recording, but Ethan spoke again.

Damn, there he is. He's catching up to me. I can't let him. . . .

Then came the noise of tires squealing and Ethan calling out, and then a terrible explosion like sound. Daniels tried to stop the recording as quickly as he could, but not before Sharon's scream battered his eardrums.

"Oh, my God. Oh, my God," she screamed as she ran from the room. Daniels knew the sound of those final seconds of Ethan Garvin's life would haunt both of their dreams for years to come.

Saturday, January 13

Despite his wanting to do so, Daniels didn't go after Sharon. Instead he checked the *Fairfax County Inquirer* that morning to see if there was a response from the kidnappers or any other useful information. Nothing. Then he looked for news about Sandra Burke's murder. A small item appeared in the *Post*. Other area media websites reported the same information. The police were still investigating and had not determined a motive for the killing.

After a while, he listened at the bedroom door to see if Sharon was stirring. He hoped she'd drifted off to sleep.

He went outside and wandered around the neighborhood thinking about where things stood and what needed to be done. He came up with some ideas and when he got back to the apartment, he sat down with his yellow pad to write them down.

The recordings were the smoking gun he wished he'd discovered much, much sooner. The problem was what to do with them. If he gave both up to rescue Maureen, assuming Knowlton was behind her kidnapping, they wouldn't be able to stop Henry Garvin from being inaugurated in a little over a week's time and all he'd gone through to determine the validity of Ethan's claim would have been for naught. He had to take care of both--rescue his fiancé and stop Garvin from becoming president and betraying America. He didn't know how he was going to do either, but it was time to put his thirty-six years of training and experience to work.

At one point he slapped himself squarely on the forehead. "I've got it," he said out loud. There were two tapes. Knowlton wouldn't know that. It seemed he'd not driven Ethan off the road, but since he was following, he must have seen Ethan's car plunge into the ditch, and he hadn't stopped. If convicted that meant prison time and the end of his political career.

The question was how to contact him and offer the first tape in return for Maureen's freedom. Daniels didn't think Sharon should make the call. Why would Knowlton agree to speak to her? He was also putting her in the position of what amounted to letting him off. Not a good idea.

Which brought him to the second tape. Was it sufficient proof for President Palmer to take action to prevent Henry Garvin from taking the oath of office? Daniels was no lawyer, but he suspected it failed that test. It would be a different story if he had the briefcase and could turn over the documents Ethan intended to bring Palmer, but all he had was what Palmer already possessed––Ethan's verbal assertion that his father was about to betray his country.

Whatever Garvin was trying to hide must be pretty terrible. What could that be? Murder would meet the test, but in all the research the media had done into his past there had never been any mention of his connection to a murder case. He certainly had never been a suspect or that would have come out at some point. Was it fraud, perjury, accepting a bribe? Whatever Henry Garvin was hiding, it was terrible enough to commit treason to prevent disclosure. Daniels knew his job wouldn't be finished until he found out.

The other problem, of course, was time. Even if he had the proof he needed, was there enough time for Palmer to do what had to be done? Daniels had no idea what that could be--go to the Chief Justice of the Supreme Court? Could a chief justice overturn an election and declare the results null and void on the basis of something the president-elect intended to do? It seemed unlikely, but that wasn't Daniels' problem. He had enough to do and needed to prioritize.

First priority was to free Maureen. He was through with secrets, which meant he'd better speak with Sharon before he offered Knowlton the trade. He'd let her sleep long enough. They had to come to an understanding.

His plan was to threaten to go public with the recording if Maureen was not released by a set deadline. That might work, but what could go wrong, Daniels asked himself. What if Knowlton tried to stall him? He supposed he could release the first recording, then threaten to release the one that proved Knowlton had not stopped to help Ethan or call for help.

First, he had to clear things with Sharon and then write up something that would result in Knowlton's taking a meeting. How he was going to get the message to Knowlton was another issue. Email was out. Too unreliable. So was faxing or messaging. He doubted the man would take his phone call. He had to deliver it in person.

Daniels felt better than he had in days. There was a light at the end of the tunnel--a way to get

Maureen back. Once he'd accomplished that he'd worry about the implications of Ethan's accusation and stopping Henry Garvin from becoming President.

Daniels wasn't the most religious person, but he took a minute and prayed.

'Dear God. I know I haven't been talking to you lately or listening for that matter. I haven't made the time to go to church. I could promise to do better, but I wouldn't blame you if you don't want to hear any of my promises. Like my grandmother always told me "don't say what you're going to do, do it."

'The thing is that some very bad people have taken my Maureen. She doesn't deserve to be a victim here. It was my failure to keep her safe. Please, God, keep her safe. I'm going to try to bring her home. Then I'll try to be a better son, brother, father, and hopefully one day a good husband.

'In Jesus' name. Amen.'

Daniels found some leftover soup in the refrigerator and put it on the stove, then went to wake up Sharon. She told him she needed a few minutes. While waiting he checked the emails sent to their website. He was not surprised to find the answer to his post offering to trade himself for Maureen.

"Re: Trade Offer" was the subject line.

"No dice." was the full extent of the text.

When she came out of the bedroom Sharon had washed her face and brushed her hair, but her eyes were still red and her mouth was turned down. "Thanks," she mumbled sitting down in front of the bowl of soup.

"Are you ready to listen to my plan?" Daniels asked.

Sharon nodded and put down the spoon.

Daniels explained that he planned to offer Gary Knowlton the first recording from Ethan's phone in return for his releasing Maureen.

"Are you certain he's behind the kidnapping?" Sharon asked.

"It has to be him. Who else had motive?"

"True."

"The next step depends on whether Trey's friend can retrieve files from Ethan's phone that are proof positive of his father's duplicity."

"Like what?"

"Like communications with someone in the Chinese government, or barring that an exchange with Gary Knowlton or someone else confirming his intent to give in to the Chinese in the upcoming talks."

"What if there's nothing else on the phone?"

"President Palmer may have to bluff. I'm not sure he's willing to do so, but based on the second recording and their attempts to prevent you from finding the truth of what happened to Ethan, he certainly could demand Henry Garvin answer some tough questions."

Sharon nodded.

"So what do you think?"

"If you give them the first recording, Knowlton gets off, right?"

Daniels thought for a couple of seconds. "Yes and no. We give up that particular piece of evidence, but we can include a demand that he step aside or something like that."

"That's not enough. Ethan would be alive today if not for him."

He was afraid she'd go there.

Sharon got up and went over to the kitchen window. "He's got to pay. He's got to go to jail for the rest of his life for what he did."

"Sharon, I wish we could make that happen, but if we don't use this recording . . . I need to free Maureen. Every minute they have her is too long. You get that, right?"

"Of course, Mr. Daniels. I feel just as bad as you do."

He doubted that, but didn't want to argue the point. "Think of it this way: Knowlton gets away scot free if we do nothing. We need to use the recording."

Sharon walked to the counter, lifted a spoon of soup to her mouth, tasted it, and put down the spoon. "I'm not saying do nothing. We need to go to the media. Give them the recording. We'll tell them he's got Maureen. Let the police and the FBI rescue her."

Daniels sighed. He wanted to argue, to pull rank, but restrained himself. That had backfired before. It would probably do so now. "That's an option, certainly, but let's examine it more carefully."

Sharon turned back from the window.

"Let's think about what would happen if we released the recording and with it the message concerning Maureen. Yes, the media would ask Knowlton about it, but it also exposes President Palmer. They'll start asking him about what kind of help he's been giving you, and my name will come up, as will Trey's who would certainly lose his job as a result of doing things that go against his NSA contract. The result would be a media circus which would not necessarily result in Maureen's being freed unharmed or in Knowlton's paying for his crimes."

Sharon had listened to him as he recited his arguments against her suggestion. "I just want him to pay, Mr. Daniels. It won't bring Ethan back, but he's got to pay."

"He will, Sharon. I promise you. He's tied into this China business, I'm sure of that and once we get Maureen back, we'll throw a monkey wrench into their plans and they'll all pay."

Daniels left Dupont Circle that afternoon at the regular time, having made arrangements with Chaz Nelson, one of the weekend agents, to come in the next morning while he was trying to track down Gary Knowlton. He still hadn't written the statement he planned on delivering to Knowlton--assuming he could find him. He would try to talk to Knowlton one on one, but doubted Garvin's aide would agree. Putting a trade offer in writing and getting it into his hands was his backup. He just needed to figure how to deliver it.

Daniels stopped at his favorite diner and worked on the statement. The first sentence came easily.

Release Maureen Thornberry by noon tomorrow Sunday January 14th or I'll release the recording Ethan Garvin made the morning of November 10th that proves you were following his car and failed to stop when he drove off the road.

He realized he had to do something to prove to Knowlton that there was such a recording. What if Trey could post the first few seconds on the Web--just long enough for Knowlton to recognize his own voice.

He called Trey's house.

"Just got in. What's up?"

"Emergency. They've kidnapped Maureen."

"What the--"

"Please just listen. I need you to post on a secure location the first twenty seconds of the first recording. Then send me the link. Can you do it now?"

"I'm on it."

"Oh, and don't tell Brianna."

"Of course not."

"Sorry. Just wanted to make sure."

Daniels needed to print out several copies of the statement in case he had to leave it at locations where Knowlton might be hanging out. By the time he'd returned to the P Street apartment and printed out four copies, Trey sent him the link to the start of the recording. Daniels added the URL in longhand to the bottom of each page. He also looked up the addresses for Knowlton's Bethesda home, the Garvin's transition team headquarters, and the Garvin's family compound in Georgetown. He planned on visiting all three that evening.

Daniels was not surprised to find Knowlton's mansion protected by a private security service. The security team refused to let him approach the front door.

"It is extremely important that I speak to Mr. Knowlton today," he told the cop in charge.

"We can't help you," the cop replied. "You'll have to contact him through normal channels."

"What does that mean?" Daniels asked.

"That means if Mr. Knowlton wants to hear from you, you already know how to reach him. If you don't know how to reach him, he doesn't want to hear from you."

"He'll want to hear what I've got to say," Daniels insisted.

"Then go through normal channels," the man said.

Seeing no alternative, Daniels asked the rental cops to deliver his envelope to the house.

The head man took the envelope. "We'll give this to someone on his staff. They'll decide whether Knowlton needs to see it."

"Let me talk to that person. It has to reach him today," Daniels said.

"Again, if they wanted to hear from you, you'd already know who to contact. Given that you don't seem to know the procedure, we're going to have to ask you to leave the premises."

"Call up to the house. I'm sure they'll want to talk to me--"

The rent-a-cop started to lean on Daniels trying to maneuver him back towards his car, which was blocking the driveway. "You need to leave, sir, or I'll have to notify the D.C. police that they need to come down here."

"I'm not doing anything threatening," Daniels said. "I'm just trying to deliver an important message--"

"And it will be delivered. Now it's time to leave or face the consequences."

Daniels had no desire to tangle with the D.C. police. He left without any confidence that Knowlton would get his message. He'd have to try the other locations, starting with Garvin transition headquarters in case Knowlton was there or someone knew where he was.

At the transition office, Daniels gave his envelope to one of the staffers who told him she'd try to get it to Knowlton although the latter was not a transition official and she didn't know when it would reach him.

His next stop was the Garvin's Georgetown compound. As he approached the address, he detected Secret Service agents staked throughout the area. This was the first time during the investigation he could use his true identity to his advantage. He showed the agent manning the booth at the bottom of the driveway his credentials and explained he had an important document that needed to be delivered to Mr. Knowlton in person. The agent called up to the house and was told Mr. Knowlton was not present at the time.

"I'd like to leave this here for him if that's okay with you," Daniels told the agent.

"I can't guarantee that he'll receive it," the man replied. "Perhaps you should keep it and try elsewhere."

Back in his car, Daniels tried to control his frustration. Those were the only locations he knew where he might reach Knowlton and it looked like none of them were going to work. Now what? Where else could he be?

Given that he was having zero luck finding Knowlton, Daniels sat in his car trying to come up with some way of discovering where Maureen was being held. If he knew that he wouldn't have to wait for Knowlton to get his message. He could call on his Secret Service brothers and they'd . . . what? Go in shooting? Probably not a good strategy.

While he was sitting there Nate Parenti called him.

"I've been trying to reach you, man."

Daniels glanced at his phone. He'd turned it off so that it wouldn't ring while approaching the Garvin's compound and forgotten to turn it back on.

"What's up?"

"Your girl is gone."

"What?"

"I was in the bathroom. She was acting cool--too cool as it turned out. As soon as I turn my back, she split."

"Gone where? Did she leave a note?"

"Nothing man. Maybe she emailed you. Better check."

Daniels opened his email and indeed there was a terse note from Sharon. "I'm sorry. I had to do it. Thank you for everything you did, but justice has to be served."

Did what? What . . . Oh, shit! He clicked on the browser icon and entered *Fairfax County Inquirer*. Sharon had posted a new entry under the title, "Proof Gary Knowlton Left the Scene of Ethan's Accident." He opened the document. It was a transcript of the first recording.

"Oh, no. How could she do this to me?"

"What, man? What'd she do?"

Daniels forgot Parenti was still on the line. "She released something to the public that I told her not to release. All hell is about to break lose and my lady may be the one who pays the price."

Saturday, January 13

Daniels didn't have time to worry where Sharon Washburn had gone or whether she'd be safe. She must have known he'd be royally angry at her for releasing the transcript of the recording Ethan made of his conversation with Gary Knowlton. It was small consolation that she was probably no longer in any personal danger.

Sharon's rash action undermined his plan of offering Gary Knowlton a trade of the recording for Maureen's release. Given the kidnappers' instructions to stop digging, whoever ordered Maureen's kidnapping was going to think he'd intentionally ignored their threat. If they did something to Maureen as a result . . .

Daniels squeezed his hands into fists and swore out loud. Sharon's betrayal made it even more urgent he find out where Maureen was and free her.

He still had the second recording where Ethan not only identified Knowlton by name, but explained why he was trying to get to the White House that morning. Daniels didn't want to have to trade that tape for Maureen's freedom, but if it was the only way to free her, he'd do it in a heartbeat. That the tape wasn't incontrovertible proof of Henry Garvin's duplicity didn't mean Knowlton and whoever else was involved wouldn't do almost anything to suppress it.

Given he'd no idea where they were holding Maureen or how to discover that fact, the second recording was his best chance to free her. Standing in the way of his taking any action, however, was his lack of knowledge about how to reach Knowlton. He needed a proxy and the first name that came to mind was Cynthia Renfro. She'd been the one reporter, other than Randy Dodd, who had been willing to investigate Ethan's death, but what he needed her to do now was not broadcast a story but deliver a message. He wasn't sure she'd go along, but it was worth a try.

Given that it was nearly midnight, Daniels was not surprised that he couldn't reach Renfro at her station, but he had her cell phone and email. He sent an email first, and then called her. She called him back thirty minutes later, just as he was pulling into the parking lot at his apartment complex.

"Mr. Johnson. What in God's name is going on with you guys? I keep telling you not to release this kind of information to the public before you've talked to me, but you don't listen. Then you call wanting my help. Don't be surprised if I tell you to buzz off."

"I must apologize, but it was not my decision. Sharon Washburn released the recording against my wishes. Now I've got to pick up the pieces."

"That's too bad, but I don't see why I should hear you out. You guys have not proved trustworthy or honest with me in the past."

Daniels knew he'd better get right to the point. "Two reasons, Ms. Renfro--"

"Cynthia, Mr. Johnson. Call me Cynthia."

"Thank you and you may call me Tucker Daniels. That's my real name. Joe Johnson was an alias."

"How interesting. Better late than never, I suppose. What are your two reasons? And they'd better be good."

"First, there's a second recording which explains what happened to Ethan Garvin."

"Do I get to hear it?"

"That can be arranged at the right time."

"At the right time--what does that mean?"

"Let me tell you the second reason before we discuss the recording. People who I believe answer to Gary Knowlton have kidnapped a member of our team and threatened to harm her if we continue the investigation or contact the police."

"Kidnapped!"

"Yes, kidnapped," Daniels repeated, choking on the word.

"You're not making this up, are you, whatever your name is?"

"Daniels. Tucker Daniels and no, I'm not making it up."

"Prove it."

"I gave you my name, but what I didn't tell you is that I'm an active agent with the United States Secret Service."

"The plot thickens. So, why is the Secret Service involved in this matter?"

"I can't answer that question right now, but I promise you will have the full exclusive story, if our associate, a woman by the name of Maureen Thornberry, is released unharmed."

"Is she Secret Service, too?"

How much should he tell her? "No. She's a personal friend who has been assisting in the investigation."

"And someone has kidnapped her?

He took a deep breath. "They have."

"And you have proof of this?"

"I can send you the email, but please don't publicize it yet or the kidnappers will harm her, but you can help and get an exclusive in the process. All you need to do is contact Gary Knowlton with a message."

"And that message would be?"

"What will happen if he doesn't release Maureen Thornberry by noon tomorrow."

"And, if he denies any involvement, what then?"

"He'll probably do so, but I'm confident he'll do what I ask to save his skin."

"What threat do you hold over his head given that he's now looking at a possible murder charge?"

"He didn't murder Ethan Garvin. Knowlton was following Ethan when he went off the road. The most he can be charged with is leaving the scene of an accident."

"That's a pretty serious crime," Renfro stated.

"It's a felony, which means he's looking at a minimum of one year in state prison if convicted."

"You still haven't answered my question. What threat do you hold over his head that's going to make him want to cooperate with you and release your friend, assuming he's connected with those who kidnapped her?"

Daniels, who had been standing, sat down. "All I can say at the moment is that it has to do with what's on the second recording made by Ethan Garvin."

"Let me see if I've got this straight. What you're saying is that to prevent you from revealing his role in the death of the president-elect's son, he committed the crime of kidnapping, and that instead of a year behind bars for leaving the scene of an accident, he's looking at a decade or more! Does that make sense to you?"

Daniels sighed. "I understand what you're saying, Ms. Renfro, but you'll have to take my word that Knowlton was involved in a crime much more serious than leaving the scene. The proof of that crime is what Ethan Garvin was trying to bring to the White House. That's why Knowlton and Ethan's mother wanted to prevent him from going there that morning. That's also why Knowlton insisted on taking Ethan's briefcase. He knew the evidence Ethan was bringing to President Palmer was in that briefcase."

"And you won't tell me what that evidence consisted of, and for that matter how you came across these recordings? As I recall, no cellphone was recovered from Ethan Garvin's car."

"You're correct. They didn't recover the phone. They were in such a hurry to crush the car that the police failed to do a thorough job searching the vehicle. We had it cracked open at the salvage yard and found the phone under the back seat where it must have ended up in the crash."

"I'll want to see the phone and talk to the people who recovered the recordings. But my main question is what was Ethan Garvin bringing the President?"

"I actually don't know the exact nature of the information, but it must have been damaging to Henry Garvin because his wife and top aide went out of their way to prevent Ethan from exposing it. Please, Ms. Renfro. Call Knowlton. Tell him Ethan made a second recording mentioning him by name and if he doesn't want us to go public with it, he must release Maureen Thornberry by noon tomorrow."

"That's a pretty big ask, Mr. Daniels, but I'm going to do it because I have you on tape promising me that exclusive, and your ass is grass if you fail to come through."

Sunday, January 14

Gary Knowlton was getting impatient. He had been sitting in his dark blue late model Mercedes near the top level of a Wisconsin Avenue parking garage for almost an hour. "Finally," he muttered under his breath when a black SUV with tinted windows backed into the space next to him. Eliot Agnew, a Secret Service supervisor with a buzz cut in the standard navy blue suit got out of the van and opened the passenger side of the thin man's car.

"This isn't smart," Knowlton said to Agnew.

"Did you want to discuss this on your cell?"

"Of course not."

"Then, tell me what you want done and I'll get the hell out of here."

Knowlton grimaced. He hadn't thought things would have reached the point where they had to mess up the woman. Didn't Daniels realize he was serious? Didn't he care what happened to her? It was time to show Mr. Secret Service he meant what he said.

Same Day

Daniels owed the President an update. After a few fitful hours lying awake, he'd finally fallen asleep and then slept later than he'd intended. It was highly irregular for a Secret Service agent to request an appointment with the President, but Edwin Palmer had left word that he be notified whenever Daniels asked to speak to him. Knowing he might have to wait, Daniels settled down in the White House Secret Service office with a large coffee, a bagel and that morning's *Washington Examiner.*

He was surprised when his phone buzzed not fifteen minutes later.

"I'm sorry, Agent Daniels," the woman who'd called him said. "The President is not available today."

"Maybe I didn't make myself clear. It's extremely important. Can you try again?"

"I'm sorry, Sir," the woman said, "but the President has answered your request. You'll just have to try again another day. He's pretty booked up tomorrow, too. I'd wait until the middle of the week."

"Did he say he wasn't available today or tomorrow?"

"He didn't specify. I'm just suggesting the middle of the week might be better."

Daniels was in shock. He sat there a few moments not sure what to do. On the drive back to his apartment in Alexandria he tried to come up with reasons Palmer had refused to see him. *Okay*, he told himself, *maybe he can't see me today, but why didn't he say 'try me tomorrow'?*

For a moment Daniels felt betrayed. President Palmer had asked him to conduct what he described as a one- or two-week investigation. He'd stuck with it after it snow-balled out of control, even involving his son and fiancé. Now when Maureen's life was in grave danger, it appeared that Palmer was bailing on him. In so doing he was destroying Daniels' faith in a man whose character he believed was beyond reproach.

"Naw," Daniels said out loud. That can't be right. *There must be a reason he can't talk to me.* Further, this turn of events couldn't stop him from doing what he needed to do. Being angry at Palmer didn't solve anything, nor could he let things play themselves out. He had to free Maureen and do what he could to prevent Henry Garvin from being inaugurated and betraying the U.S. to China.

When he got back to his apartment he found a text message from Cynthia Renfro stating she had not been able to reach Knowlton, but would keep trying.

Small consolation was the media play given to the transcript of Ethan's conversation with Gary Knowlton. While the mainstream press was reporting it as an alleged conversation pointing out they had yet to obtain a copy of the recording, Internet media outlets and hundreds of individuals jumped on the *Fairfax County Inquirer*'s assertion that the person talking to Ethan the morning of his death was long-time Garvin aide Gary Knowlton. Many commentators repeated the questions Sharon had added at the end of the tape: What did Gary Knowlton know about Ethan's accident? Why didn't he come forward? Did he force Ethan's car off the road? If not, did he see it leave the road? If so, why didn't he stop?

Sharon pointed out in her post that leaving the scene of an accident could lead to a felony conviction. She even cited the section of Virginia law concerning that crime. At the end of her post, Sharon asked Knowlton to reveal what was in Ethan's briefcase that he was planning on bringing to the White House. Those were the right questions, but what incentive did Knowlton have to answer them?

As Daniels considered what to do next, he realized he needed to update the retired agents who were guarding Sharon.

An hour later, after having spoken to each of the four agents who'd helped guard Sharon and the two who'd been watching his son's house, he did a quick email and message check. While there was nothing from Cynthia Renfro, there was a message that had been sent to the *Fairfax County Inquirer* website with the subject line 'we warned you.'

Daniels stomach lurched as his thumb hovered over the link. Dare he read the message? It included an image. He put the phone down and buried his face in his hands for a second, then opened the email.

It was worse that he'd expected. There were two photos of Maureen curled up in a ball on the floor of a carpeted room, her top arm was bent in a way that arms shouldn't bend. If her arm wasn't broken, her shoulder was dislocated. Daniels had suffered a dislocation as a kid after falling off a roof when playing cops and robbers with some neighborhood kids. If they didn't pop the arm back in place quickly, the pain would get worse and the damage more lasting.

Daniels wanted to throw something across the room. They were going to pay. He didn't care what happened to him. He'd find them and they'd pay.

He almost forgot to read the message.

"Your finance had a little accident, Mr. Daniels," it said. "She keeps falling down from the top of the stairs and unless you put out a press release by noon today saying the tape was a hoax, the next time she might break a leg."

No matter how angry he was, Daniels knew he had to comply with their demand. Thanks to Sharon they had won this battle, but they were going to find out that the war was not over.

He had to call Sharon. She'd released the recording. The retraction had to come from her. If she knew what was good for her, she'd do what he asked. He couldn't be responsible for what he might to do if he had to chase her down.

Fortunately she answered her phone.

"I knew you'd be pissed," she said, after thirty seconds of silence while Daniels implored her to speak to him.

"Let's not go there, Sharon. What you did was wrong. It put Maureen's life in jeopardy and for what?"

She didn't answer.

"I need you to post a retraction ASAP," Daniels said knowing he had to control his anger if he was to save Maureen.

"I've already written it. I was going to call you first."

"Put it out."

"Okay. It's out."

Daniels didn't feel any better. The enemy was still in control. Whatever he did had to be done without their knowledge. His options were limited.

"What are you going to do?"

He had forgotten he was still connected to Sharon. "I don't know. I just don't know, but I'm pretty angry so I'd better hang up."

Despite the overwhelming urge to go someplace and do something, Daniels stayed in his apartment the rest of the day waiting to hear from Cynthia Renfro, the kidnappers, or both.

The mainstream media acted with glee at Sharon's announcement that the transcript was a hoax. Even their supporters on the website directed all kinds of invective at them for doing such a thing, although a tiny few questioned the retraction, wondering if it, rather than the original statement, was the hoax.

Late that evening he told himself he needed to try to get some sleep. Instead he tossed and turned for a couple of hours, got up and took a hot shower, then tried to sleep once more. At some point he dozed off, sleeping until the alarm told him it was six a.m.

Daniels didn't need a calendar to remind him that Henry Garvin's inauguration was just one week away.

Daniels was pacing his apartment late Monday morning when Cynthia Renfro called. He had to hold his cell an arm's length from his ear while Renfro lambasted him with every description ever levied against a phony, two-faced, double-speaking fraudster. He didn't even try to apologize.

"I still owe you that exclusive," he said when she slowed down to catch her breath.

"I don't want it, Agent Daniels. Don't call me again. You've blown your credibility. Do you hear me?"

She disconnected the call. Daniels wished he could have told her the whole story. Maybe someday he would.

Sharon emailed him midday to ask if he'd meet her at Dupont Circle that afternoon so she could recover her belongings. She told him she didn't feel safe going there by herself. Daniels didn't want to, but he agreed. He met Sharon Washburn in the lobby of the P Street apartment complex and let her into the apartment. While she packed, he scrolled through messages and comments on the website. He found nothing of interest. When she was done, he helped her pack up her car. Neither said much until her car was loaded.

"Going back to your apartment?" he asked.

"Do you think it's safe?"

He nodded. "One week from today, the Garvins won't give a hoot about what you tell the media. Henry will be President with all the power to control the media as well as the FBI and the Secret Service."

Sharon looked down at the floor. "Can you ever forgive me? I realize now I shouldn't have done it, but I couldn't bear to let him get away--"

Daniels swallowed the choice words that came to mind. He shook his head. "I don't know what to say to you."

"I feel so bad about Maureen. They won't hurt her any more, right?"

He hesitated. *Better tell her what she wants to hear.* "I think they'll release her as long as we do what they tell us and nothing stops Henry Garvin from taking the oath."

But what incentive did they have to let her go? He had to face reality--given that Knowlton and his cronies had already shown themselves capable of murder, why would they be willing to leave anyone alive who might implicate them? That meant Maureen, Trey, and himself were all in danger.

Knowledge is power, Daniels told himself. If Knowlton thought it was going to be easy to finish the job, he had seriously underestimated who he was dealing with.

After Sharon left, he returned to Mrs. Palmer's apartment and started packing up his things, including the computer equipment that he intended to donate to an orphanage or school. He was about halfway done when the house phone rang.

"Daniels . . . I mean Johnson here."

"Mr. Johnson. You have a visitor. Can I send him up?"

"That depends. Who is it?"

"He says his name is Palmer, but he doesn't look like the president to me. Maybe he's a relative."

"Sure, why not. I'll open the door for him."

It's probably a family member who's taking over the apartment now that the Palmers were heading back to Nebraska. Perfect timing!

Daniels waited at the door. An elderly, stooped man got off the elevator. He was wearing a faded University of Nebraska jacket, baggy jeans, dirty sneakers, and a wool cap with Nebraska's cream and scarlet colors pulled over his ears.

The man marched into the apartment without speaking. Daniels let the door close behind him.

"Agent Daniels," the man said as he moved the cap, revealing a familiar, albeit unshaven, face.

"Mr. President?"

"Pretty good disguise, don't you think?"

Monday, January 15

"That explains things," President Palmer stated after Daniels told him about Sharon's decision to release the transcript of the first recording, effectively sabotaging his plan to win Maureen's freedom.

Daniels noticed the President's mug was empty. "That was the last of the coffee. I can get some fresh from across the street."

"No time. How about a glass of water?"

"I'm drinking hot water with lemon," Daniels said.

"Make it two," Palmer told him. "My wife tells me I need to drink more water. All I can see that it's doing is making me pee more often. Speaking of which I'll be right back."

Daniels refilled their mugs from the kettle.

"I'd like to listen to the recordings," Palmer said when he returned.

"I take it you've no idea where your female friend is being held?" Palmer asked, after listening to both twice.

"None and I can't figure out where Gary Knowlton is hiding out either," Daniels admitted.

"Let me see if I've got this straight," Palmer said after taking a sip of hot water. "Ethan's death was an accident. Apparently he was driving too fast or not looking where he was going while trying to get away from Knowlton. Correct?"

Daniels nodded. "As far as I can tell, that's what happened."

"Knowlton may or may not be liable for the accident," Palmer said after taking a sip of the hot lemon water, "but he's certainly on the hook for leaving the scene of an accident, assuming this tape will be admitted into evidence."

"I'm not a lawyer, sir."

"Sometimes I wish I weren't," the President said with a wink. "I can't say what the courts will do, but the court of public opinion matters. Even were a court of law to reject the recording, it's already out. Weighing against that is Sharon's retraction, which you can explain was due to the threat to your friend's life."

Daniels nodded. "I'm with you, sir."

"Turning to Ethan's evidence against his father, it's clear that Knowlton took the briefcase and must have destroyed the contents. We don't know, however, if those were the originals or copies, which means there's still hope we can find out what Ethan was bringing me. Could there be copies on his phone?"

"Possibly. My people are still trying to recover the files. I'll let you know if they come up with something. If not, perhaps the FBI can recover the files from wherever Ethan backed up his data files."

"It's critical, Agent Daniels, that you follow up on that lead. I'll try to get the FBI on it, but it may not happen overnight. My director left two weeks ago and the temporary doesn't jump when I call."

"I understand."

"Push the people who are working on Ethan's phone," Palmer suggested. "Tell them you'll quadruple their normal rate if they can give you an answer, let's say, by tomorrow midday."

"Will do," Daniels said.

"Don't think I'm forgetting Ms. Thornberry," Palmer said. "Here's what I'm thinking. I'll ask Henry Garvin to bring Gary Knowlton to the White House tonight. I'll offer them the deal you were going to offer--suppression of the second recording in return for her immediate safe return. Otherwise, I'll tell them we'll release the second recording to the media at 10 a.m. tomorrow morning."

"And if they deny any connection to her being kidnapped?"

Palmer messaged his chin. "Good question, agent. How do you suggest I respond if they take that tack?"

"Can you get the FBI to probe Knowlton's phone and text conversations since last Thursday? He must be communicating with those he hired to do the job, and he must have distributed a large sum of money upfront to whoever picked up Maureen. Can that be traced?"

Palmer shook his head. "Not possible. I'd have to get the special court to okay it. There's not enough time. We need a backup plan."

Daniels paced the room for a few seconds. "Bluff. Tell him we know who he hired and the FBI is already looking for them. Tell him once they're arrested, they'll no doubt rat on him, and he'll be on the hook for kidnapping plus a dozen other charges.

If you tell him that, I'll bet he confesses then and there."

Palmer stood up. "Let's hope so. I can't think of anything better at the moment."

"How do I communicate with you, sir, now that I'm not allowed back at the White House?" Earlier Palmer explained why. Apparently, the Secret Service had received a tip that he was filing false time sheets and revoked his security clearance.

Could someone over there be working for the Garvins?

"I haven't figured out how to quash that, but your not being allowed into the White House gave me a reason to get out of the damn place."

Daniels laughed. "Glad to oblige."

Palmer smiled. "In any case, there's no need for you to come to the White House. I'll send you a courier pouch with updates every eight hours starting this evening. You can send it back letting me know what you've come up with. If we need to meet use the code I showed you and I'll come back here."

"That works for me," Daniels said.

"Good." The President put his knit cap back on his head. "My military aide is probably having a cow by now. I'd better get back."

"Thank you, Mr. President. I recall what you said about bringing in the answer at the last minute, but I'll give it my all until it's over one way or the other."

Palmer patted Daniels on the shoulder as he donned his University of Nebraska jacket. "You've done a remarkable job, Agent Daniels. I've every confidence you'll finish the deal."

Daniels felt only slightly more confident after his meeting with Palmer, but it was time to bring Trey in on his plan.

"Did you ever consider someone might be following you?" Trey asked. They were sitting in Trey's car in the parking lot at Ruby Tuesday's on Route 301 in Bowie, Maryland, roughly halfway between their homes.

"I can't say I wasn't followed, but I didn't want to talk on the phone. I'm trying to keep you from being caught up in all this."

"I'm afraid that's water under the bridge. I've been to Mrs. Palmer's apartment several times. You've been to my house. If someone's watching you, they're onto me."

Daniels grimaced. He couldn't bear to think his role in President Palmer's investigation might harm his son, given what already happened to Maureen. How could he ever forgive himself!

Trey handed him a flash drive. "Here's a drive containing everything we could get off the phone. I'm afraid there's not much there--a lot of incomplete files. Nothing exciting, and lacking Ethan's passwords, my guy couldn't access what he had stored in the cloud."

"Okay. Helping us find the phone and then retrieving those recordings was a tremendous help."

"Speaking of which, what was that retraction all about?"

"Sharon thought releasing the transcript was the only way this Gary Knowlton fellow would pay for what he'd done to Ethan. No sooner had she done so, however, than the people holding Maureen took it out on her and demanded we retract."

"What? What did they do?"

"Sent me pictures showing they'd done something to her arm or shoulder. I was ready to kill the bunch of them then and there, but of course they threatened to harm her severely if we didn't put out a statement admitting the recording was a fake."

"That was pretty awful of Sharon," Trey ventured.

"I'm pretty steamed about it, but there's too little time left to worry about spilt milk or should I say spilt bytes."

Trey shook his head. "Don't try to get technical, Dad. It doesn't suit you."

Daniels smiled and then hated himself for doing so. How could he joke when Maureen was in pain?

Trey, who'd been looking out the side window, turned back to face his father. "Given that I don't seem to have what you need, what's your plan?"

"The President is going to offer Knowlton the second recording in return for Maureen's release. I should find out how that went shortly."

"I hope she's okay," Trey said quietly.

"I pray she'll forgive me. I tried to keep her out of it, but--"

"More spilled bytes?"

Daniels cringed. "All I can do is keep working and hope at the end of the day we come out on top."

After a quick review of the files taken from Ethan's iphone, Daniels concluded none contained any material that incriminated Ethan's father. He wrote that up to put in the courier pouch the President had promised to send to his apartment.

When it arrived it contained more bad news.

Gary Knowlton had resigned his position as a personal aide to Henry Garvin. As a result, Garvin sent a message to the White House saying he could not order him to come to the White House.

Palmer included a video in the courier bag describing his attempt to haul in Knowlton. "When I called Henry Garvin, Mrs. Garvin came on the line and demanded I put a muzzle on Sharon Washburn. She told me Ms. Washburn has received unprecedented and unwarranted support from the White House, and it had to stop immediately or legal action would ensue."

Daniels stopped the video. He was not surprised at their latest maneuver. The Garvins would do anything to keep the truth from coming out. He re-started the message.

"I told Katherine Garvin I had not had any direct contact with Ms. Washburn, and I wanted to talk to Henry in person about the information Ethan had provided me the day before his unfortunate accident. Of course, she asked what kind of information.

"I did what you suggested. I bluffed. I told her she knew what I was talking about and that I'd go public unless Henry came to the White House personally to answer Ethan's charges. She hemmed and hawed, but eventually said she'd try to clear his schedule and would let me know when they could come in."

Daniels added to the document he'd prepared for the President a note asking that he be present if and when the Garvins came to the oval office. Then he closed the pouch and gave it to the messenger to take back to the President.

Daniels wasn't sure where that left them. Perhaps Garvin would agree to require Knowlton give up Maureen, but he couldn't count on that. Hope for the best, he'd read someplace, but prepare for the worst. All he knew was he wasn't going to sit around and wait any longer.

Tuesday, January 16

Free Maureen. Waking before sunrise, Daniels had only one thought in mind and that meant compelling Gary Knowlton to release her in order to save his own hide. It came down to which one of them was smarter and more resourceful, and he was highly motivated to demonstrate there was no contest.

Although he didn't think Knowlton was staying at his Bethesda home, he couldn't rule out the possibility that he was sneaking in and out, perhaps in disguise, perhaps late at night. Just in case, he decided to install digital, motion-detection cameras around Knowlton's mansion in hopes that they would enable him to catch Henry Garvin's top aide going in or out of his house.

Few people are aware that the Secret Service maintains a large collection of disguises, consisting of various uniforms and outfits for use by agents working undercover. Daniels requested a telephone repair getup that looked reasonably authentic and fit his frame. When filling out the form explaining his intended need, he wrote "classified undercover operation." Someone up the chain of command might challenge his request, but by the time the form wound its way through the bureaucracy, Daniels expected to have returned the uniform and to be on his way to Hawaii.

Next, he visited the agency's electronics unit to obtain the camera equipment. Using the same wording to explain his need for the equipment he found a helpful technician who outfitted him with half a dozen cameras and the monitoring software. A quick demonstration gave Daniels confidence he could install the equipment and set up the software to record every movement that was detected in selected zones.

"This is all legal?" the tech asked him.

"Absolutely," Daniels replied. "The paperwork will be here in a few days."

That seemed to satisfy since more often than not the paper justifying a monitoring operation was days behind the actual need.

Daniels installed the software on the computer at Mrs. Palmer's apartment rather than drive to his apartment, a trip that would cost him a couple of hours at minimum. Then he used a mapping program to scan Knowlton's neighborhood for telephone poles that would give him the desired views of the mansion. With that information acquired, he headed out to Bethesda.

It took over an hour to install cameras on four telephone polls--two covering the driveway and one each on the front and back entrances to the building. Coming off the fourth pole, Daniels decided to put a fifth camera on a pole that would give him a view of the back of the upper levels of the house at a different angle from the other pole. It would only be of value if someone left a curtain open enough for him to identify Knowlton. Not a likely prospect, but given his prior investment of time, he figured he'd add that camera as well.

When he first arrived in the neighborhood, he had noticed a white van with red signage for a plumber parked opposite Knowlton's house a few houses down. Now that van was pulling out and a second van was replacing it. Daniels watched the first van turn at the corner and reappear two minutes later on the street where he'd parked his own rental van. Oddly, no one got out of the van.

This had to be some form of surveillance. Were they watching Knowlton's house? It was possible someone had hired a security firm on a personal matter. Knowlton might be watching his own house or it could be someone who Knowlton owed money to or who knew what.

Then he recalled a brown van like the one that was now parked on Knowlton's street had been parked down the street from the Garvin's compound when he stopped by there Saturday evening. Could they be following him? Did they switch assignments hoping to go undetected? If so, who was doing it and why? Perhaps Knowlton had hired someone to keep track of him.

It was also possible it was just a couple of workers stopping to eat their lunch, but he needed to find out. Finishing the last installation, he climbed down the pole and walked around the block to his van. He put his equipment bag inside and drove off slowly as if he didn't have a care in the world. He needed a destination and chose his favorite diner-- the Metro 29 on Lee Highway in Arlington--even though it was at least an hour away. He wasn't surprised when as he took the ramp to I-495 that a white van with red signage appeared in his rear view mirror. It stuck with him the whole time it took to fight through noontime traffic into Arlington.

So someone was surveilling him. He needed to find out who.

When he got to the diner, he pulled into a spot near the back of the parking lot. He didn't expect the occupants of the van to follow him into the diner's lot. They had to park someplace where they could observe his car. The bank parking lot next door was the obvious choice.

Presumably the driver of the van would look for a parking spot that would give them a view both of his car and the entrance to the diner, but the bank lot was pretty full. Pretending to make a cell call standing in the lot, he noticed the van pull into the bank lot and circle looking for an open spot. He didn't wait to see where they stopped not wanting to let them know he'd spotted them.

Daniels entered the diner through the back entrance, but instead of waiting to be seated, he went out the front door, waited a couple of minutes, walked to the corner, and then proceeded into the bank parking lot.

The white van was parked near the back of the bank lot facing the diner. Daniels hoped no one in the van was watching out the back, which meant he could approach it undetected.

Reaching the van, he banged on the back door, and then crouched behind the car next to the van so the people inside couldn't see him.

He heard some scrambling around in the van, but no one got out.

He waited a minute, then banged on the door a second time--harder this time.

That brought results. A man possibly in his thirties got out of the passenger door. He was of Asian descent and was wearing a black suit and tie. Clearly despite the signage on the van he was not in the plumbing profession.

"Why do you bang on car?" the man asked cautiously approaching Daniels.

"Who are you and why are you following me?" Daniels demanded.

The man took a quick look at whoever was sitting in the driver's seat and looked back at Daniels. "We no follow."

"Yes you were. Don't deny it. Who are you? Who do you work for?"

The man didn't reply, but got back in the van as the driver started the engine. Daniels had to jump to avoid being hit as the van backed up and drove towards the lot entrance.

Daniels had just enough time to see the driver was also Asian. He wrote down the van's license plate, then cut through to the diner parking lot, hopped into his car and sped to the exit to see if he could detect which way the van had turned. Fortunately the traffic light had been against the van. Only now was it able to cross Lee Highway going east on North Glebe toward I-66. Daniels pulled into the left lane on Lee and waited for the left turn arrow. They had a good minute's lead. He'd have to hustle to catch them.

When the light changed, Daniels wove through traffic, earning a few angry scowls and horn blasts. For a moment he feared they'd gotten away, but he spotted them as they were making a left onto the I-66 ramp. He followed. Now it was a matter of staying far enough behind the van not to be detected, although he doubted they were even thinking about being followed or knew what to do if they detected him.

Daniels followed the van as they exited I-66 onto Virginia State 110, then made a series of quick lane switches putting them on US1 going across the Potomac River into the District.

Daniels thought he'd lost them at one point, but picked them again as they ran into a red light after making a right-hand turn off 14th Street. He stayed a couple of cars behind the van which made two more right-hand turns putting them on Maryland Avenue where they pulled up to the valet parking stand in front of the famous Mandarin Oriental hotel.

Daniels kept going around the circle. It was past one o'clock and he still hadn't heard from Cynthia Renfro. Did that mean Knowlton hadn't returned her calls? He was torn about releasing the second tape. If Knowlton got the message and still refused to release Maureen, he'd do it, but what if Knowlton never got his warning?

He put that issue aside for the moment. First he needed to find out who had been following him and why.

Same Day

Daniels used his Secret Service badge to pull aside one of the people at the registration desk in the lobby of the Mandarin Oriental.

"Did you notice several Asian men in black suits come into the hotel a few minutes ago?"

"No, sir." He shook his head vehemently. "I didn't."

"There were at least two and possibly more. I doubt they stopped at the registration desk. They are either registered here already or were going to see someone who is staying here."

The man shook his head again.

"Okay, then. I need to see the video of the elevator area. Now!"

The young man chewed on his lip and then nodded indicating he had decided to cooperate.

"This way," he said motioning for Daniels to follow him into an office behind the registration desk. On the wall were half a dozen video monitors.

"Which one shows the elevators?" Daniels asked.

The young man pointed to the third monitor. "That would be this one."

"Rewind it back fifteen minutes," Daniels instructed.

The young man stood over the keyboard for a second perhaps trying to recall the training he'd been given in the use of the equipment. Then he punched a few keys and the display on which the time was imprinted started to search and then begin to replay.

At first, nothing. A few people getting on and off the elevator, but no one who looked like the men who had been following him. Then three men came into view.

"There," Daniels said.

The clerk stopped the playback. That had to be them. They seemed nervous and quickly jumped into the elevator when it arrived. Daniels watched the display above the elevator door as the numbers indicated what floor the elevator was on. It stopped at 9.

"Okay. I need a list of everyone who is staying on your 9th floor," Daniels said.

The young man startled. "I don't know--"

"I don't have time for warrants, son," Daniels said. "Get the list and bring it here, and don't tell anyone what you're doing."

Daniels wasn't sure if the clerk was going to cooperate, but he'd probably already broken a dozen house rules. In for a penny?

A few minutes later the young man came back with a print out. Only eleven of the thirty rooms on that floor were occupied. A quick scan confirmed Daniels' fear that none of them would stand out. He started scratching out non-Asian names, which cut the list down to seven names.

While following his followers, Daniels had speculated on who might be following him and why. The obvious answer was either Zhai Qi or Zhang Heijing, the men whose presence Ethan Garvin had questioned during the campaign. They must be helping Gary Knowlton interfere with the investigation into Ethan's death.

"Are any of these remaining guests associated with the Chinese government?" Daniels asked the clerk.

"Possibly," he replied. "Wait. I registered this one. His identification showed him to be a Chinese government official."

Daniels didn't recognize the name at first, but then it made sense. He'd forgotten that for the Chinese the surname was listed first. The registration listed a Mr. Zhang under surname. That had to be him.

Mr. Zhang was registered in room 909.

"Perfect. Okay. I'm going up there. Call up to the room and tell them there's a problem with the plumbing in their room and you're sending up someone to fix it. Can you do that?"

The young man looked like he was unsure.

Daniels read the nametag on the clerk's uniform. "This is crucial, Brent. I'm counting on you."

Daniels waited to the side of the registration area while Brent returned to the registration area and appeared to be looking up some information on the house computers. He then picked up his phone and spoke for less than a minute. When he'd completed the call, he gave Daniels a quick nod.

Four minutes later Daniels stood outside the door to 909. He waited until the sound of the elevator door closing indicated that a woman who'd left her room while he was in the corridor had gotten on. Then he knocked on the door.

At first, nothing happened and Daniels was about to knock again when the door opened about four or five inches.

"Yes," a man said without showing his face.

"Plumbing repair," Daniels said loudly.

"Not today," came the reply.

Daniels put his shoulder to the door. It gave way knocking whoever had been on the other side to the floor. Daniels barged into the room. "Secret Service. Everyone stay where you are." He hoped his Secret Service badge would elicit cooperation and that no one was packing.

He didn't recognize the man on the floor. He was younger both than his recollection of the man who had gotten out of the van and his fleeting image of the van's driver, both of whom now stood up looking shocked to see that the man they had been pursuing had found them. A fourth man sitting apart from the others was talking on a cell phone. He had turned to see what the commotion was all about and continued speaking rapidly into the phone.

"Who's in charge here?" Daniels demanded.

Daniels followed the eyes of the driver, who briefly looked in the fourth man's direction. The man put down his phone and stood up.

"Mr. Daniels," he said, "you surprise us."

The man Daniels presumed to be the group's leader looked to be in his late forties. He was slight and dressed in a loose-fitting black suit with a white and blue-stripped tie. His hair was longer than his compatriots and he comported himself as if he knew he was important.

"Zhang Heijing at your service," he said with a slight bow.

Finally we meet. "Why were your men following me?"

"Have no fear. I will answer all your questions. Please have a seat. May we order you some coffee?"

"I just want answers," Daniels replied.

Zhang said something in Chinese to the man who had gotten off the floor. He led the others out of the room.

"Have a seat, please," Zhang said motioning to a chair next to the table where he'd been seated. "We will not be disturbed."

Daniels still wasn't sure what Zhang's game was, but having the others leave the room put him at ease.

"If you prefer, I can order you some hot water with lemon?"

Daniels shook his head again. *How'd he know? They must have planted listening devises at Mrs. Palmer's apartment.*

"No? Then we shall, as you Americans say, get down to business."

Let's, Daniels said to himself as he sat opposite Zhang.

"It may surprise you, but let me assure you that we are on the same side," Zhang began.

The same side! This ought to be interesting.

"I represent Mr. Wan, the President of the State Council of the People's Republic of China."

China's Premier, Daniels translated. *Impressive, if true.*

"Mr. Wan sent me to America last year to observe Mr. Garvin's presidential campaign. He was concerned about Mr. Garvin's ties to Vice Premier

Shen Wei. Mr. Wan suspected they were not the normal ties of two high-ranking officials."

"Not normal?" Daniels said. "What do you mean?"

"I will try to explain. Mr. Shen is what you Americans call a hardliner. He has opposed Mr. Wan on a number of issues. Some say he is campaigning to become the next premier."

"Okay, but--"

Zhang paused.

Daniels wanted to ask what that had to do with anything, but realized he'd have to be patient let Zhang continue. "Sorry. Go on."

"Thank you. As I was saying, Mr. Shen has been extremely cautious about revealing his ties to Mr. Garvin, but we discovered they are close allies indeed."

"Close? In what way?"

"Every time Mr. Shen has had an opportunity to meet Mr. Garvin in person, he has made an excuse not to do so. This made Mr. Wan suspicious and so he began to investigate. That is how he discovered Mr. Shen has provided millions of dollars to Mr. Garvin for decades and has received information your government considered classified in return."

Daniels was taken aback. Classified information! This was more serious than he'd imagined--much more serious than negotiations about CO2 emissions, but it didn't explain what role this Zhang was playing.

"That's quite an accusation," Daniels stated.

Zhang nodded. "We hoped there was some other explanation, but we now know when and why this exchange began."

"Why? Why would Henry Garvin commit what amounts to treason? Did Mr. Shen hold something over Garvin's head?"

"Good guess, Mr. Daniels. It took deep digging, but we found the answer. Are you aware that your Mr. Garvin spent a year in China when he was a college student?"

"Yes, we knew that. It was an exchange program of some sort."

"Yes. Your Oberlin College in Ohio has the longest running cultural exchange program with China. It goes back to 1908."

"Why is that important? Did he meet Mr. Shen while he was in China?"

Zhang smiled and nodded. "Mr. Shen met Mr. Henry Garvin when he was investigating the suicide of a young woman."

"A suicide, but--"

Zhang paused and took a sip of what looked like tea from a fancy hotel cup. "We Chinese do not like discussing such matters, but in this case I must."

"Please, tell me."

"It appears your Mr. Garvin, while he was in China with the Shansi program, entered into an illicit liaison with a young woman from a good family by the name of Zhu Jinling. In his report Mr. Shen concluded she committed suicide when she became pregnant rather than embarrass her family."

"I'm sorry to hear that," Daniels said.

Zhang nodded his agreement. "Mr. Shen was not able to determine who was responsible for getting her pregnant."

"Then what is the connection to Henry Garvin?"

"In order to answer that question, you must think like Mr. Sherlock Holmes."

"Sherlock Holmes?"

"Yes, if you look at all the evidence, you will arrive at the right conclusion."

Daniels was getting anxious. This was taking too much time. What if this was all a ploy? He would play along another minute or two, but not much longer. He thought about the information Zhang had revealed. What did it mean?

"I suppose Mr. Shen believed Henry Garvin was the person who impregnated the young lady. If so, why wasn't he charged?"

"You are correct, Mr. Daniels. Whether consensual or not, and we believe it was not, it is a grave crime in our country to have sexual relations with an unmarried woman of her age. If he had been convicted, he would have served many years in a Chinese prison."

Now we're getting someplace. Shen was blackmailing Garvin.

"By committing suicide, " Zhang said, "Mademoiselle Zhu was hoping to protect Mr. Garvin as well as her family."

"So, why didn't Shen have Garvin arrested?"

There was a knock on the door. Daniels jumped to his feet ready to defend himself.

"Not to worry," Zhang said. He went to open the door for a man dressed in a hotel uniform carrying a room service tray. Zhang pointed to the table. The tray contained a teapot, a plate of sliced lemons, and a cup with a hotel logo. Zhang gave the man a tip and returned to his side of the table.

"Help yourself," Zhang said.

Daniels didn't want to appear impolite although he'd have preferred that Zhang hurry up with his story. He poured some hot water into the cup, squeezed in some lemon and sat back indicating he was ready.

Zhang nodded. "No one knows for sure, but it's not hard to imagine the scene when Mr. Garvin was being questioned by Mr. Shen. He is quite ruthless today and I imagine he was not less so then."

"That's interesting, but--"

Zhang held up his hand. "Can you picture Mr. Garvin begging Mr. Shen not to arrest him? What promises might have been made at the time?"

"An offer of money perhaps?"

Zhang shook his head. "Mr. Shen would have turned that down because he knew he could not get away with accepting money. Money is too easy to trace. Maybe Mr. Garvin made a different kind of promise. Maybe he said he would help Mr. Shen come to the States or help him in a business deal. Our guess is that Mr. Shen extracted something more valuable in return for allowing Henry Garvin to avoid being arrested."

"I'm not following," Daniels said. "Spell it out please."

Zhang nodded. "Certainly. The evidence suggests Henry Garvin agreed to provide information to Mr. Shen--information that would help him advance his career."

"Didn't you say they did not meet in person all those years?"

"That is correct. Like many of my countrymen, Mr. Shen is sensitive about who he is seen with. If he had he met frequently with Mr.

Garvin in person, it would have been noticed. People would have started asking questions. They would have investigated and discovered that Mr. Shen was protecting Mr. Garvin, resulting in a scandal that would have ruined both men."

"How then did they communicate?"

"We have uncovered a pattern of Mr. Shen's associates meeting with Henry Garvin and members of his staff. In recent years, Mr. Shen's emissaries met with Mrs. Garvin or his aide Mr. Knowlton, not with Mr. Garvin."

"Mrs. Garvin?"

"Yes."

"As well as Gary Knowlton?"

Zhang nodded.

Daniels rubbed his chin. "Do you think Mrs. Garvin and Mr. Knowlton knew why Henry Garvin was so anxious to do what Mr. Shen asked him?"

"I cannot be certain," Zhang replied, "but why else would they go to such lengths to prevent that information from becoming public?" Zhang took a sip of his tea. "I observed Mr. Knowlton and Mrs. Garvin during the campaign. They acted very formal in public, but they met in private with several members of the American Chinese community who were big contributors to Mr. Garvin's campaign. I believe those individuals also conveyed monies from Mr. Shen to the Garvin campaign."

"That would explain a great deal. Do you have documentary evidence I can bring to President Palmer?"

Zhang reached into a brief case and handed Daniels a folder. "It is all in there, but you must never reveal where it came from."

"I understand."

"I hope I have answered all your questions," Zhang said, looking at his cell phone.

"Not entirely. Why were your men following me?"

Zhang nodded as if he'd been expecting the question. "We have been monitoring your investigation for several weeks. We had no idea how much you knew and thought to discover that before contacting you."

That didn't quite ring true, but he had another question.

"How did Ethan Garvin tie into all this?"

"I believe young Mr. Garvin suspected his father's loyalty was divided. I had a couple of conversations with him during the campaign that led me to believe that was the case. When I asked him about certain positions his father was taking that did not make sense based on his prior views, Ethan admitted he was perplexed as well."

"But that's not proof, and as you say, this Mr. Shen was cautious and did not have direct contacts with Henry Garvin."

"That is correct."

Daniels stood up. "So what now?"

Zhang stood up and gave Daniels a brief bow. "Use the information carefully. Mr. Shen is extremely powerful, and quite ruthless. He will not hesitate to harm anyone who gets in his way. Your reporter friend's death is proof of that."

"Shen was responsible for Dodd's death?"

"I have reason to believe so. We contacted Mr. Dodd to let him know Mr. Knowlton had been sent to retrieve Ethan Garvin the morning of his death. I believe he contacted you to give that information to you."

"He did, but how did they find out?"

"They planted someone in my office who told them. He's been arrested, but too late to help Mr. Dodd."

"Damn. Why did you tell Dodd and not contact me directly?"

"I knew someone was helping Ms. Washburn, but did not know at that time who it was or how to contact you. Later we sent the same information directly to you."

"So that was you who sent that note?"

"It was."

"Things are starting to make sense." Daniels started for the door, but stopped. "Why give me this information today?"

"Mr. Wan is concerned about our relations with your country. He does not want your leaders to feel China is interfering in American politics. That would be very bad. That is why I was sent to America to observe the Garvin campaign."

Daniels rubbed his chin. "Does Mr. Wan oppose Mr. Shen's policies or just his way of doing business?"

"Both. Mr. Shen has been taking a strong position on the South China Sea, demanding that your country accept Chinese hegemony. That could weaken your economy, which might benefit China in the short run, but Mr. Wan thinks such victories only backfire and would damage the world economy. That is why I sent you those messages."

"It seems I have a lot to thank you and your Mr. Wan for."

"I wish we could have been more helpful. It seems there's little time left for you to act, but I hope what I've provided you today will be enough."

Same Day

Convinced he now understood the big picture, Daniels retreated to his apartment to mull over what Zhang Heijing told him as well as to study the data in the folder that showed a pattern of financial support Henry Garvin had received from a high-level Chinese official. He planned to summarize what he'd learned for the President along with a brief statement of how he planned on using the information. Maureen's situation remained his foremost concern, and Zhang's revelations gave him confidence he'd finally be able to free her.

As he pondered how to proceed, Daniels could not escape the worry that his personal interests conflicted with his obligation to the President. Every minute Maureen was being held ate at his stomach, and tested his will to do the right thing with regard to the information he'd uncovered. Could he get whoever had kidnapped her to release her and still stop the president elect from betraying America? It had to work out that way. He wasn't going to sacrifice Maureen or hope the kidnappers released her unharmed, but he also needed to stop Henry Garvin from being inaugurated.

Complicating matters was the fact that he was due at the Secret Service's Rowley Center in two days to turn in his firearms and other equipment. A ceremony for recent retirees was scheduled for one o'clock Friday afternoon, to be followed by a dinner. If Daniels knew his colleagues, dinner would be followed by a night "on the town," and he would be vilified if he didn't participate. He wasn't worried about missing out, but attending the compulsory events would leave him precious little time to execute his plan to win Maureen's freedom and expose Henry Garvin.

While he still lacked a way to reach Gary Knowlton, Zhang's information gave him an alternative--approach Mrs. Garvin instead. Given what he had just learned, it shouldn't be hard to persuade her to hear him out. She would not need him to explain the damage revelation of her husband's role in the rape and suicide of a young Chinese woman many years ago would have on Henry's reputation.

He would initiate a trade. In return for suppressing the fact of his past treasonous record, Henry would have to step aside. He could claim it was a health issue. Daniels didn't care what excuse they made up as long as Henry Garvin did not take the oath of office.

By the time President Palmer's courier arrived, Daniels had written it all up. He inserted a copy of the financial records given to him by Mr. Zhang into the pouch along with a memo that explained a prominent member of the Chinese government had been financing Henry Garvin's political career for the past thirty years. He provided an outline of what he intended to do, but skipped some of the details. If Palmer needed more information he knew how to set up a meeting.

That done, Daniels needed to bring his son in on his plan. He not only needed Trey's help in executing the plan, but he knew Trey would not hesitate to point out any weaknesses. He couldn't afford any mistakes. They were running out of time and he was running out of options.

Evening rush hour traffic was in full swing raising Daniels' blood pressure. It was a stop-and-go ride to Trey's house in Millersville, but, as it turned out, Trey had only arrived a few minutes before Daniels hit the doorbell.

"I hope I'm not interrupting," he told Brianna who answered the door with LeBron in her arms.

She motioned him to come into the house. "As a matter of fact I was just in the process of putting dinner on the table. Can I add a place setting for you?"

Daniels shook his head. "You don't have to feed me. I just need a few minutes of Trey's time."

"Take off your coat, Dad," Brianna said. "There's plenty of food."

Daniels hung his coat up in the closet. "I really didn't mean to barge in, but shame on me for not bringing anything."

"You look a little stressed, Dad. Isn't Maureen feeding you these days?"

Daniels cringed. "You've touched a sensitive subject, Brianna."

Brianna motioned to Daniels to follow her into the kitchen. "You two are not fighting, are you?"

Daniels had to decide whether to tell his son's wife the truth. "I wish we were . . . I mean I wish we had the opportunity. I don't want to scare you by telling you this, but the people we're after have er . . .

Well, Maureen has been detained by the people who want to make us stop the investigation."

Brianna put the baby in a high chair. "Oh, my god. Detained? How? When?"

The baby started to fuss.

"I've got a plan to free her. That's why I need to talk to Trey."

"Talk to me about what?" Trey asked entering the room.

Brianna went over and grabbed Trey by the arm. "Maureen's been kidnapped, Trey. Your Dad needs your help."

Trey stopped in his tracks. "Kidnapped? You're kidding me. This has gone too far."

"You're right. It has," Daniels said, admiring Trey's acting job since he already knew about Maureen.

"Does the President know about this?" Trey asked.

"He does," Daniels answered. "He's working with me to get her freed."

"Thank goodness," Brianna said from the kitchen.

"You probably already guessed why I'm here," Daniels said to his son.

"Of course he'll help, won't you, Trey," Brianna said before Trey could answer.

Trey had been quietly shaking his head and staring at his father. "What do you need?"

The baby quieted as he took to the bottle. "Dinner's still fifteen minutes away," Brianna said. "Why don't you boys go in the back while I feed LeBron."

"You know I've been skeptical," Trey said after Daniels outlined his plan and explained what he needed from Trey, "but this beats all get out."

"I know. I know, but I can't see any other way to do it. When I meet with Mrs. Garvin, I'll give her a set time period to bring about Maureen's release and Gary Knowlton's surrender, but in return for my not going to the media with the China story, she'll have to persuade her husband to step aside."

"I'm thinking she won't buy that deal," Trey said.

"Why not?"

"Because once you get what you want, what's to stop you from telling the world anyway? Plus, if he gets inaugurated, he'll make up some story about your plotting against him, have you killed while resisting arrest and label all your evidence part of a plot against him."

"That's why we can't allow him to be inaugurated."

"I get it. I'm just worried Mrs. Garvin is so close to getting what she wants. She's not going to give up without a knock-down, drag-out, below-the-belt fight."

"You're probably right. My guess is that she'll threaten to hurt Maureen again or my family."

Trey frowned. "Me in other words."

"Which is why I've got guys watching you and your house."

Trey didn't look happy. "Do I need to buy a gun?"

"Do you know how to use one?"

"I've had the training, but haven't been to a range in years."

"I'll leave you my Glock and some ammo just in case. I've got a backup."

Daniels didn't have much appetite when Brianna called them to the table, and he left Trey's house later that evening feeling only slightly better about his plan. At least Trey agreed to play the part Daniels needed him to play.

"I'll do it on one condition," Trey had told him.

"What's that?"

"Once this is all over, take Maureen on the best honeymoon any woman has ever seen."

Daniels laughed and then gave his son a bear hug. "Only if some day you let us baby-sit LeBron while you two go someplace Brianna is dying to go to."

The next morning Daniels taped the tiny device Trey had given him to the inside of his shirt. The latest in such technology, it would transmit the conversation he planned on having with Katherine Garvin to a cloud-based storage location where he counted on its existence to record her agreeing to persuade her husband to step aside.

Thursday, January 18

Wired to the max, Daniels arrived at the Garvin's Georgetown family compound at nine the next morning. The mansion was set well back off the street with a tall fence fronting a row of thick pines.

He informed the Secret Service agent at the front gate that the documents he was carrying from the White House had to be delivered to Mrs. Garvin in person.

The agent appropriately contacted the White House. Daniels held his breath until the agent came back to him stating the White House had confirmed his story. The request he'd sent the President the previous evening had yielded the desired result.

It still took another thirty minutes before he was escorted inside the mansion to a small first floor alcove overlooking a side garden.

Daniels stood up when Mrs. Garvin came into the room. She looked extremely put out. Her lips were pursed and the lines around her eyes were tight with anger. She reminded Daniels of Nancy Reagan- -thin, wound tight and dangerous.

"What's this all about?" Mrs. Garvin demanded, as she sat on the window seat forcing Daniels to remain standing, as there were no chairs or benches in the room.

"I have some documents you need to see, Mrs. Garvin, before I release them to the press," Daniels said, offering her the pouch that contained copies of the documents he'd received from Zhang.

Mrs. Garvin put her hand up. "I don't care what you have. The press won't give you the time of day. They've been made aware of your scheme with that Washburn bitch to sully my son's name. It won't work. So you'd best go home and take your documents with you."

"This isn't about your son, Mrs. Garvin. It's about your husband and his relationship with a Chinese official by the name of Shen Wei."

She sniffed.

Daniels continued. "The documents include financial records that show your husband received millions in illegal gifts and contributions--political and personal--over more than three decades from Mr. Shen and his allies. They also document a number of times when Mr. Shen received classified information from your husband."

Mrs. Garvin's eyes blazed. "Poppy-cock. Those must be forgeries. Further, every contribution my husband ever received was legal and reported."

Daniels took a sheet of paper out of the pouch. "Not true. Here's one detailing tens of thousands over the contribution limits from George Lee, the Seattle businessman?"

"Let me see that," she said grabbing the paper.

"They're marked."

She studied the paper for a few seconds and then handed it back to Daniels. "Some are from his wife, some are from his son, and some are from Mr.

Lee. They're all under the limit. There's nothing illegal about that."

"Not true. The courts have ruled such patterns are prima facie evidence of collusion."

"If so, the Lees are in trouble, not us. If this is all you have, you're wasting my time. I'll excuse you for interrupting my morning if you leave quietly right this very minute. Otherwise, I'm going to have you arrested for attempted blackmail."

"We also have emails showing your husband lied when he told the voters he will resist China's ongoing maneuvering for hegemony in the South China Sea. That combined with these donations will show the public that your husband is on the take from China."

"Bullcrap," she exclaimed, her jaw jutting out. "The public doesn't understand either issue, and the media will interpret your evidence as manufactured out of motives driven by Sharon Washburn's having been rejected by my son." She stood up suggesting the meeting was over. "I'm not going to ask you again. Leave this minute or I'll have you arrested."

"What about your husband's involvement in the suicide of Zhu Jinling? Will the press ignore that?"

"More bullcrap."

"Really?"

She turned to face him. "I don't know what you're talking about."

"I think you do, Mrs. Garvin. That's what Henry has been hiding all this time, isn't it?"

Mrs. Garvin's eyes darted left and right as if she was struggling to find the right response.

"None of this has to be made public, Mrs. Garvin."

"Don't play games with me, Daniels. What do you and that bitch want?"

"I want my fiancé released by 5 p.m. today and I want your husband to step aside and allow his V.P. to take the oath. If you comply with both, I will not release any of this information to the press."

"Step aside. You're out of your mind, and what makes you think I know anything about your fiancé?"

"I think you do. You and Gary Knowlton are working hand in hand. Tell him to release Maureen Thornberry today or I'll go to the Fairfax County D.A. with evidence that will put him on trial for kidnapping, not to mention leaving the scene of your son's accident."

"Why are you talking to me about this? Go tell him your story."

"I think it would be more effective if it came from you, and while you're at it, tell Mr. Knowlton we know about the classified documents Henry shared with Shen Wei over the past decade. I'm sure Congress and the media would be fascinated to learn the man they elected president has been committing treason for years. I'm confident Knowlton will agree resigning before Monday is your husband's only option."

Mrs. Garvin's lower lip quivered. Daniels hoped that meant her iron demeanor was beginning to crumble. It was time to press his advantage.

"Do nothing and Knowlton will go to prison while you and your husband will be charged with treason, the penalty for which is death. That is unless Maureen Thornberry is freed today and your husband announces he's stepping aside."

Mrs. Garvin sat back down on the window seat and looked out the window for a second.

What is she thinking?

"If this Thornberg woman--"

"Thornberry."

"If Thornberry is released, how can you assure me that you won't go to the press anyway or come back here a year from now and demand money?"

"If she's released and your husband steps aside, I'll provide you all the documentation I have in my possession. After that, I'd have no more leverage."

Mrs. Garvin got to her feet. Some color had returned to her face. "Your claims don't hold any water, Mr. Daniels, so here's what I have to say. I concede none of the accusations you have made are true. Nor do I have any knowledge of Ms. Thornberry's whereabouts. I will ask Mr. Knowlton if he knows anything about her being missing. If he does, I will implore him to convince whoever is holding her to release her, but only on the condition that you provide us originals and copies of all the documents you possess. Further, I want you and everyone else with knowledge of your information to sign an affidavit agreeing never to speak of these accusations or to write anything concerning them for the rest of your lives. Is that clear?"

"What about your husband?"

"You can't be serious."

"Deadly."

"It seems you have a choice to make, Daniels. Get your woman back or not. My husband will become president on Monday no matter what you do. So do you want her back or not?"

"And you have a choice as well, Mrs. Garvin. If your husband tries to take the oath of office, the world will learn he's worse that Benedict Arnold. Congress will impeach him so fast you won't even have time to unpack at 1600 Pennsylvania Avenue. Better contact Knowlton and make up your mind. I've left my contact information in the folder. Remember, you have seven hours to release Maureen Thornberry, and I'll give you an hour after that for Henry to make his announcement."

Daniels set the folder down on the table, turned, and left the room. Outside a Secret Service agent he didn't recognize was waiting to escort him to the front gate.

Same Day

"What do you recommend?" Katherine Garvin asked Gary Knowlton, who had been listening in on her previous conversation in an adjoining room.

Knowlton was livid. "Henry's not resigning. That goes without saying. As far as their information goes, the media has been warned, but I don't want to let it get that far. We need to round up everything they have and make sure no one hears from them ever again."

"We need a plan," she said after considering his answer. "To start with, delay them. Re-negotiate the time and place for tomorrow instead of today. Then, when the time gets close, delay them again by changing locations."

"What if they release part of their information, starting with those recordings? They incriminate me, not you or Henry," Knowlton stated.

"Don't worry. The chain of possession is fuzzy. You can claim they've been tampered with, and I'll make sure the judge in the case will not allow them to be admitted as evidence."

Knowlton's mouth was dry. He wished he had a glass of water or better yet a scotch. "Okay. I'll tell them we need to amend the arrangement to include the originals and copies of the two recordings as well as Ethan's phone and anything else they recovered from the phone. That will take them at least another twenty-four hours. Then, I'll tell them we need another six hours or so to bring Thornberry back to D.C. That'll postpone things until Sunday."

Mrs. Garvin took a sip of the coffee that had grown cold since she'd ordered it. "Then you'd better make sure the trade takes place at a location where neither Daniels nor his woman comes out alive."

Knowlton nodded. "My thinking exactly."

"The agents will do what you tell them, right?"

"They will," he replied. "I've told them these people are connected with International terrorists, and that we're not going to give them the luxury of spreading their propaganda during some trial."

Mrs. Garvin stood up. "Keep me up to date by the minute."

Knowlton nodded. "There's one more loose end we'll have to deal with after we get the documents and the recordings and after we get rid of Daniels, his girlfriend, his son, and Sharon Washburn."

"Palmer?"

Knowlton nodded.

"How are you going to do that?"

Knowlton scratched his neck. "I'll set up a meeting at the White House Monday morning. It seems President Palmer is about to take ill and miss the swearing-in ceremony."

Katherine Garvin smiled broadly. "I never liked that man. Now get going. You've got a lot to take care of and no slip-ups."

"Not to worry," Knowlton replied. "We haven't come this far to leave any loose ends."

Same Day

After meeting with Katherine Garvin, Daniels spent two hours at the gym with a goal of wearing himself out while waiting to hear from Knowlton or Garvin with the time and place for the swap.

He knew they'd try something--probably delay turning over Maureen or ask for something else, but he was ready to escalate his demands as well. He told them he'd back down if Henry Garvin stepped aside, but if they balked or demanded something else, he'd tell them Garvin would have to confess and face the consequences. No way would Katherine Garvin stand for that.

He knew given the chance they'd try to kill him and everyone else connected to the investigation. Would he be protected by the fact that Edwin Palmer was ready to release copies of the documents and the recordings to the media if he didn't check in thirty minutes after the swap meeting? Time would tell.

Daniels also worried when this was all done how Maureen would feel about him and their impending marriage. It was possible she'd tell him she couldn't go through with it. If that happened, he didn't know what he'd do with his life, but he knew he would do it the same way if he had to do it all over again. He'd been right not to tell her about the investigation. Had he come up with the answers in a week or two, it would have been done and she'd never have gotten involved. His mistake had been not doubling her guard. He still hadn't forgiven himself.

Finishing his workout, Daniels went to his apartment to await a call about the exchange. It came at 1:30 while he was eating leftovers from the refrigerator.

"Daniels?" the person on the other end asked.

Daniels recognized Gary Knowlton's voice from Ethan's recording. "Speaking."

"I'm calling about the deal."

"Good. Name the time and place."

"Not so fast. We need to make a change."

Here it comes. "What change?"

"I want the originals and all copies of every recording and document you got from Ethan's cell phone as well as the remains of the phone itself."

"Isn't it too late for that, Knowlton? The public has already heard--"

"That's not the recording I'm worried about. You left me a message about a second recording. I want the second recording, too, or no deal."

"There's definitely a second recording," Daniels said. "Ethan recorded it while driving ahead of you that morning. He explained what he was trying to bring to the White House and how you and his mother were trying to stop him."

"Whatever. The point is I want it all or no exchange."

"Listen, Knowlton. I'm not changing the deal Katherine Garvin agreed to. If you want to make a separate deal, I'll tell you what I want in return."

"You're not hearing me, Daniels. If you want your woman returned free from further injury, bring me any and all recordings and the cellphone."

"And you're not hearing me, Knowlton. If you want those recordings, here's what I need from you: a signed, notarized statement that you fled the scene of Ethan's accident. Make up whatever excuse you want, but we'll see what a judge decides to do with that."

Knowlton didn't say anything.

"My guess," Daniels continued, "is that your boss won't be able to give you a cushy job in the White House and you'll be doing six months in the big house instead."

"No deal. Now, you listen to me, Daniels. You fail to bring me those tapes and your woman will pay the price. Your deal didn't say what kind of condition she'd be in. A bullet in each knee, or maybe a broken neck."

"You lay another finger on her Knowlton and--"

"You have 'til noon tomorrow. Take it or leave it."

Another delay. Damn. "Where?"

"I'll call you an hour before the meeting with the location. Bring it all, Daniels, or Ms. Thornberry pays the price."

"Knowlton...Knowlton, you shit."

Dial tone.

Daniels wasn't surprised. He figured they'd try something like that. Now the question was how should he respond. Meanwhile, he needed to get the materials Knowlton was demanding. He didn't have the original of the recordings or the cell. He didn't even know who had them.

He'd have to wait until Trey got home from work. The next five hours passed like people sick of winter wait for a sign of buds on the trees in their backyards. At six-thirty he dialed his son's home number.

Trey answered. "What now?"

"I'm in a bind, son. They are willing to trade Maureen, but they want the original of the recordings and the remains of his cellphone."

"By when?"

"Noon tomorrow."

"Okay, I should be able to get what you need. Can you meet me someplace?"

"Sure. Call me when you have it all together and I'll come and get it."

Daniels headed to his apartment. He had to turn the tables on them. That meant showing Mrs. Garvin he was serious about her husband's resigning.

A post on their website might just do the trick. He put in a call to Sharon Washburn, but had to leave a message. He wanted to use her writing skill to get the wording just right. He started drafting the post himself. If she didn't call back by eight, he'd do it without her.

He'd just dug into a sandwich he'd scrounged from his refrigerator when his phone rang. It was Ricardo Alvarez, probably looking for an update on the situation. He didn't want to answer it. What could he say? He chose the option that said he was busy.

He'd taken another bite out of his sandwich when the phone rang again. Ricardo's name came up on the screen. He punched accept.

"Ricardo, what's up?"

"I think I've got something for you, boss."

"What's that?"

"I think I know where they're keeping her."

Friday, January 19

"Maureen? You know where they're keeping Maureen? Spit it out. Tell--"

"Whoa. Slow down."

"Sorry, sorry. I'm listening. Talk."

"A guy I know--a Mexicano--calls me up, says he's been baby-sitting a Yankee senora, but they need a second guy for overnight duty--tonight and maybe tomorrow. Pay's real good. Cash. Am I interested? I said sure. How do I sign up?"

"Good thinking."

"I'm supposed to meet him tonight at midnight outside a bodega on Wilson Boulevard."

"Where's that, Arlington?"

"Yes. He's going to drive."

Could it be her? "Did he say anything else about the woman? What she looked like? Her age? Why they were keeping her?"

"I didn't want to ask him anything specific. He'd get suspicious. You never want to know too much in these situations."

It was a few minutes to nine. Not a lot of time, but enough. "Okay. Here's what I'd like you to do."

Daniels' mouth was dry. He was starting to worry something had gone wrong. It was past midnight and he along with former Secret Service agents Sam Freeman and Nate Parenti had been waiting almost an hour in Parenti's van for Ricardo Alvarez' friend to pick him up.

Daniels' backup handgun was tucked in his belt behind his back. He'd turned in his equipment earlier that day including his service weapon. He wasn't officially retired until 5 p.m. Monday, but he was free of any assignments or responsibilities.

Maybe it was a trap. Maybe Ricardo's phone had been tapped. He was about to send Parenti into the bodega where Ricardo was waiting for his ride, but hesitated when a beat-up silver Hyundai Elantra pulled up across the street from the bodega and blinked its lights. A few seconds later, Ricardo exited the store and got in the car.

Nate, who was driving the van, waited until they had a head start and then slid away from the curb. He drove without his headlights on for several blocks until the Hyundai merged into Arlington Boulevard where there was enough traffic to follow without being detected.

The Hyundai was heading towards D.C. Nate stayed back as much as he could without losing touch.

"Stay with him," Daniels said as the Elantra merged onto 395.

"I've got him," Nate replied.

Minutes later the Hyundai left the freeway heading into D.C. Nate shortened the distance to avoid losing it.

"Where the heck are they going?" Daniels demanded, knowing neither of his colleagues knew the answer.

Suddenly, the Elantra pulled into a parking garage. Nate drove past the garage and pulled over.

"Check to see if there's more than one entrance," Daniels told him.

Nate pulled out and turned left at the next intersection, and then twice more, now approaching the garage from the other direction.

"That's the only entrance for vehicles," Nate said, "but there are exit stairs on both sides."

"Pull over," Daniels instructed. "Sam. Get out here. Go to the other side of the building so you can watch in case they exit on foot on that side."

"Will do," Sam Freeman said, hopping out of the van.

Daniels ask Nate to try to find a place to park where they could watch the front and side entrances. All the while he considered their location. It was a commercial area, which meant the captive could be in any building--a garage, warehouse, even the back of a store. The only way they'd find out was stick to Ricardo and his friend.

No cars entered or left the building for ten minutes. Then a white utility van pulled out of the garage and headed north.

"Should I follow them?" Nate asked.

"Not sure," Daniels answered. "What do you think?"

"What if they transferred cars?" Nate ventured.

Daniels buzzed Sam Freeman. "Anything?"

"No sign of them."

"We think they switched cars," Daniels said, not wanting to let the van get too far a jump. "Stay there. Call me if you see them. We're following a van."

They followed the white van for twelve minutes before it pulled into a parking space on a residential street. A woman got out and went into a house.

"Shit," Daniels said. "It's not them. Go back."

When they got back to the garage Sam Freeman reported that he hadn't seen Ricardo leave the garage on foot.

Daniels slipped out of the vehicle. "I'm going in." He crossed the street walked up a block, crossed the street and then headed back towards the parking garage. The man in the booth ignored him. He doubted he'd find the Hyundai on the lover level so he walked up the stairs to the second level. He walked around that level and the next three before he found it on the top level. There was no one in the car.

Daniels reported back to the others.

"Looks like they gave us the slip," Freeman said.

"Do you think they knew we were following them?" Parenti asked.

"Hard to say," Daniels replied. "But it looks like we're stuck here for a while. They probably won't be back until morning."

The three men took turns napping in the back of the van while the ones on watch duty consumed coffee and made small talk. There was little activity in the garage during the next six hours. Around six thirty, area residents began emerging from their homes. One or two retrieved their vehicles from the garage. Shortly after seven, a late model dark blue BMW pulled into the garage.

"Check that out," Parenti said.

"I've got the license plate," Freeman replied. He'd set up a wireless digital camera on a telephone pole across from the garage entrance that he controlled from a laptop in the van. Every time a car entered or left the garage he snapped the plate.

"Wake up, Tuck," Parenti called to Daniels who was snoozing in the back.

"I'm up. What have you got?"

"BMW. Late model. Could be them."

Ten minutes later the BMW left the garage. It drove past them. Nate tried to get a picture but the windows were tinted

Five minutes after that the Elantra belonging to Ricardo's friend exited the garage and headed back toward Arlington. They could see Ricardo sitting in the passenger's side up front with the driver who ostensibly was Ricardo's Mexican friend.

Nate stayed farther behind the Hyuandi on the trip back to Arlington, since it was daytime and they pretty much knew where they were going. Ricardo's friend dropped him off at his house instead of the bodega.

They parked across from Ricardo's apartment building and waited for him to join them.

"Ola," Ricardo said, when Sam let him in the back of Nate's van.

Daniels, who had been in the front passenger seat, slid into the back of the van, and sat opposite Ricardo. "Well?"

"It's her," Ricardo said.

"Is she . . .?"

Ricardo nodded. "I waited until I was sure she was asleep before going into the room. I only met her once or twice, but worried she might recognize me and spill the beans."

Daniels nodded. "Good thinking."

"They did something to her shoulder or arm. They've got it taped to her body."

Daniels felt sick to his stomach.

"The room was dark. I couldn't see much else."

"So where are they keeping her and how'd we miss you guys leaving the garage?"

"When he parked the car in the garage, Victor told me they'd have to blindfold me. I was pretty nervous. He put a blindfold on but kept talking friendly-like, so I didn't resist. After a few minutes I heard a car pull up next to us. Sounded like a big engine."

"BMW?" Daniels asked.

"Could have been. It smelled new. Anyway, they moved me into the car. Victor sat next to me talking the whole time about life back in Mexico."

"I thought you were an American," Sam said.

"I am. Born here, but my sisters and I used to stay with my grandparents every summer in the village my family is from. That's how I met Victor. He snuck into the country and tried to sign up for the Secret Service."

"You're kidding," Nate said, looking over to Daniels.

"He thought he could get his citizenship that way," Ricardo said.

"Worth a try, I suppose," Sam said.

"Let's get back to Maureen," Daniels said.

Ricardo wiped the smile off his face. "Sorry, boss."

"You were in this car. How long?" Daniels asked.

"Not long. Twenty minutes tops."

"Then what?"

"They parked in an underground garage. I could tell by the echo as they walked me into the building. I worried that it was some kind of setup, but if there was a chance we could get to Maureen, it was worth it."

Daniels beamed. *What a guy!* "Thanks, Pal."

"Once in the elevator, they took off the blindfold. There was one other guy besides Victor. I recognized him. He's Service, but I couldn't place the name. I don't think he recognized me."

"Describe him."

"Six-two, two fifty if an ounce. Big head. Starts lecturing me about the job. Says this is government black ops which is why they had to go through the blindfold procedure. Their captive is dangerous, a spy. They're holding her, he says, until they can make a deal to exchange her for an American."

"What!"

"It's all bullshit. I could tell he was making it up. Victor was looking at him like he'd never heard the story."

"Amazing," Daniels said. "Continue."

"We arrived at floor nine--the top. Got out of the elevator. It was a second-rate hotel."

"Which one?" Daniels demanded.

Ricardo reached in his pocket and pulled out a bar of soap. The label said Georgetown Harbor Suites.

"Good job. Then what?"

"They led me to the room. The big guy opened the door with one of those keyless entry cards. It was a suite--a large sitting room with bedrooms off both sides. He told me I was to stay in the middle room. My buddy was the only one allowed in with the prisoner. He reminded us not to allow anyone else into the suite. No room service; no cleaning people; no one. We also had to stay awake the entire time. The relief team would be there ready to take over at six a.m."

"Seems like they're running four six-hour shifts," Sam said.

"Takes a lot of people," Nate commented.

Daniels nodded to Ricardo to continue.

"The head guy went over the procedure for dealing with the prisoner. She could have any of the food in the refrigerator. If she needed the bathroom, someone had to be in there to make sure she didn't try anything. While she was in the bedroom, she had to be secured to the bedpost by a plastic chain linked to an ankle bracelet.

"How did you confirm it was Maureen?"

"I told Victor I wanted to see who they were holding. He said it was a bad idea. So, I dropped it. About two a.m. the buzzer went off which meant she needed something. Victor went to get her. I stayed in the middle room like they wanted, but Victor left the door open. He winked at me as he led her into the bathroom. I could hear her object, but she gave up when he yelled at her. A few minutes later I heard the toilet flush and he led her back into the bedroom. I stood in the doorway to see how they had her secured."

"Did she seem in much pain?" Daniels asked quietly.

"A little I suppose," Ricardo answered.

Daniels grimaced, swallowed, and then sighed. "That was it?"

"Yup. Nothing else until the next crew showed up."

Daniels opened one of the water bottles they'd stacked in the back of the van and took a long drink.

"I recognized one of the new guys. Definitely Service."

"He recognize you?" Daniels asked.

"Yeah. Older guy. Must have retired five, six years ago. We chatted a bit. I made it seem like I was pissed I had to do extra work to pay my bills. He agreed, said not like they told you when you signed up. That kind of stuff."

"Nothing about the job?"

Ricardo shook his head.

"You hired for tonight?"

Ricardo nodded. "I guess I passed their test. They want me the same time. He gave me the address. No need for the charade. One small problem; well, maybe two."

"What?"

"First, they rotate. Victor's moving to one of the daytime slots. I'm on the night shift with someone I haven't met yet."

"Second problem."

"They said they might move her. If so, they'll let me know the new location. I'm to show up unless I hear from them."

Daniels considered the additional information. "The fact that Ricardo won't be on with Victor could be a problem, but more importantly I have to think about the fact they are prepared to move her."

"Explain?" Ricardo asked.

"They're supposed to hand her over to me at noon today. Yet they're prepared to keep her another night. That suggests they'll try to delay the handoff a second time.

"Makes sense," Sam said. "The longer they put you off the closer they are to sealing the deal."

"Exactly," Daniels said.

"I see what you're saying," Nate said. "They ask for more stuff. Meanwhile, they have what you gave them and keep Maureen."

Daniels took a deep breath. "Okay. Decision time. I can't rely on them coming through with the swap."

"What then?" Ricardo asked.

"That means we're going to have to rescue her ourselves––tonight, when you're in with her."

"Isn't that risky?" Nate asked. "Maureen could get hurt."

Daniels clapped his friend on the shoulder. "I'm aware of that, but think of it this way. They don't know we know where they're holding her. If Ricardo is right and there are only two men on the job, and he's one of them––seems like it should be easy as stealing candy from a baby."

"I hope you're right," Sam said.

"We'll plan it out to the second," Daniels said.

"Keep in mind I don't know anything about the guy I'll be working with," Ricardo reminded them. "It won't be easy to get him to let me open the door."

"What if you unchain the door while he's in the other room?" Daniels suggested.

"That might work," Ricardo said, "but what if he notices?"

"We need a distraction," Daniels said. "Wait a second. I've got an idea. I need to make a phone call."

Same Day

"I told him I need the originals and all copies," Gary Knowlton told Katherine Garvin using a secure phone connection. "The new time is noon today, but I'm going to postpone again until midnight."

"Good," she replied. "How are you going to handle it at that point?"

"Get rid of him and his girlfriend both."

"No loose ends this time. This guy isn't likely to show up by himself."

"For sure. We'll be prepared."

"Good. What about Sharon Washburn?"

Knowlton had been puzzling over a variety of possibilities for dealing with Ethan's fiancé. "She shouldn't be a problem."

"I hope so. Just be ready for anything, Knowlton."

"Don't you worry. I will."

Saturday, January 20

At two a.m. sharp Saturday morning a couple who had registered in the Georgetown hotel where Maureen Thornberry was being held left their fourth floor room and got on the elevator. Instead of going down, however, the man pushed the button for the next to the top floor.

The couple got off the elevator, checked to make sure no one was wandering around the hall, and ducked into the stairwell where Tucker Daniels and Nate Parenti were waiting.

Parenti whistled. "Nice get up!"

Sharon Washburn blushed. The uniform they'd purchased for her to wear that evening was short and tight. She was carrying a room service tray containing a pot of coffee and pastries.

"You should have seen how the desk clerk looked at us when we checked in," Sam Freeman said. "I could see the expression 'robbing the cradle' flashing through his mind."

Sharon blushed again.

"Everyone ready?" Daniels inquired.

The others nodded.

Daniels opened the stairwell door to make sure the ninth floor hall was empty, then motioned them forward. The others followed, Sharon carrying the room service tray.

When they got to room 909, the three men stationed themselves as Daniels had drawn it up-- Sam and Nate on the right side of the door, Daniels on the left.

Sharon was about to knock on the door, when Daniels phone buzzed. He looked down to see a message. *They're getting ready to move her. Two guys are downstairs waiting for us to bring her down.*

"Hold on," he said. "Complication."

"What?" the others said almost in unison.

"I just got a text from Ricardo. He says they're getting ready to move Maureen. Two of their guys are downstairs."

"Now what?" Nate asked.

"Either Sharon knocks on their room like we planned or we wait for them to bring her out," Daniels said.

"It could get messy if we wait for them to come out," Nate said.

Sam nodded his agreement. "I like the original plan."

"Okay," Daniels said. "It's settled. If the second guy is in the bedroom getting her ready to move, Ricardo can let us in and we'll have the upper hand."

Daniels motioned for Sharon to go knock on the door.

Sharon did so and called out "room service."

Daniels felt sweat break out on his forehead. If the guys waiting downstairs got impatient and came up to help out, all hell could break loose.

"Knock again," he told Sharon.

The door opened a couple of inches to the end of the chain.

"Room service," Sharon announced.

"We didn't order anything." That wasn't Ricardo's voice.

Whoever was behind the door closed it.

"Knock again," Daniels whispered. They'd gone over the possibility that Ricardo's partner would refuse to open the door.

Sharon obeyed.

"Go away," she was told.

"I need you to sign the check," she called.

Nothing happened for a few seconds; then the door opened.

"Hand it in."

"Go," Daniels said as he kicked into the door with his right boot, his Glock 19, cocked and ready, in his right hand.

The person on the other side of the door had not been ready. The force of the door swinging into the room knocked him backwards.

Daniels barged into the room. "Not a word," he commanded pointing the Glock at the man's forehead. Ricardo came up from behind the man and relieved him of his weapon.

"Lock the door," Daniels said, after Sam, Nate and Sharon entered the room.

"Let's move," Daniels said to no one in particular. Each person had a job to do. Ricardo removed a set of keys from a table next to one of the bedroom doors and motioned to Sharon who followed him as he unlocked the door to the room where Maureen was being held.

Nate used a set of plastic handcuffs to secure the second man's hands while Sam covered the man's mouth with a bandana. The two of them then dragged him into the second bedroom where they intended to secure him to the bed so he couldn't rejoin the party.

Although he wanted to go into the bedroom and comfort Maureen, Daniels realized he had to take into account the existence of the extra men waiting someplace downstairs. Their original plan had been to bring her out of the hotel through the service entrance, but that's probably where the kidnappers were waiting.

The key question was how would the men downstairs react when they realized something was amiss? When Ricardo and his partner didn't bring Maureen down, they'd probably call up, but what if they came upstairs on their own? He needed Ricardo to answer their call or the knock on the door. They probably didn't have five minutes to prepare either way.

Daniels took a deep breath--fearing how she would react when she saw him, he headed for the bedroom where Maureen was being held.

Ricardo was standing by the door. Maureen was sitting on the side of the bed, her right arm in a sling, looking dazed. Sharon was sitting beside her.

"Ricardo, do you have the other guy's phone?"

Ricardo pulled a cell out of his pocket.

"Good. If the guys downstairs call up to ask why the delay, tell them there's a problem and you need them to come up. While they're coming up, we'll be on our way down. That should buy us some time."

"What if they ask what the problem is?" Ricardo asked.

"Make up something. Tell them it's taking longer than planned to get the prisoner dressed."

"Okay, boss," Ricardo answered.

Maureen must have noticed Daniels' voice. "Am I dreaming?"

"No, it's really me," Daniels replied hurrying over to sit next to her. She folded into his arms. "We've got to get you out of here. Can you walk?"

"I'll try," she answered.

"Good. Sharon will get you ready." Daniels got up. "Stay in here until we tell you to come out," he instructed Sharon.

Daniels headed back into the suite's main room.

Ricardo, Sam, and Nate were waiting, having accomplished their tasks.

"Now what?" Sam asked.

Before Daniels could answer, however, he heard the front door's key mechanism unlock. Daniels motioned wildly for the three of them to disappear. He couldn't watch to see if they'd gotten the message, but rushed to the side of the door.

A large man came into the room his hands empty. He must have seen Daniels out of the corner of his eye because he turned back toward the door intending to warn his partner, but for the second time that evening Daniels put his weight into the door, this time knocking whoever was on the other side into the door jamb at the same time motioning with his Glock for the big man to raise his hands.

Ricardo Alvarez, who had pushed Sam and Nate into the second bedroom a split second before the front door opened, came back into the room both hands wrapped around a Browning handgun.

"Hands up," he yelled to make sure both of the newcomers were aware of his presence.

Daniels grabbed the arm of the second man and dragged him into the room. "On the ground," he commanded, his Glock aimed at the man's face.

Sam and Nate, both of their personal weapons out and visible, joined Ricardo.

"Secure them," Daniels commanded.

Minutes later the kidnappers were securely handcuffed to stationary furniture in separate locations in the hotel suite. With that accomplished Daniels motioned for Sharon to bring Maureen out of the bedroom where she'd been held captive for more than a week.

Daniels needed to get Maureen to a hospital as soon as possible, but first they needed to get down to their van and away from the hotel. "Ready? Let's do it."

Same Day

"What are you going to tell the docs?" Nate Parenti asked Daniels as they approached the entrance to George Washington University hospital.

"I'm not sure," Daniels replied. He'd been asking himself that same question during the drive from the hotel. The hospital staff would ask the cause of her injury and could probably tell her mental state was not the result of a fall or some other accident. He couldn't exactly tell them Maureen had been held captive for a week and he'd not reported it to the police. Kidnapping crimes fall under the FBI's jurisdiction and he didn't want to have to answer to them at this point in the game. "I'll tell them it's a Secret Service operation."

"How so?" Parenti, who was driving, asked.

"I'll flash my credentials and explain we rescued her from terrorists."

"That might work."

"I'm also going to tell them we need to register her under an alias. I want to do that anyway to prevent the kidnappers from finding her."

"Works for me," Parenti said as he pulled his van into the emergency entrance.

Finally! It was past 8 a.m. before the doctors would let Daniels in to see Maureen.

"She should go to physical therapy for that shoulder," the doctor who examined her stated, "and I've sent some blood to the lab to tell me if there are any other problems we need to worry about."

After thanking the doc, Daniels peeked into the room.

Maureen teared up when she saw him and he had to blink back his own tears when he saw the effects of her week from hell. She looked half her normal healthy size as she lay in the hospital bed tubes attached to her arm while monitors tracked her vitals.

"Can you forgive me?" he asked after sitting in the chair next to her bed and covering her hand with both of his.

"You didn't do this, Eugene," she said, her voice stronger than her appearance.

"Still, I feel like I should have. . ."

She shook her head.

"I'm going to make it up to you," he said after wiping a tear from her face.

"Just make them pay," she said.

He nodded. "If it's the last thing I do. Do you feel up to answering some questions? I need to learn as much as I can about who did this to you."

She told him she'd heard enough chatter to confirm his belief that Gary Knowlton had hired a security firm under the supervision of an active Secret Service agent to guard her, but they weren't the ones who'd taken her.

"I was going down to the garage," she said in a halting voice. "An Asian woman got on the elevator with me. I was surprised because there are no Asians living on my floor. I assumed she'd been visiting someone."

"What did she look like?" Daniels asked.

"I noticed her clothes. Traditional Asian. Straight dark pants and a matching top. She was carrying a large cloth bag. When the elevator stopped in the basement she motioned for me to get off first. When I did, two Asian men appeared on each side of the elevator door and grabbed me as the woman--it must have been her--pulled a bag over my head. I started to scream, but felt a needle going into the back of my neck. The next thing I knew I was strapped to a bed."

Her story seemed to confirm what Zhang Heijing had told Daniels about Henry Garvin's blackmailer--that he was ruthless. He'd killed at least two people and wouldn't hesitate to add to the total.

Because the doctors wouldn't say how long Maureen might have to stay in the hospital, he decided to ask his friends to work out a schedule to monitor her. He wouldn't put it past Gary Knowlton to send some of his goons into the hospital to make sure Maureen didn't live long enough to identify them in court. He was not about to give them that chance.

As if he couldn't get any angrier at what the kidnappers had done to her, Maureen told something that made him cry tears of rage.

"Did Ricardo tell you they shot me up?" she asked him.

"What? When? Where?"

She pulled back the sleeve of her robe to expose needle marks. The doctors hadn't told him about that. Daniels could see the alarm in Maureen's eyes. He had to pretend it was no big deal.

"Did they say what it was?" he asked her, trying to keep his voice neutral.

She shook her head, tears clouding her eyes. "It made me hallucinate."

Daniels pulled her into his arms to hide his own tears. He held her tightly until she pushed him back, laid her head back on the pillow, and closed her eyes.

"I'll be back later," he whispered to her. "I've got some business to attend to. You rest. Ricardo or one of the other guys will be outside your door the entire time and I'll be back this afternoon."

"Go do what you have to do," she replied, turning her head away from him. "I just want to sleep."

What could they have used to drug her? Daniels asked himself. He wasn't an expert in narcotics, but knew enough that the damage could be long-lasting. He stopped at the nurses' station on his way out of the hospital. They told him they hadn't heard back from the lab.

Having left his car at his apartment the night before, he used a ride-sharing service to drop him off at Secret Service headquarters where he phoned the White House using the code he'd worked out with Palmer requesting a meeting.

After grabbing a large coffee from the cafeteria, he sat at his old desk reviewing where things stood. He had to assume Gary Knowlton would soon discover Maureen had been rescued. That left him and Mrs. Garvin with zero leverage. It could make them desperate. He buzzed the men watching Trey's house to make sure they were on the job.

"Stay on your toes," he told them after warning them to be extra careful if they saw any suspicious acting Asians. "These people are dangerous and the next forty-eight hours are crucial."

An hour later one of President Palmer's secretaries contacted him with a message that the President would see him at the game––code that meant Palmer would come to his wife's P Street apartment at 1:00 that afternoon.

"You did the best you could," Edwin Palmer assured Daniels when he arrived at the apartment. He'd used the same disguise to enter the building after convincing his military aide that he'd only be gone for thirty minutes. Daniels had hot water with lemon ready when Palmer arrived.

"Maybe we can't stop Henry Garvin from being inaugurated president," Palmer said, "but nine a.m. Monday morning I'm turning the data you retrieved over to the Justice Department and order them to begin an investigation into Garvin's relationship with this Shen Wei. Then, at ten, the heads of the appropriate Congressional committees will be given enough details to make sure Justice under a Henry Garvin attorney general doesn't bury the information."

That sounded good to Daniels' ears.

"So, what you and Miss Washburn uncovered will not have been in vain."

"That's very gratifying," Daniels said, "but what about stopping the inauguration?"

Palmer shook his head. "I can't think of a way to do so."

Daniels didn't press the issue. "What about the possibility Gary Knowlton used active Secret Service agents as part of his scheme?"

"I talked to the head of Secret Service earlier today urging her to investigate Gary Knowlton's use of the agents assigned to Henry Garvin. There's no doubt in my mind some agents will wind up losing their jobs and one or two might end up in prison when it's all over."

Daniels tried to repress the fury he felt knowing members of the Secret Service had allowed themselves to be used by the Garvins to commit multiple crimes. "It's likely that agents of Shen Wei and not members of our Secret Service killed Sandra Burke, the retired agent who was guarding my fiancé, but at least one active agent was involved in holding Maureen against her will."

"Those who killed Miss Burke most likely left the country," Palmer suggested.

Daniels nodded. He had the same thought.

Palmer offered his hand. "I've got to get back to the White House. They've got a traditional last night dinner planned. All my relatives including some I've yet to acknowledge I'm related to will be there."

Daniels laughed. "Enjoy it, Sir, and enjoy life back in Nebraska. You deserve it."

Maureen was asleep when Daniels returned from his meeting with Palmer. Nate Parenti was posted outside her room. "Ricardo's still here," Parenti told Daniels. "I think he's in the cafeteria."

He found the former agent nursing a large coffee. "I can't thank you enough, amigo."

"Least I could do," Alvarez answered. "It's over, right? Case closed?"

"Not quite. They win if Henry Garvin is inaugurated Monday at noon."

"But what can we do? Isn't it too late?"

"I could release to the press the material I have showing how Garvin got millions from China along with evidence he provided them classified information in return, but I'm sure they warned the media to expect something like that. Plus, President Palmer is going to turn the documents we got from the Chinese over to Justice and Congress Monday morning before the inauguration ceremony."

"Then the good guys win, right?"

"Not necessarily. Once he's president Garvin has enormous power. He can come after me, claim I manufactured the evidence and tried to blackmail him. He can lock me up and throw away the key or worse--tell the media I died trying to resist arrest."

Ricardo looked up. "Ouch."

"Not just me, but Maureen, Sharon Washburn, my son."

"We can't let that happen, boss."

"But that's not the worst of it. Ethan Garvin was onto something. He feared his father was going to concede to China's demands on the South China Sea, CO_2 emissions, and currency manipulation. That would be a disaster and it would betray our allies Japan, Australia, and the Philippines."

"That would be a disaster. What are you going to do?"

"I'm thinking about offering Gary Knowlton another swap deal. He's still on the hook for leaving the scene of Ethan's accident. Maybe in order to get him to meet with me I'll offer the materials in return for their granting us some kind of immunity."

"Are you sure that's what you want?"

"What I want is to get him into a room where I can get him to confess on the record everything he and the Garvins have done and then release that to the media."

"Will he admit what he did?"

"If he thinks there's nothing I can do to hurt him, I'll bet his ego's that big."

"Then what?"

"Then I survive whatever plan he has to eliminate me and the truth comes out, maybe not in time to stop the inauguration, but there's always impeachment."

"Whatever you do, you're going to need us to make sure he doesn't double-cross you . . ."

"Thanks, amigo. I know where to find you."

Daniels napped on and off in Maureen's room Saturday night into Sunday. Each time he awoke he checked to make sure one of the agents was on duty in the hall and they'd not seen any signs of trouble.

Sunday morning, Maureen objected when told her doctors wanted her to stay another day. "I'm going home today whether they like it or not," she told Daniels.

"Okay," Daniels replied, "but wait until I have someone check out your apartment and set up a schedule for someone to watch you for a few days. I might not be able to stay with you the whole time."

She agreed to stay in the hospital until that afternoon to give Mary Broussard, the retired agent who'd been Sandra Burke's partner, time to check out her apartment.

Daniels knew his scheme of offering Knowlton a trade--the recordings for immunity for himself, Maureen, Sharon and Trey--was not worth the paper it would be written on. Further, he knew he represented a loose end Knowlton and the Garvins needed to tie up. By agreeing to meet with them he was giving them what they wanted--an opportunity to take him off the board, which would pave the way for eliminating the rest of his team as well. It was a risky maneuver, but he couldn't see any alternative.

Daniels had no desire to sacrifice himself, but if that's how it turned out--well, no one could say he shirked his duty. On the other hand, he wasn't going to let Knowlton and the Garvins get away with their crimes without a fight. Whether President Palmer's way of solving the problem--turning the evidence over to Congress and Justice--would succeed was unclear. The Garvins might be able to squash the information or make it look like he and Sharon Washburn had made the whole thing up. No, it was up to him to stop the Garvins and that meant getting face to face with Gary Knowlton.

He used one of his burner phones put in a call to Gary Knowlton's cell. After listening to the taped greeting he left his message. "This is Daniels. There's still reason for us to meet. I've got something you need and you've got something I want.

"I've got copies of the materials I've collected on the money Shen Wei provided Henry over the past three decades, plus evidence Henry provided classified materials in return, and I've got the recording that will put you in prison for leaving the scene of an accident, but I'll turn it all over to you in return for immunity for me and the members of my team on one condition. That we make the trade before Henry Garvin is sworn in. Once he's president, I hand everything over to the press."

An hour later Knowlton called back.

"We're open to a discussion, but today's out," Knowlton said. "I'm busy all day with media events. I might be able set something up for late tonight or first thing in the morning. I'll call you with the location and time."

Daniels had no choice, but to agree to Knowlton's terms. He banked on his need to get his hands on the evidence of Henry's treason and take him out in the process.

Daniels devoted the rest of the day to taking care of Maureen. It was a typical January Sunday in D.C. A cold brisk wind kicked up the remnants of a light snow that had fallen during the night along with plastic bags and other pieces of trash that some residents found too much of a bother to secure in trash receptacles.

Daniels had driven Maureen to her apartment the previous day after Mary Broussard confirmed it was safe to bring her home.

"You can spend the night, right?" Daniels asked them. She agreed. Sam Freeman agreed to relieve Broussard the next morning in case Daniels got the call to meet with Knowlton.

Daniels also decided to bring Sharon Washburn up to speed. Now that he'd gotten Maureen back, he told himself to bury his anger in favor of staying focused on making Knowlton and the Garvins pay for what they'd done. He texted Sharon that she was welcome to come to Maureen's apartment any time after six p.m. Sunday evening.

Sharon arrived a little after seven. She was dressed smartly with purple mittens and a matching wool hat.

"How is she?" she asked Daniels who came down to the lobby of the apartment building to greet her.

"She needs time," Daniels replied. "No one can go through that kind of experience and not be affected."

Sharon looked away, clearly upset.

"Her shoulder?"

"Reset and in a sling."

Sharon nodded.

He couldn't hide the rest. "And, they shot her up with some narcotic."

"Oh, no."

"She couldn't tell the doctors what it was. The hospital took some blood but we won't know for a day or two."

Sharon started to cry.

Daniels reached out and rubbed her shoulder. "You couldn't have known what they were going to do."

She nodded.

"And I blame myself," Daniels said, "for letting them take her. I should have known one guard was not enough."

Sharon shook her head. "You couldn't have--"

"I'm Secret Service. We are supposed to know how to protect people."

An hour later after she'd spent some time with Maureen talking about anything but what they'd been through, Daniels escorted Sharon back to the lobby.

She turned to face Daniels when she got off the elevator, tears in her eyes. "I can't believe the Garvins are going to get away with their crimes."

Daniels nodded that he understood her concern. "We'll see what happens." He told her about President Palmer's plan. "At least, we know the truth and soon everyone else will also. You've got to think about taking care of yourself."

Sharon wiped her eyes. "Maybe I'll go to Europe or someplace for a while. What about you guys? You're getting married a week from today, right?"

Daniels walked Sharon to her car. "You got our invitation, right? It won't be a big crowd, but we'd like you to come."

Sharon opened the driver's side door. "I'll try and thank you. I'd never have gotten half as far on my own."

Daniels nodded. They parted awkwardly. He doubted he'd ever see her again.

8:00 a.m., Monday, January 22

"Mr. Daniels. Welcome to the Oval Office."

Daniels recognized the speaker's voice although they'd never met in person. Gary Knowlton looked like Daniels had imagined—a self-satisfied weasel with a smirk on his face and the air of being the smartest man in the room. In addition to the Garvins and President Palmer, there were four Secret Service agents standing in the corners of the Oval Office at 1600 Pennsylvania Avenue.

Daniels glanced at Palmer. He looked pallid and fidgety, standing behind the famous *Resolute* desk that he had already abandoned in spirit if not in fact.

Gary Knowlton pointed to a vacant chair facing the desk next to the couch on which the Garvins were seated. "Sit down, Agent Daniels. We've some business to attend to and not much time to do it."

Mrs. Garvin was sitting erect. Her gaze sliced Daniels into little pieces. Mr. Garvin, who had not acknowledged Daniels' presence, was studying a thick printed document. His inaugural address?

Gary Knowlton motioned to President Palmer to sit in a chair opposite Daniels with the coffee table between them while he sat on the second couch. "Let's begin."

Palmer hesitated, but came over and sat down.

"A series of unfortunate events brings us together," Knowlton began. "If everyone cooperates, we'll clear things up quickly and come to a satisfactory conclusion. I assume, Agent Daniels, you brought the originals and all copies of the materials you promised."

"Right here," Daniels said pointing to the briefcase, although the originals had been handed over to Edwin Palmer days before. Only Ethan's cell phone was authentic. Trey assured him they'd removed everything of consequence in a manner that would stand up in court.

"Do I need to be present for this?" the president-elect interjected. "I need to rehearse."

"Yes, you do, Henry," Mrs. Garvin replied before Knowlton had a chance to respond. "You need to understand the price others have to pay for your indiscretion."

Garvin grimaced, but put the speech down on the coffee table.

Gary Knowlton cleared his throat. All eyes turned to him. "We are all aware why Ethan was planning to come to the White House on November 10th."

He paused. "As you apparently discovered," he said, turning to Daniels, "I went to the family farmhouse that morning to bring him to his mother, where she planned to read to him a page in the facts of life book that his father had failed to provide-- namely, that family loyalty comes first."

Daniels wondered why Knowlton was telling them this at this time.

"Sadly, Ethan did something stupid that cost him his life. He was making a recording on his phone while driving too fast and . . . well, I don't need to say any more, other than for reasons I need not go into now, I could not stop to help him."

Daniels noticed Henry Garvin look up. A brief look of hatred crossed his face. Henry apparently had not reconciled himself to Knowlton's decision to flee the scene of Ethan's accident. Based on Knowlton's knowledge of what Garvin had done while a student in China and his subsequent career doing Shen Wei's bidding, it was clear to Daniels that Garvin had been unable to hold Knowlton accountable for letting Ethan die when quicker help might have saved his life.

"I had to bring Ethan's briefcase back to Katherine where we learned what it was that he had discovered. Do either of you have any idea what he was bringing to the White House?" Knowlton asked, looking first at Palmer and then at Daniels.

Daniels had spent a good deal of time trying to come up with the answer to that question. One look at Henry Garvin told him what it must be. "A confession," he blurted out.

"Well done, Agent Daniels," Knowlton said. "You've done remarkably well with so little help, but unfortunately for you, you've chosen to play in a league above your pay grade."

Daniels knew the moment of truth was at hand. Knowlton wouldn't be admitting this if he expected it to ever leave the room. They had stopped him from exposing Knowlton's role in Ethan's death by holding Maureen, but that had come to an end. What was the alternative? They had to dispose of him, which confirmed an observation he hadn't fully digested when he entered the room. He only recognized one of the four Secret Service agents standing in the room. He couldn't recall his name, but remembered seeing him at Ethan's funeral. That agent was paying more attention to the proceedings than he should have been. The others must also be Knowlton's men as well. He decided to press the issue. "What's the point to going over all this, Knowlton? Do we have a deal or not?"

"Patience, Agent Daniels. I'm just getting warmed up."

"You may think you can shut me up," Daniels said, "but we still have the original recordings from Ethan's I-phone and financial records that prove that Henry here is on the payroll of a high ranking official in the Chinese government."

"Little good those things will do you," Knowlton said. "We've taken care of the guy who retrieved the recordings from Ethan's phone. We've doctored them up so that they no longer resemble the version you possess. So, if Ms. Washburn or your son--"

Daniels started to get to his feet, but strong arms restrained him. He hadn't heard the agents move behind his chair, but before he could resist four arms grabbed him from behind, pulled his arms behind his back, and secured his wrists in plastic cuffs.

"What's the meaning of this?" Edwin Palmer demanded, but before he could do anything he was accosted by the other two agents and was prevented from getting up. Palmer yelled in pain as his arms were twisted behind his back and cuffed.

"Keep him quiet," Knowlton said to the agents holding Palmer. One of them produced a gag ball that he stuffed in Palmer's mouth secured with tape.

"Him, too," Knowlton said motioning to Daniels who had started shouting for help.

Daniels was unable to prevent the gag from being shoved into his mouth and likewise secured.

"Is this necessary?" Henry Garvin asked leaning towards Edwin Palmer as if he were going to go to his aid.

"Sit back and shut up, Henry," his wife demanded. Henry gave her a nasty look, but complied.

"And if I see another look like that--"

"Never mind, Katherine," Knowlton said. "Let me finish my story. Then we'll do what we came here to do."

Daniels was shocked not just that the Secret Service agents were taking orders from Gary Knowlton, but they had laid hands on the President of the United States. He had foolishly assumed the agents on duty that morning would be trustworthy. That mistake could cost him his life.

"Agent Daniels," Knowlton said, turning towards him. "Perhaps you've figured where this is going. Perhaps not. Let me explain. You are about to assassinate Edwin Palmer only hours before he would have relinquished the Presidency to Henry Garvin. Then, having been captured by four brave Secret Service agents, you will die attempting to escape. A video will show both events in *super high definition* color."

Daniels struggled to get up, but the turncoat agents held him down.

Knowlton gloated. "Too bad you chose not to listen when you were warned."

Daniels tried to calm himself, but the cuffs were cutting into his wrists and he was having trouble breathing through his nose.

"Oh, and you are probably wondering about Ms. Thornberry. Did you know she was addicted to heroin? You should have warned her about taking too much at one time. Her body will be found in a day or two. An overdose will be the coroner's verdict."

Daniels tried to propel himself at Knowlton, but again the agents were ready. They held him down and one of them smacked him on the back of his head as his reward.

"Now, now, Daniels," Knowlton said. "You wouldn't want to miss the fun." He motioned to Mrs. Garvin.

"About time," she said. She opened her large pocket book, pulled out a coiled device, and handed it to Knowlton. The latter released a plastic band revealing something that resembled an old fashioned garrote, but with a thin plastic between two wooden handles instead of a metal wire. Knowlton went around behind Edwin Palmer. "Who wants to go first?"

Mrs. Garvin turned to her husband. "Henry. You're first."

"No," Henry said, finding a spark of courage someplace in his broken psyche. "You've got to stop this. You've gone too far."

"Henry, you will do this," Mrs. Garvin said, "or Mr. Daniels here will be guilty of two murders, not one."

Garvin looked at his wife as if he'd never seen her before. "Katherine," he whispered. "How--"

"Can it." She stood up and went over to where Knowlton was holding the garrote over Edwin Palmer's head. "I mean it, Henry. Don't make me do something I'll regret."

"But--but," Henry stammered.

"Watch how easy it is." She took the garrote from Knowlton, swung it in front of Palmer, and secured it around his neck. She winked at Daniels then gave the handles a violent twist. A terrible noise emerged from Palmer, his eyes bulged, and his face convulsed. After a few seconds, she released the pressure. Palmer was making, horrifying sounds trying to breath. He was still alive, but barely.

Katherine Garvin held the garrote towards her husband. "It's your turn, Henry. Show me you can be a man for once in your life."

"I'm so sorry, Edwin." Henry Garvin pushed himself off the couch. "If I'd known it would come to this--"

Mrs. Garvin grabbed her husband by the elbow and pulled him behind the president's chair. "Shut up and do it."

Henry took the handles of the garrote and gave them a light tug.

"Harder," Mrs. Garvin demanded.

Henry tugged them a bit harder.

Edwin Palmer's gasps for air were getting fainter. All the color had left his face and his eyes were bugling.

Daniels couldn't believe what he was seeing. *Wasn't anyone in the building aware of what was going on? Weren't people monitoring the Oval Office?*

Gary Knowlton took the handles of the garrote from Henry Garvin. "Looks like I'll have to finish the job like I always do for you, Henry." The latter slumped to the couch, buried his head in a pillow, and burst into tears.

Knowlton secured the garrote around Palmer's throat. "Ready downstairs?" He touched his right ear and waited. Then, perhaps after having been told by whoever was doing the recording that he was ready, he twisted the handles jerking Palmer's head back.

Daniels tried to turn his head away, but the agents forced him to face the President as Knowlton applied all of his strength. Finally, Palmer's head slumped. It was over.

Knowlton took the President's pulse. "Look what you've done, Agent Daniels. You've killed a sitting president: the first assassination since JFK. You've been a bad boy. Now it's your turn to meet your maker."

8:20 a.m., Same Day

Daniels strained to listen to the instructions Knowlton was giving Agent Darryl Agnew, the head of the four turncoat agents. He was to wait until the inauguration ceremony began before reporting that Edwin Palmer had been killed and the perpetrator had been shot and killed as he was trying to make his escape.

"How do we explain how Daniels was able to get the garrote through security?" Agnew asked.

Knowlton shrugged. "Use your imagination. It's plastic. He must have been able to get it through on a previous visit and then retrieved it this morning before coming into the Oval Office." He pointed to Edwin Palmer's body on the floor. "I like that idea. It proves this was premeditated."

Knowlton turned to give Daniels a self-satisfied smirk. "I've got a story that explains why you turned on Palmer who had been so kind to you. It turns out the President discovered that your Miss Thornberry is a heroin addict, and that you stole property from Mrs. Palmer's apartment, which you were supposed to be guarding, to feed her habit. You must have decided to kill him when he threatened to expose you to your superiors, but you needed to shoot up to get the courage to do the job."

Daniels tried to control the rage he felt. No doubt the media would buy whatever story Knowlton gave them, especially if he provided a doctored video showing him killing Palmer.

Knowlton handed a package to one of the agents. "Here's a needle and some heroin to pump into Agent Daniels before you shoot him so the medical examiner's report will confirm our story. We've got to get Henry ready to do his speech."

He turned to face Henry Garvin whose face was white and hands were shaking. "You'd better shape up, Henry. Your brother is standing by, looking quite presidential I must say."

So, it was true. They had been using Henry's twin as his stand in.

Mrs. Garvin pulled her husband to his feet. "Let's get on with it, Knowlton."

Henry groaned as he looked at Palmer's body on the floor, then he picked up his speech and followed his wife.

Knowlton turned to face Daniels. "I think that takes care of everything. Do you see any loose ends, Agent Daniels?"

Knowlton laughed loudly when Daniels refused to answer. "Of course, you do. There's Ms. Washburn and your son and his family, but you must know that gas explosions can be so devastating. Apparently an entire house and all the people inside can be blown to smithereens if someone carelessly leaves the gas on. In terms of Ms. Washburn, I think she's depressed, don't you. The coroner will have to decide whether the overdose she's going to take tonight will be an accident or on purpose."

Daniels managed to free one shoulder from the grip of the agent who was holding him down, but the agent recovered quickly, pulled Daniels back and slugged him again on the back of the head.

Daniels' head snapped forward and everything went black for a few seconds. When his head cleared, Knowlton was still going over details with the head of the renegade agents.

"Do you have any questions, Agent Agnew?" Knowlton asked the agent in charge. "If not, I'm out of here."

Agnew shook his head and closed the door behind Knowlton. "Who wants to do this?" he asked, offering the package containing a syringe and heroin packets to the others.

"I'd mess it up," replied the youngest one of the four who also looked the most shaken by that morning's events.

"I've no idea how to do it, boss," stated the only black member of the crew.

"Me either," the fourth agent said.

Were the agents wondering how they'd gotten themselves into a situation where they'd aided in the murder of a sitting President and were expected to shoot a fellow agent in the back?

"Okay, numbskulls. I'll have to do it," Agnew said. "Watch closely, but don't think about trying it. This stuff's only for losers like Agent Daniels here."

"Phew, can we open the doors?" the black agent asked. "It's beginning to smell in here."

Edwin Palmer's body had voided in response to his being asphyxiated. The smell of death was something Daniels had not experienced since his tour in Afghanistan.

"Sure, Johnson, open the doors," Agnew said pointing to the doors that led to the outside. He laid the heroin kit on the coffee table in front of Daniels and began the process of liquefying the dirty brown powder.

Daniels could hear the doors that led to the Rose Garden being opened. "We'll be right outside," one of the agents called.

"Cowards," Agnew muttered.

Daniels watched him heat the heroin in a test tube with a heavy-duty lighter.

"Get his shirt off, Lopez," Agnew commanded to the agent who had remained in the room.

Lopez unbuttoned the right wrist of Daniels' shirt and tried to roll it up high enough to expose a vein, but he had trouble with Daniels arms pinned behind him. "I need to uncuff him, boss."

Agnew studied the set up. "Okay, but then re-cuff him once you get that arm exposed."

The agent in charge turned back to his task. He was starting to fill the syringe.

Once he felt his wrists freed, Daniels kicked both legs under the coffee table lifting it up and knocking the heroin spoon and the syringe out of Agnew's hand.

Agnew hollered.

The commotion caused Lopez to loosen his grip just enough for Daniels to yank his arms free.

"Fuck!" Lopez yelled.

Unrestrained, Daniels propelled himself out of the chair head first into Agnew's mid-section driving him to the floor and knocking the syringe out of his hand.

Daniels smashed Agnew with a right to the jaw, but suffered a blow from Agnew's right fist to his head for his trouble. He pushed Agnew back with left hand and smashed him in the nose with his right.

Daniels spied the syringe that had fallen to the floor, and reached for it, but Agnew took advantage and rolled over on top of Daniels with both hands around Daniels neck.

Daniels felt his hand close on the syringe as Agnew's thumbs dug into Daniels' throat. Seconds from losing consciousness, he drove the point into the Agnew's left eye. He depressed the plunger emptying the heroin into Agnew's brain. The narcotic worked instantly. Agnew slumped forward racing towards unconsciousness.

Knowing he was not safe yet, Daniels rolled Agnew off him just as Lopez was in the process of removing the safety on his service weapon, but he'd gotten too close. Daniels kicked Lopez arm knocking the gun out of his hand and followed that with a vicious kick to the man's groin.

As Lopez fell to his knees, Daniels reached for Agnew's service weapon. The latter having been immobilized by the heroin penetrating his brain offered no resistance as Daniels pull his service weapon out of its holster.

"BAM!"

Lopez had retrieved his gun and fired it at Daniels. A bullet flashed overhead.

"BAM!"

A second round skinned Daniels' upper right arm, but before Lopez could fire his weapon a third time, Daniels discharged Agnew's weapon nailing Lopez in the chest. As Lopez fell back, a second bullet created a round cavity in Lopez' forehead and dropped him to the floor.

The sound of gunshots brought the other two agents back into the Oval Office, their weapons drawn. Daniels pulled Agnew's inert body in front of him holding the man's service weapon against his ear.

"Stay right there," Daniels yelled at them, "or Agnew dies."

The men stopped.

"Drop your weapons."

They hesitated. Daniels fired a round into the ceiling between the two of them.

Both weapons fell to the floor.

"Kick them this way."

They obeyed.

In control for a moment and ignoring the pain in his right arm, Daniels stood and backed towards the President's desk, holding Agnew's limp body in front of him. He remembered from a long-ago briefing where the alarm button was located on the underside of the *Resolute* desk, and reached down to punch the button.

Seconds later, the doors to the Oval Office burst open and three Secret Service agents entered the room their weapons drawn.

"What's going on," one of them demanded.

One of the turncoat agents turned toward the newcomers. "He killed the president and agent Lopez."

"Who?"

The agent pointed to Daniels who was holding up Agnew's increasingly limp body with the man's service weapon pointed at Agnew's right ear.

"Agent Tucker Daniels."

"Shit," one of the new agents exclaimed pointing to Edwin Palmer's body on the floor. "It's Palmer."

"He killed the President," the renegade agent said pointing at Daniels. "Kill him."

"BAM!"

Daniels fired a round into the knee of the agent who'd just spoken.

The agent howled and dropped to the floor.

"Drop your weapons," Daniels demanded, "or the next round will be fatal."

The newcomers turned in his direction. Daniels recognized the lead agent.

"Agent Andrews. I don't have time to explain, but you need to arrest those agents as accomplices to the murder of the President of the United States."

Daniels had known Eliot Andrews for two decades. He was as straight-shooting an agent as you'd ever find, but he seemed totally confused, turning left and right, at a loss for words.

"Agent Andrews. Do you recognize these men? They're all part of Henry Garvin's personal unit. They helped him kill Edwin Palmer and they were going to frame me."

Andrews found his voice. "Put the gun down, Agent Daniels, and we'll sort this all out."

"There isn't time. Someone's got to stop the inauguration."

Andrews blanched as if hit in the face with a baseball bat.

Daniels knew he had to move. "I'm not going to say it a third time. Drop your weapons or someone else will join President Palmer in paradise."

The two agents who'd come into the room with Andrews looked to their supervisor.

"Don't do anything you'll regret, Agent Daniels," Andrews barked.

While he was talking Daniels had been maneuvering Agnew towards the door to the corridor. He opened it with his gun hand while keeping his other arm around Agnew's neck. As he stood in the doorway, he pointed Agnew's gun at the traitor's shoulder and pulled the trigger. Agnew fell forward and landed on his face. Daniels fired twice more into the ceiling causing the other agents to duck for cover, pulled the door shut, and ran towards the main part of the building. He knew he only had seconds before three agents would be on his heels their weapons drawn with safeties off.

8:30 a.m., Same Day

On a normal day the West Wing of the White House buzzes with activity. The President's personal secretary, chief of staff, press secretary, and dozens more would be in their offices, on their phones or moving through the corridors processing the hundreds of documents that circulate for signatures, forwarding and filing. Staffing on inauguration day, however, was a different story. All of the non-civil service people had cleaned out their desks and departed in advance of the arrival of Henry Garvin's replacements, and most of the civil service people were in the Capitol assisting with the inauguration ceremony.

That made it easy for Gary Knowlton's chosen Secret Service agents to control the environment, which Daniels realized must have included taking control of the sub-basement room where Secret Service agents monitor the security cameras that record the comings and goings throughout the White House.

Recording the Oval Office was on an as-needed basis. The President typically only requested video coverage when welcoming international guests. On the other hand, the room was monitored whenever the President was in, which Daniels realized meant someone had observed the proceedings of the past thirty minutes, and most likely had recorded key moments in order to piece together a video that would implicate Daniels in President Palmer's murder.

Daniels was conflicted. He could try to get to the Capitol and do something to stop the inauguration, but he had no idea what. Plus, his chances of succeeding would be one in a billion. Who would believe him if he showed up claiming the Garvins had just killed Edwin Palmer? There had to be another way. What if he could get to the monitoring room and stop whoever was doctoring the video or at least retrieve the original recording showing the Garvins and Gary Knowlton killing Edwin Palmer? Then perhaps, justice could be served.

The monitoring room was in the sub-basement. Taking the elevator would be a mistake. Not only could it be controlled by whoever was in the monitoring room, but the agents pursuing him would know where he was going. Fortunately, Daniels knew how to access the emergency stairwell.

As he descended the stairs towards the sub-basement level, Daniels knew he might not make it out of the White House alive, but if he could stop the doctoring of the video, the truth might still get out. He hoped his pursuers would think he'd try to get to the Capitol, which might buy him a little time. That also assumed the people in the monitoring room were not in touch with the agents who were hot on his trail.

As he descended the staircase, Daniels felt dizzy. He feared he was near to passing out due to the loss of blood from the bullet that had grazed his right arm. He transferred Agent Agnew's gun to his left hand because the bullet had caused the fingers on his right hand to go numb. Noise from the stairs above him meant Andrews' team or some other agents were close. If he was to live another five minutes, much less another day, he had to get to the monitoring room before they caught up with him.

He opened the door to the sub-basement, but didn't step into the corridor, worrying that one of Knowlton's men might be waiting for him. He flashed Agnew's service weapon part way out of the door, but nothing happened. Crouching down, he peaked around the corner. The corridor was empty. The sound of a bullet striking the door above his head told him he had no choice but to move. He ducked into the corridor. It was empty. The monitoring room was a few steps away.

He tried the door to the monitoring room. It was unlocked. He opened the door cautiously, gun first. Normally three or four agents would be monitoring the outside area, the gates and different parts of the building. The first two bodies he saw were clearly dead--one leaning over the console his neck covered in blood, the other on the floor a hole in his chest. A third man was sitting in front of a bank of monitors, his back to the door. Presumably he was the one assigned to create the video that showed Daniels garroting Edwin Palmer.

The third man turned at the noise of someone coming into the room. Daniels pointed the gun at the man while locking the door with his right hand.

"Hands up! On your feet!"

"What? How?"

"Never mind. Do as I say or you're a dead man."

The man raised both hands. "Okay, okay. Don't shoot."

"On your feet and turn around."

The man obeyed. Daniels planted a blow with the butt of the gun to the back of the man's head, driving him to the floor unconscious.

Banging on the door told him his pursuers were trying to get into the room, but when he closed the door, Daniels had activated the room's emergency locking system. He was safe for the moment until someone showed up who had override authority. The more important question was had he stopped Knowlton's man soon enough to make it clear who really killed Edwin Palmer?

Pushing the unconscious man aside, Daniels sat down at the console. It took a few seconds, but he figured out how to play back the segment the man had been working on. The scene of Palmer's execution taken from a camera stationed above the door exiting into the secretary's office showed a man behind Palmer twisting the garrote. Knowlton's man had done his job well. Daniels had no idea if an expert would be able to prove the video had been doctored, but that wouldn't matter if he, Maureen, Trey, and Sharon were all dead!

He had only one chance to come out of this alive. Even if the original video of what actually happened in the Oval Office remained in the system, if he wasn't able to retrieve it and show it to the world, one of Knowlton's lackeys could delete it, replacing it with the edited segment.

His only hope was to broadcast the segment showing what really happened. That might be possible for someone who knew the technology, but Daniels didn't have either the ability or the time to find that segment, much less figure out how to broadcast to the world. Further, the loss of blood meant he was in danger of losing consciousness and eventually the agents banging on the door would find an official with the necessary rating to open the door. Whether he'd be alive or dead by that time was immaterial. Knowlton's renegade agents would likely empty their weapons into Daniels' body the minute they accessed the room.

Stopping the bleeding was his first priority. He tore the shirt off the unconscious man and used it to bind his right arm as best he could. Next he opened the half empty water bottle that had been left on one of the monitoring stations and drank it down. Doing so might give him a few more minutes. Finally, he pulled one of the burner phones Trey had provided him out of his jacket pocket.

He punched in the ten-digit number and prayed once more. *It's me, Jesus. Don't let me down now.*

"Trey Sharp."

Thank God. "Trey, it's your father. I've got a situation here."

Sharon Washburn had not wanted to go to the Mall that morning to join the inauguration crowd. It was bitter cold and she knew watching Henry Garvin get sworn in as president would put her in the sourest of moods, but Agent Daniels had texted her yesterday evening begging her to attend. He told her he needed her to perform one more task. After Henry Garvin was sworn in, she was to hand flash drives of the materials containing Ethan's recordings and the financial records provided by the Chinese government agent to as many members of the press she knew as she could find. The flash drives she created with the materials he'd emailed filled both pockets of her winter coat. Yet, as she surveyed the crowd, she wondered whether she'd be able to get close enough to the press section to see if she recognized anyone much less get their attention.

She was surprised she'd gotten as close as she had. Daniels had somehow forged a pass that got her through security into the public section closest to the Capitol steps where the inauguration would take place in a matter of minutes. She pulled her hat down over her ears and began to work her way towards the elevated platform that housed the reporters with their cameras and workstations. How the print people could type with bare hands in twenty-degree windy, ice cold conditions was beyond her.

"Where do you think you're going?" an angry man said to her as she bumped the chair he probably planted in that location the previous day. Skirting his chair she earned a growl when she stepped on a woman's blanket.

"Sorry, sorry." She knew it was futile to explain. She kept moving slower now hoping not to piss off too many people.

Daniels had texted her that Gary Knowlton had told him to come to the White House at 8 a.m. supposedly to trade the materials for immunity for her as well as Daniels and his family.

"I find that hard to believe," she'd texted back.

"I realize that it's most likely a trap."

"Then don't go," she told him.

"I've got to," he replied. "No matter what happens to me, I've got to go. Meanwhile, I've an assignment for you."

Sharon realized she was as close to the media section as she was going to get. People were packed in tight and no one looked like they were willing to make room for another body. She turned to face the podium where the inauguration would take place in just a few minutes time. Presidential terms begin at noon. Prior to the swearing-in would be the usual preliminaries--starting with the pledge of allegiance and the playing of America the Beautiful.

She couldn't spot President Palmer on the stage. He would be coming out shortly, followed by the leaders of Congress and then the Garvins. Charlotte Palmer, whom she recognized from pictures she'd discovered in one of the bureau drawers in the master bedroom, was already seated. Next to her were her daughter and a man who presumably was the daughter's husband. Two children sat between the adults.

Sharon read that the Palmer's only son had died during the war in Iraq a dozen years ago. Would she be able to recover should such a fate befall a child of hers? Would she even get married? In recent weeks she'd turned down two men who wanted to date her. Didn't they understand that she hadn't gotten over Ethan Garvin!

"I'm in," Trey said.

Daniels, who'd been searching for a first aid kit returned to the chair where he could view the monitors.

"Can you find the original?"

"Give me a minute," Trey answered.

"I may not have a minute," Daniels muttered. He could hear people outside the door. Did one of them have the combination that would open the door?

"Got it."

"Great. Capture it and see if you can spread it around to the media…and don't forget our website."

"I can do better than that," Trey answered.

"Oh, oh," Daniels said, turning to the door. "They're in. If I don't make it, Trey--"

"Hands up! Move away from that computer!"

Daniels didn't hesitate. "I surrender. Don't shoot."

Sharon felt her phone buzzing in her pocket.

It was a text from some unknown source. "Henry Garvin killed Edwin Palmer."

"Oh, my God," Sharon said out loud, earning her nasty looks. She thought of texting back, but didn't know who it was from or why they'd texted her.

Another text: "It's me, Trey Sharp. Tell the media. Henry Garvin killed Edwin Palmer."

"Will try," she texted back. Sharon tried to move closer to the press gallery, but no one was willing to let her by. She recognized a woman who worked for McClatchy.

"Abigail," she called out. "Abigail Dewater."

The woman reporter turned in her direction.

"President Palmer has been killed," Sharon yelled.

"What?" Dewater called back. "Say it again."

"President Palmer. Henry Garvin killed him."

"What are you saying?" someone nearby demanded.

"It's true," Sharon said turning to the people around her. "Henry Garvin killed President Palmer. Listen up, everyone, Henry Garvin killed Edwin Palmer."

People started shouting all around her, the rumor spreading throughout the crowd.

"What are you trying to do, start a riot?" a man yelled at her.

"Look," someone shouted. "The screens."

Sharon turned back to face the podium. Something was happening on the giant screens that had been broadcasting welcome messages and precautionary instructions all morning in between video clips of shining moments in recent American history. The video feed seemed to be breaking up. People's attention was focused on it as the images fluttered and disappeared. A few moments of white static followed. Someone shouted out "technical difficulties." There was general laughter from the huge crowd.

Then a new image appeared. Sharon tried to make sense of it. It must be from the Oval Office. Sharon recognized the President's *Resolute* desk from a tour she'd taken with her association as well as the special carpet that had been installed at the beginning of Edwin Palmer's term with images of Americans--farmers, truck drivers, teachers, policemen, and factory workers--arrayed in a circle around an eagle holding an American flag in its beak.

There was President Palmer seated in a chair. What was that in his mouth and what was that man doing behind him? It looked like Henry Garvin. He was doing something to President Palmer.

The crowd gasped. Someone screamed and pushed someone else. Someone else tried to move. The people were packed in so tight the movement snowballed. Sharon tried to resist the flow, but found herself almost knocked to the ground. She grabbed onto a stranger's coat to keep from falling and being crushed. It felt like a riot was about to break out all around her. Then the band started playing the Star-Spangled Banner. People came to a stop, but the video kept playing.

Tuesday, February 13

The porter had to wait for his tip while Tucker Daniels struggled to remove his money clip from his left front pants pocket. He tried to ignore the twinge in his arm caused by reaching with his right hand before he remembered to use his left. Extracting the clip, he transferred it to his right hand, which was still in a sling, and took a twenty off the top.

"What a view!" Maureen was standing by the windows.

Daniels was glad he insisted on a room facing the ocean. It was a view he didn't think either of them would live to see, but he knew better than to remind her. It was time to forget the nightmare-- time to celebrate.

His wife of less than forty-eight hours turned to him. "Tucker Eugene Daniels. Are you sure we can afford this?"

Daniels laughed, went over to his bride, pulled her close, and planted a kiss on her forehead. "This must be paradise because I'm here with an angel."

"I didn't realize they charged $600 a night in paradise."

Daniels gave her another kiss. "Rumors say Congress is going to give us a medal. Maybe we can pawn it to pay our bill."

She gave him a gentle push and sat down on the bed testing its firmness.

He felt his phone buzz in his jacket pocket. Maureen tried to take the phone away from him when he pulled it out.

"Don't answer it. We're on our honeymoon."

"It's from Alexander Worthington. Don't you think I'd better see what he wants?"

"I guess so. You do that while I check out the bathroom."

Daniels opened the sliding door to the balcony and settled down in a padded deck chair.

"The Secret Service has dropped all administrative charges," Worthington said. "You're a free man. Enjoy your honeymoon."

"Great news. I don't know how I can thank you enough."

"No need to thank me. I'm just doing what Edwin would have wanted."

"And the Garvins? What's the latest?"

Despite Trey's having managed to cut into the video feed to the Mall and the ensuing near riot, the Garvins with Gary Knowlton behind them had mounted the podium as if nothing had happened. They stood in the practiced locations while Knowlton threatened the Chief Justice of the Supreme Court with all kinds of repercussions if he did not conduct the swearing-in ceremony.

When the Navy band started playing the Star Spangled Banner, most of the crowd stopped moving and faced the podium. As a result they saw the text that scrolled across the screens.

This video is real. Henry Garvin, his wife, Katherine, and top aide Gary Knowlton took turns choking Edwin Palmer until he perished because President Palmer had uncovered the truth that Henry Garvin is a traitor. Stop the inauguration. Stop the inauguration.

That message prompted renewed turmoil People were yelling; some were trying to leave, but it was too crowded to get far. The confusion was multiplied when the video re-started at the beginning, showing Katherine Garvin garroting Edwin Palmer, followed by Henry and then Gary Knowlton.

The reason the inauguration was not consummated, however, was due to the head of the Chief Justice's security team who whisked the Chief Justice off the stage back into the bowels of the Capitol over Gary Knowlton's protesting howls.

"I still can't get over the brutality of those people," Daniels said after Worthington informed him the Garvins, Knowlton, and a dozen other people including the renegade Secret Service agents were being held in custody while the charges against them mounted daily.

"Ambition and greed cause people to do terrible things," Worthington said.

"Apparently it all started rather innocently. An American college student falls in love with a Chinese girl who rejected his advances."

"True enough. In any case, stop by my office when you get back. I'll need you to sign a few dozen documents."

Daniels heard Maureen come out of the bathroom. "Hey, babe. The Secret Service has dropped the administrative charges. I'm a free man."

She didn't reply. She must not have heard him, but it didn't matter. He'd tell her in a few minutes. He just wanted to sit there and take it all in--the warm breeze, the smell of the flowers, and the ocean view.

Things had happened so fast since that morning three weeks ago he still hadn't processed it all. Once the door to the monitoring room had been opened, he'd been placed under arrest for the murder of President Palmer. Thankfully, whoever was in charge of the Secret Service agents who had opened the monitoring room door, had instructed the agents to take him alive. At the hospital, while barely conscious, officials from the Justice Department, Homeland Security, and the Secret Service crowded into his room along with a federal judge to read off a criminal justice textbook's worth of crimes and violations that he was being charged with.

He learned later that the live broadcast of his charges was only cut off when the Supreme Court announced that Janice Lawrence, Henry Garvin's vice presidential candidate, had been sworn in as the 47th President of the United States pending the results of a full investigation.

Despite the fact that the medications for his wound caused him to fall asleep in the middle of sentences, Daniels did his best to respond to questions thrown at him from the FBI and other agencies. Finally, Alexander Worthington got a court to accept him as Daniels' attorney and put a stop to the interrogation.

Then, overnight, Daniels went from villain to hero, from being charged with Edwin Palmer's murder to being one of his honorary pallbearers when the video Trey had broadcast on the mall was proven to be real and one of the Secret Service agents who'd been in the room corroborated Daniels' version of events.

Although he was not able to help carry Edwin Palmer's casket during the burial ceremony at Arlington Cemetery given his right arm was in a sling, Daniels had been positioned with other dignitaries, and walked to the burial spot on his own power.

Prior to the funeral, Alexander Worthington and a team of attorneys had not only appeared in court with mountains of documentation on his behalf, but they'd convinced a federal judge to dismiss all criminal charges against Daniels.

"This man's a hero of the first order," every major news outlet quoted the judge as saying when he signed the order.

That still left a list of administrative charges the Secret Service drew up, but Worthington had been on the ball there as well, first getting them to allow Daniels to get married and fly to Hawaii on his honeymoon, and then, as Worthington promised, getting those charges dismissed in their entirety.

"Edwin Palmer documented everything you did for him," Worthington told Daniels in his hospital room three days after the events that cost the President his life--the first president to be assassinated since John F. Kennedy. "When we present that to the agency you'll be exonerated of all charges."

The Thursday after Inauguration Monday Daniels was released from the hospital and driven to Arlington for Palmer's funeral and burial.

After the burial, Worthington offered the assembled domestic and international news media a brief summary of what had taken place. Daniels read a brief statement honoring Edwin Palmer for his courage, but refused to take any questions.

Stories continued to appear daily on different aspects of the ten-week investigation. On the flight over to Hawaii, Daniels caught a number of errors in an *L.A. Times* story about Henry Garvin's relationship to an official in the Chinese government citing the figures contained in the flash drives Sharon Washburn handed to reporters at the mall. As the story of a young Chinese woman's suicide had not come out, reporters speculated on the origins of the relationship between Garvin and Shen Wei. No one had discovered the truth yet, but Daniels suspected it would come to light one day as well.

Another wire story delved into the corruption of Henry Garvin's Secret Service unit, speculating that the Garvins had bought off the members of that team with promises of being promoted once Garvin was in office. Daniels was not surprised. Given that the Secret Service had long been the step-child of Homeland Security, resentment over lower pay and more demanding working conditions made agents susceptible to doing things they might otherwise not be willing to do. Once you bend one rule at the request of the people you're supposed to be guarding, you no longer maintain the ability to say no to someone like Katherine Garvin.

"I've posted a picture of the view to Facebook," Maureen said, sitting down next to Daniels. "Sharon Washburn has already shared it."

"She'll be fine," Daniels said. When her role in the story came out, Sharon had been inundated with interview requests, marriage proposals, and job offers. "I'll wait to decide which job I take until I come back from Europe," she'd told Daniels at the wedding reception. He told her he approved her decision.

"I'm ready for a Mai Tai," Maureen announced.

"Room service or should we test out one of the seaside bars?"

"I'm ready to explore. You?"

"Absolutely. We can check out the dinner menu while we're at it. I think my appetite is returning."

"Mine never left, but I don't think I'll ever eat another tuna sandwich."

When she finally had a chance to tell the story of her capture and captivity, she made light of various aspects of how she'd been treated, but her captives' shooting her up with heroin was not to be taken lightly. Once the drug they'd used had been identified, Maureen's doctors explained the need for her to enter a rehab center where they monitored her vitals and counteracted the effects of the opioid.

She agreed once Daniels promised their wedding and honeymoon was postponed not cancelled. He was amazed at her ability to handle two weeks in rehab with courage and humor.

"Dishwater coffee and stale cornflakes for breakfast, a tuna sandwich with wilted lettuce at midday, and rice with vegetables in the evening. I think I lost five pounds."

Daniels got up and followed Maureen back into their honeymoon suite. "You know, I was thinking about ordering us Ahi tuna steaks for dinner tonight."

She gave him a shove. "You would, wouldn't you, Tucker Eugene Daniels."

He shrugged. "I would, unless you're offering a roll with honey in bed instead."

-30-

Made in the USA
Columbia, SC
24 July 2018